THE GATE

By
Rachel Selwan

For my mom and aunt—
without you, this book would still be in my head!

THE GATE

First Edition. October 1, 2016

Written by Rachel Selwan

HARRIS

Table of Contents

Prologue 1
Sam 6
The Park 10
Clair 12
Emily 30
Clair 34
Dorthea 42
Clair 45
Chris 48
Clair 50
Sam 57
Clair 63
Chris 67
Clair 71
Chris 91
Clair 99
Emily 106
Clair 115
Dorthea 122
The Airport 125
Dorthea 127
Clair 130
Emily 146
Clair 148
Sam 154
Clair 158
Emily 161
Clair 163
Clair 172

Emily....184
Clair....187
Chris....193
Clair....197
Emily....204
Dorthea....211
Clair....213
Emily....223
Dorthea....229
Clair....233
Chris....240
Clair....245
The Bar....248
Joe....249
Emily....251
Clair....253
Chris....260
Emily....262
Clair....269
Clair....274
Clair....279
Acknowledgements....290
Biography....292

PROLOGUE

Clair woke up screaming.

It wasn't the first time.

Sweat poured out around the edges of her face, arms, and legs, making the soft silk sheets cling to her body. Even with the small lamp on, her room felt dark and cold. She was always so cold now.

She couldn't go back to sleep after that . . . after reliving the horrors of that night in the rain, her ex-boyfriend, her ex-best-friend.

She sat up, turned to her open laptop, and paused the relaxing music that she had set to repeat. Music was the only thing that could coax her to sleep lately; not even the sleeping pills could keep the night terrors away.

During the day her mind would play those scenes out over and over again, trying to see what she could have done differently, but her dreams were out of her control, pulling the memories to the surface in the most real way possible.

Clair shook her head to clear the last fragments of the dream. Peeling the sheets off her legs, she stood and headed to the bathroom across the hall. She lived with her grandmother, who was sleeping soundly on the other side of the house. She wouldn't hear the bath water running.

Clair turned on the lights and stood in front of the dirty sink, placing her hands on the cold ceramic. She wasn't sure how many hours of sleep she'd lost over the last few weeks, but in the mirror was the face of a stranger. Her normally tan complexion was blanched white, her heart-shaped face gaunt, muscles weak under the baggy sweatpants and sweatshirts she continually wore because getting dressed in the morning took too much effort and she just didn't see the point anymore. Her long brown hair fell in thin lengths past her shoulders around her dirt-brown eyes.

She hadn't seen it coming.

Clair joined the Christian club at the beginning of her sophomore year in high school. She thought it would be good to experience something new. None of her friends or her boyfriend wanted anything to do with the idea of God, and neither did Clair, but there was just something about the club that drew her in.

The first time she stepped into one of their meetings, she was greeted by smiling faces, and everyone seemed to want to get to know her. She wasn't left alone once in the entire two hours they sang, listened to a speaker talk about God, and discussed their bible study sessions that happened once a week at different students' houses.

So she went to another meeting, and then another. Eventually, Clair was asked by the adult leader of the club to become a leader—teaching people about the Bible and holding general after-school discussions.

Clair learned a lot in those first few months about the Hebrew God, and then the New Testament Jesus. She was an outgoing person and enjoyed bringing people together, and the club members eventually started coming to Clair for advice, not the adult leader.

She even convinced her boyfriend to join the club, and he eventually became a leader.

But Clair got so involved that school became her second priority. Her friends that were not in the club and her grandmother became less important. Her entire life was the club, a behavior encouraged by the adult leader. Clair was engrossed with being one of the main facilitators at the center of it all.

So she didn't see it happening until it was too late.

Her boyfriend started spending more time with her best friend, another leader. Clair was so busy trying to juggle everything in her life that she didn't think anything was wrong. Then her boyfriend left her—to be with the other girl. When Clair tried to confront her friend about the issue, the adult leader of the club said it would be a good idea for Clair to take some time to heal, away from the pressures of leadership. But Clair knew better; the adult leader of the club was threatened by her and was using the rift in the leadership team as a way to get rid of Clair.

She was being asked to leave.

After everything she had done, they were kicking her out. Exiled by the one place that was supposed to accept and take a person in no matter what.

So she walked away: out of the club, out of school, out of her life.

The friends she had before the club didn't speak to her anymore, she was failing almost all of her classes, and she was completely alone.

Clair was sixteen but felt forty.

She looked back into the mirror, watching the tears slip out of her eyes and down her face. She grabbed the bottle of sleeping pills from the cabinet in the wall. Pouring out half the bottle, she popped them into her mouth and swallowed. She walked over to the bathtub, turned on the water, and climbed in, lying on her stomach and listening to the loud thud of the tub slowly filling.

She felt the water rise to her chin, warm and loose, filling her body with a heat that never quite hit her bones. It had been three weeks, and she still couldn't bring herself to return to school, unable to face the pieces of her broken life.

As quickly as her anger had come that day, it left, leaving her colder and emptier than she had ever been—exchanging the heat of hatred for cold night terrors.

So she just lay there, dwelling on her mistakes and giving herself over to bitterness and despair.

Clair let the water rise.

Past her lips, past her nose, above her head.

She felt the pills kicking in, and her body grew heavy, her mind slowing.

Her body was telling her to breathe, but she was so tired, so tired of everything.

She could sense her mind relaxing, heartbeat surprisingly slow, as if it was tired too. She could feel everything slipping peacefully away.

"No, there's more."

Clair leapt from the bath, spraying and coughing up water.

5 years later

SAM

veryone has a purpose.

Even angels.

To say Samuel liked books would be a drastic understatement. Sam loved books.

Currently he was researching Maria Sibylla Merian, a book on insects depicting her trip to Surinam.

Merian would collect and observe the insects in order to create a visual of their lifecycle. The images were hand drawn and colored by the scientist, with historical references, quotes, and footnotes placed by the editor on each opposing page describing the insects' qualities and the relationship of the author to them.

Sam was particularly interested in Merian's work on the Tevian Owl Butterfly, discovered originally by Linnaeus in 1758, whose wings are whose wings are patterned to resemble an owl's eye, in order to deceive predators. The butterfly, considered one of the giant species, developed from a plain brown caterpillar with a red underbelly.

Merian's use of color and the details within her plates showed an artist searching for the greatest understanding and acknowledgment of each specimen collected.

Sam had never been the biggest fan of historical bug analysis, but his recent discovery of a *Cephalcia tannourinensis* while walking the streets of Beirut, Lebanon, had encouraged him to spend some time in Pier's Love Books shop.

A few years ago the insect, a cousin of a common bee found only in Lebanon, was discovered as the cause of death for many of the national trees. They would lay eggs in the branches of cedar trees, and once hatched, their larvae would devour the needles of the trees.

Sam hoped this particular bug was a very distant cousin.

He closed the book and pressed the palms of his hands into his blue eyes, rubbing to clear the sleep. The light pouring through the bay window signaled high noon, the sun warming the wooden desk he had been sitting at for over a day.

The owner, a kind old Lebanese man named Pier, felt so comfortable with Sam being in the shop every day that he even let him continue his studies overnight. Pier would simply lock Sam in the shop when he left, and return in the morning to find him still pushing through the texts, head bent and eyes bleary.

Sam looked out and watched the ocean as it hit the bay beach, the people sunning themselves and laughing in the warm weather. When he looked down at the cement sidewalk just below the window, he saw a lizard bobbing up and down, a common territorial offense, before it retreated into a bush.

The animal society was not so different from the human; both required survival through gifted traits. The only thing humans got stuck on was searching for purpose and meaning.

And what did Sam have? Too many years waiting to atone for a life he couldn't remember.

Sam got up and stretched his arms, hearing the bones crack. He returned the book to its shelf and thanked the smiling owner for his hospitality, before walking out into the sunlight.

It's been too long, he thought for the millionth time. The last few centuries he'd been wandering the world, reading and waiting for his time to come. Waiting was the hardest part. He had met some like himself before, but most had stories of friends whose purposes were fulfilled within a few years, while others took only days. So when Sam was asked how long his time had been, they were always shocked.

It has been too long. Maybe he has forgotten me, Sam thought, remembering the last eight hundred years.

As he walked, Sam noticed children running along the shore of the beach, the braver ones swimming out into the bay and catching urchins, cracking them open, and eating them raw.

The Lebanese, rich in culture and history, shared bloodlines with the Greeks and early Mezzanines. The society was thick with Maronite Catholicism, Hinduism, and Greek influences in their food, architecture, and fashion. Sam was enjoying his time living amongst the bustling culture.

“رحبلا ذفنق ةجزاطلا”

Sam turned to his right to see a street peddler holding out a plate of fresh sea urchin, and his stomach rumbled. He purchased half an urchin and ate quickly, the smoky flavor of the uncooked meat spongy in his mouth. The last time he had anything to eat was more than twenty-four hours ago, and the meat took effect on his senses immediately.

He could *see*.

Not, after all of his reading had confirmed, as well as some higher-ranking angels, but the world was more beautiful through his minor angel eyes after fasting. The sun was brighter, the people walking changing into beacons of light, their souls all touching. Even without his sight, it existed, secretly, this web of collective conscience that floated on even after the body could not.

It was always such beautiful experience that Sam decided to stop and sit on a bench along the sidewalk, watching, until the effect faded. He wondered if it ever faded for the higher-ranking angels. It was a subject he longed to study.

The theology of many religions pointed toward a creator: a divine being that, by whatever cause, developed the universe in a way to leave it self-sufficient—at least in part. All the stories led him to the conclusion that should any life form choose to believe in the divine being, by any given religious name, and seek out the truth about that being, while living morally upright, that being would welcome that individual into some version of paradise. Sam thought this was all debatable (especially within the Hebrew and Christian religions that spoke most often of, what he believed, was his designation—an angel) considering the wars, natural disasters, and general evil that plagued the world.

Sam was pulled from his thoughts by the sight of a young girl walking along the beach with her parents. She glanced over at Sam just as the effect wore off, and smiled. She spoke a few words of Arabic to her mother, who walked her over to Sam with an expression of kind confusion. The little girl held out a small piece of paper.

It was a page from the local newspaper, written in Arabic and covered in dirt; she had most likely found in the street and plucked it up. Her mother watched as Sam took the paper and thanked the girl in Arabic. She smiled shyly at him before dragging her mother back to the rest of their family.

Unfolding the paper, Sam read about the governmental issues plaguing the world, about his homeland, England, and a piece about the latest scandal regarding the new princess. Apparently everyone thought she was pregnant already, which was considered improper because she had been married only a short while.

Laughing to himself, Sam moved on and found some interesting columns about the price of gas and responses by the resident advisor to questions posed by readers.

It wasn't until he flipped to the back, to the section with the crosswords and help wanted ads that he found a picture.

In the photo was a woman with brown hair and bright eyes, holding an antique. The picture was dated over fifty years ago. The caption beneath described her as the discoverer of an Egyptian Mau vase, a local treasure once thought lost to the culture. It also said that a museum in Cairo would be featuring the Mau for the next few weeks.

Sam was shocked.

The effect from his blood had worn off completely, but the woman in the photo was glowing.

The Park

She was close.

There had only been one angel guarding the entrance to the park, and she stepped over his dead body feeling giddy, caressing the snake pendant hanging from her neck and enjoying how the golden scales warmed at her touch.

We are close, my love, she thought.

The other angels would be on their way soon, but she could handle them, kill any who would dare try to stop her.

Her blood was pumping through her veins, the liquid churning for its origin as she crossed the inner barrier—edging ever closer to the throbbing pulse of The Gate.

The sun was rounding the edge of the earth in her direction, but she was too close now. It wouldn't escape this time.

The earth around The Gate smelled like her blood.

"Stop!"

She turned.

Another guard was standing behind her holding a gun out in front of him, with trembling hands. An insignia on his shirt read NYPD.

Human, she thought with a snarl. So he was not a guardian of The Gate. His life would be forfeited for a purpose he may never know.

She felt for his weaknesses, watching his body grow rigid as she used her mind to explore everything within him that made him vulnerable—greed, vanity, and pride—anything to hold onto.

She stretched her hand toward his face, squeezing the air until she made a fist, hearing his neck bones snap.

Easy, death was so easy.

She collected his life in the air, feeling it fill her and give her a taste of power she lacked without enough human essence. The sweet taste of his newly extinguished energy kept her going, an invisible force that only humans possessed, just as the first rays of light filled the world.

She turned and screamed as The Gate vanished.

Clair

Clair wished that the drive back to her grandmother's house, soon to be her house again too, would have taken longer.

The last few months of college had been the best time in her life. She was able to get into all the classes she wanted, and most of them were purely for fun because she had managed to finish the necessary courses ahead of schedule.

It helped when the professors enjoyed what they were teaching. It sucked trying to sit through a class where the instructor was hell-bent on teaching directly out of a textbook, usually because they had gotten their degree in something completely different but the state school was low on funds and didn't have enough high-level professors to teach the correct classes.

Yet here *she* was, driving up the interstate, a college graduate with a degree in art and a minor in spiritual studies, moving back home. She had picked up the minor at first because of some lingering anger at the organization that had caused her so much pain, but eventually became interested in the idea of a divine being—just not religion or any specific organization.

It wasn't all that uncommon for a graduate to move back home, but it still bugged her. She graduated at the top of her class for heaven's sake. She thought there should have been at least one job opening to keep her from having to move home.

But there wasn't.

Clair could still see her two best friends smiling, their hair curled into perfect ringlets under the black, scholarly graduation caps.

"It's okay, Clair," Zelda had laughed, her dirty-blond hair blowing in the breeze while they all waited in line to cross the stage. "Everyone takes time off before working."

"Yeah," said Nastran, who was always more practical than Zelda but still less practical than Clair, with her light brown hair and oval eyes. "Get a part-time job, save some money, and then join us in the Bahamas—or in DC!"

Clair smiled as she remembered watching Nastran tuck a curl behind her ear. Nastran preferred her hair straight to wavy, but Zelda had convinced both of them to have their hair the same for the pictures. Both Nastran and Zelda would be moving to DC to complete law school after spending the entire summer in the Bahamas.

Clair laughed at the dashboard, remembering the frat party they crashed that night and the look on Nastran's face when one of the hottest guys in the graduating class complemented her curly hair. It looked as if she would have a conniption. Clair encouraged her to go for him, stating that this was one of their last nights as uncommitted young adults before joining the real world.

Zelda had laughed, arms wrapped around her long-time boyfriend, and said that Nastran would have a better chance at getting a career as a lawyer *before* law school than she would at bagging the hottie.

Zelda always knew how to motivate Nastran.

From that moment on, Nastran put on her resolved face and pounced, asking him about his last football game where he had scored the winning touchdown—which, of course, gave her his full attention for the next hour. Zelda turned to Clair after Nastran had walked away.

"So, Miss Accomplished," she said with a wink, "who's next on *your* touchdown agenda?"

Clair laughed, taking a sip of her tequila sunrise. Usually she preferred vodka, but that night was special. "I think I am going to lay off the dating scene for a while, Zel."

She had smartly broken up with her most recent long-term-dating relationship about four months before graduation. They weren't going to be heading in the same direction, and Clair didn't want things to get emotionally messy when she was trying to focus on creating a new life somewhere else.

Unfortunately, with her lack of employment, she wouldn't be creating much of a new life walking back into her old town.

"Well," Zelda said while she and her boyfriend stared longingly into each other's eyes, "I think I'm done with the dating scene for a while too."

"You better be," he said, hand under her chin. They were so damn cute it was annoying.

Clair was shaken from memory lane when a semitruck decided it wanted to pass another semi, and her temper flared up. She hated it when they did that. What was the point? They were all basically going the same speed—ridiculously slow. Why pass each other?

To drown out the thought of tailgating the guy, Clair stuffed a new CD into the console and listened to the pop-country music fill the car. There was no way someone could be mad with pop-country playing; it was just too happy, even the sad songs.

It had been almost five years since she had been in Healdsburg. Years ago, after that night in the tub, Clair transferred to a different high school, graduated, and sailed off to college, with the intention of never looking back.

She tried not to think about the mysterious voice from the tub, and mostly that worked. But sometimes it slipped through her mind unbidden. In fact, the voice—her conscience as she dubbed it—had become very handy. It helped push her through college and was especially opinionated when it came to her spirituality classes. It was like a part of her brain had opened up—almost like a sub-personality. It specialized in finding knowledge, using both her heart and mind. The voice loved all the spiritual classes, easing her into certain concepts that had sent her to the top of her class and into her professor's office hours for literally hours of conversations on topics that intrigued all three of them.

Having the voice was like having an extra brain to think with, every day.

Still, she liked going against her self-dubbed conscience every once in a while. She had met Zelda when she switched into a government class even though she was supposed to be taking pottery. She didn't know why it happened, why she had that idea, but it worked out. The voice said it wouldn't progress her art degree but didn't give an opinion after that.

In fact, the voice was almost as relaxed as her grandmother, who preferred the simpler life of Healdsburg to Clair's college town. Dotty had made the trip to see Clair at graduation, but she only stayed long enough for them to discuss her return home and how she was moving her belongings.

It wasn't that they weren't friendly. They spoke on the phone sometimes while Clair was away at school, but never really had anything in common. Her grandmother liked collecting antiques more than selling them and was very quiet about her past and even more tight-lipped about Clair's parents.

Clair remembered asking about them once, when she was in kindergarten. She would always remember how her grandmother had knelt down in front of her, the wrinkles around her eyes only beginning to form, and said that they had died suddenly in a car crash when Clair was still an infant, but that she would be there for Clair for whatever she needed.

And for the most part, Clair never felt like she was missing anything.

Her grandmother was both strict and loving, fulfilling both parental roles, and since Clair never attended anything that required one parent or the other (and the fact that she never knew either of her parents because she was so young when they died), it didn't really affect her as much as people thought it should. Dorthea just got cards on Mother's and Father's Day (a comical tradition Clair still kept, preferring the hilarious booby cards for Father's Day and half-naked men cards for Mother's Day).

All in all they had a great system.

Clair didn't realize how close to home she was until she saw her exit on the sign, four miles away.

Wow, she thought. That was fast.

Clair liked to drive fast, so it shouldn't have been a surprise. She enjoyed the way the speed felt—how her adrenaline would pick up as she scanned the mirrors for hiding cops.

You should slow down. You know there are more as you get closer to town.

Yeah, yeah, Clair thought, lifting her foot off the gas a little.

As if on cue, she hit the speed limit just in time to catch a particularly hidden police officer under an upcoming overpass. It was like the voice was her instinct sometimes.

She didn't thank it.

As she pulled off the exit, Clair felt her heart squeeze.

Everything looked the same—the exact same.

She turned down Main Street, looking at all the shops, each owned by a family in town, and the people walking around. Strangers weren't unusual here. Typically, tourists would come to see the wineries or boutique shops, but everyone looked at her car as she drove through, much too fast.

At least I am keeping with outsider tradition, she thought sarcastically.

At the end of the street was a three-way stop sign, and another smaller sign, painted red with green letters that read, "Antiques Ahead!"

Her great-uncle had painted the sign when he and her grandmother first opened the shop in town. The letters were peeling a bit, but mostly Dotty kept repainting it (probably because they had to have the income). Clair had had to work through college, but she didn't mind it much. She learned how to make Excel worksheets at her assistant position for a chiropractic office, and that pretty much paid for everything besides her tuition. She had taken a few loans out to pay for the rest of her college expenses and to cover the tuition she didn't want to bother her grandmother about, and would now be paying them off with a new job. Hopefully soon.

Taking a deep breath, Clair gassed it up the road and through the trees to where her grandmother's house sat at the edge of the forest.

It was worse.

How can it be worse than it was when I left? Clair thought as she pulled into the driveway and turned off the car, killing the country music.

The house was a two-story, country-style green, with a wraparound porch and enough space for a lawn to go around the entire two-acre property—if there had been a lawn. Instead there was only enough dead grass to hint that a lawn had once existed, the black dirt hard and coarse as if someone had taken a shovel and dug up the whole plot up and then left it to dry in the sun. Instead of a fence in the backyard, the open woods of the forest served as the end of the property, allowing creatures of all sorts to wander near to the house from time to time. On the right side was the small one-story building that connected to the house, a sign above the shop indicating the separate store attachment, with just enough room in front for some gravel parking spots outlined with white paint lines that were fading. The rest of the house was so consumed with dead vines that it appeared to be growing from the shrubbery.

Clair got out of the car and walked up the front steps.

It was hard for her to believe that the yard had once been a wonderful garden. But that was before her time, when her great-uncle James had been alive. Apparently, the garden had been the best in town, sporting flowers of beautiful shades and exotic scents. But after James died, her grandmother let the garden rot, until it became a wasteland. Now the only flowers she kept were painted on antiques.

The door opened, and Dotty hurried out for a hug, her spiked gray hair flattened by the purple, rectangular reading glasses she kept like a headband. She smelled like tuna salad and spice, and Clair leaned into the embrace. It felt good to be held after such a long time.

Dorthea pulled back and examined her. Clair never thought about what she did or felt when she was away, until that moment, but they were both independent, and she had never once made Clair feel like her absence was an insult. They had separate lives. When they were apart, they thought of each other, but both were concerned with their immediate situations.

"Clair," she said, "you look good. I'm so proud of you."

Dotty had said this multiple times at Clair's graduation, congratulating her on her achievements and showering her with hugs. Dotty was an affectionate woman, albeit private. But that was okay; Clair was private too.

"Thanks, Grandma," Clair said, "and thanks for letting me move back home. I can't believe there were *no* job openings."

"I know, dear, but that's life," Dotty laughed, amused by her frustration. "I'm sure you will find a job here. And in the meantime," she looked at Clair's car, which was overflowing with things from her college life, "you will have a hell of a job trying to fit all that stuff into your room."

"Yeah," Clair looked back to the car, her forehead creased with the thought of unloading all the crap. "Things start to accumulate after three years of living somewhere else."

Dotty rolled up her sleeves, gave an encouraging smile in Clair's direction, and started toward the car.

It took them about an hour to get everything into her old room, along with some special finagling by Dotty to stuff most of the boxes into the closet, but they managed. After sitting in her old bedroom and staring at the boxes for five minutes, willing them to unpack themselves, Clair decided she needed energy for organizing and headed to the kitchen for some food.

The afternoon sunlight was pouring through the window above the sink, making the teal cabinets a seafoam green. Clair wandered over to the old refrigerator and peered inside: half a carton of orange juice, cheese, eggs that would expire tomorrow, and leftover Chinese food—not a promising start.

Dotty walked into the kitchen, glanced at Clair with her head in the fridge, and chuckled.

"There are a few cans of tuna, and some black beans in the cabinets above the toaster." She grabbed Clair's keys off the small wooden table in the middle of the kitchen. "I don't eat much, but now that there are two of us again and your car is here, I'll run to the store."

Dotty didn't like to drive and would normally walk to the supermarket with her little basket and only get the essentials.

"Don't worry about it, Grandma. I can go," Clair said, closing the refrigerator.

"No, it's okay," Dotty was twirling the keys on her finger. "It could be fun to get behind the wheel again. It's only been a few years." And with a wink, she walked out the door.

Clair didn't like the idea of Dotty behind the wheel, but the supermarket was close, and she was so hungry she let it go, opting instead to eat some tuna salad she found in a plastic container in a pocket of the refrigerator door.

Once satisfied, she walked back to her room and observed the damage. Her stuff barely fit, and the pink painted walls were beginning to peel. Clair looked down at the little lamp on her bedside table, covered in what looked like cobwebs, and shuddered. She didn't want to start unpacking yet.

Instead, she wandered the house, making her way to the garage. The air was stale, and it smelled like mold. Clair pushed the button to open the garage door about fifty times before deciding it was broken. Sighing, she walked outside and approached it from the front, putting her hands underneath and lifting with her legs, trying to force it open.

For a second she wondered if any customers would be coming to the antique shop while her grandmother was gone, but when she glanced over to the front door, a little sign was posted on it that read Closed.

That would serve, she decided, and continued to pull at the door. It finally relented, and she could almost see the shadows fleeing from the sunlight behind all the old boxes. In the garage, she found some gloves, shears, and weed killer and began work destroying the shrubbery around the house.

As she was yanking the dead plants from the ground, Clair thought about what type of job she could hope to find. Her art degree had been fun—throwing objects together in order to create some small sense of meaning—but most artists were starving or gave up and pursued other jobs in the business field. Clair had never really thought about a specific career, but the idea of one in the business world was intriguing.

Once she made it halfway around the front of the house, Clair paused to survey her work. The bright sun was warming her back, and a light summer breeze was chilling the sweat on her neck and face.

After looking at the rest of the house, she decided to complete the task today; it needed to be done. This was their home, had always been their home, and Clair wanted to feel proud of it, even if Dotty didn't care how it looked.

It took the rest of the afternoon, but Clair managed to clear the overgrowth from around the edges of the front of the house and around the sliding door leading out from the back. She piled the dead shrubs in a corner of the backyard, vowing to make a fire pit at some point to get rid of them. Her grandmother had returned when she was in the middle of the war, stared at her for a few minutes, and then unloaded the groceries from the car.

Clair could smell chicken cooking from the open kitchen window, and by the time she finished, her stomach was growling so loudly it sounded like a wild animal. Clair surveyed her work one last time before running into the house, shouting to Dotty that she was going to shower, and hopping up the stairs.

She turned on the faucet in the small bathroom; grabbed her pink pack containing her bathroom essentials from her backpack, throwing it onto the bathroom counter; and began undressing, listening to the shower running. She glanced at the tub in the corner of the room, and a small shiver ran down her spine. It had been so long ago, but the thought still made its way to her core.

It was years ago, the voice said. *You were a different person.*

Clair shook her head and decided it didn't do any good to think about that night. Plus, her hunger and the growling noises from her stomach were making her irritated. She jumped into the shower and was back downstairs in the kitchen ten minutes later. The chicken smelled like barbecue sauce and pepper, and she could see broccoli steaming in a pot on the stove.

"Mmm." She salivated while Dotty pulled potatoes from the microwave. "Smells great."

"You didn't have to clear the yard," Dotty said, cutting the potatoes in half lengthwise and spreading butter on them. Clair grabbed plates and silverware and placed them on the table with some napkins.

"I know, Grandma, but you know how much I like manual labor."

In truth, Clair just didn't want to feel like she was living in an abandoned house. She also knew Dotty would never hire someone to do it.

Dotty narrowed her eyes at the sarcasm in Clair's voice, but shrugged, letting the subject drop.

"Well thanks, dear," she said, pulling the broccoli off the stove and placing it in a bowl.

Dinner was a quiet affair.

Clair ate and asked Dotty questions about the town, but mostly the answers weren't surprising. A couple people had changed, a few had moved, and some new ones had arrived. Dotty didn't keep up with town gossip—she was not very social with anyone—so she didn't have much to say in that regard. When they were done, Clair put the leftovers in a plastic container and washed the dishes while Dotty dried.

"Heading to bed soon?"

Clair hadn't thought about her unorganized room until right then, and wasn't eager to get started after working in the yard all day. A thought struck her.

"Is the Brown Bear still open?"

Dotty laughed. "Yes. Need a good stiff drink before job hunting?"

"Yeah," she said, flicking water at Dotty and sticking her tongue out. "I'm just so excited about it that I need alcohol to contain myself."

They both laughed, and Clair thought it was nice to spend time with her grandmother.

As Clair went to grab her car keys, Dotty tossed her a new house key.

"Don't forget to lock the door when you come home."

Dotty was always so obsessed with locking the door.

Clair was instructed to lock the door like every other child, but unlike normal families, she made her lock the door during the day—and it was a small town, as in nothing bad ever happened here. The one night Clair had forgotten to lock the door, Dotty had come barging into her room in the middle of the night, telling her she was grounded for the next two weeks. Clair never forgot after that.

Clair promised that, yes, for the millionth time, she would remember to lock the door.

As she was walking to the living room, Dotty turned to look at Clair, her smile crinkling the corners of her eyes. "I'm really glad you're home."

Clair felt moisture behind her eyes, but held it back.

"Me too, Grandma."

Clair walked into the Brown Bear fifteen minutes later. It was one of the only places in town that was open past eight on a weeknight.

The bar, which took up half of the space in the small room, looked like a tree cut in half lengthwise. It was situated on its side atop a thick metal base. A few round cocktail tables dotted the floor, with tall wooden chairs, and booths lined the edges across from the bar and next to the small hallway leading to the bathroom. The stuffed bear from which the Brown Bear got its name was at the back, standing on its hind legs, arms swiping at an invisible attacker. There were more people in the bar than she thought would be for a weekday in Healdsburg.

Clair decided against a table and went straight for the bar. Most of the after-hours townspeople were less than savory individuals. Clair recognized a few faces of the kids she went to high school with, who either didn't recognize her or pretended not to; the local cemetery gardener who was always mumbling to himself; the pawn shop owner; and a few other people she didn't recognize, who were either getting drunk or making out.

"What would you like, sweetheart?"

The bartender was standing in front of her behind the bar, cleaning a glass with a raggedy towel and throwing glances at a couple displaying too much affection in one of the booths at the back. His nametag said "Joe." Clair looked behind him to the rows of bottles. There were about ten taps of different ales surrounded by two bookshelves of hard liquor. Clair preferred the latter.

"I'll take a lemon drop please."

Joe tore his attention away from the couple and eyed Clair. "Can I see some ID?"

I never thought you'd ask, she thought sarcastically.

Clair pulled out the small rectangle and passed it to Joe. He put the glass down to examine it with both hands, looking from Clair to her picture on the card and back again. They always did that to her, as she looked younger than most people. A few minutes later, Clair was sipping the best tasting lemon drop she had ever had. The tartness of the lemon was quelled by the sugar on the glass, and the top-shelf vodka sent a warm tingle down her throat.

In less than three sips, she could feel the heat spread through her whole body, a dull numbness taking a firm hold of her senses. It was the one thing she both loved and hated about drinking: she was such a lightweight. Beer was never an option because it filled up her stomach without providing the heated touch that hard alcohol brought. But being a lightweight also meant she didn't have to spend as much money on liquor as her friends did when they would go out.

Thinking about her friends made Clair realize that she was sitting in a bar on a weeknight, alone. It wasn't the best thought.

She needed a snack before she could finish the drink. There were no taxis in Healdsburg, and she would need to drive home. She saw a menu sticking up behind the bar. Clair reached to grab the laminated paper, and even though Joe didn't move from where he was at the other side of the room, Clair saw his eyes flick toward her.

He was not the type of man to be easily robbed.

Clair browsed the options. The Brown Bear had the typical list of fried food, but the menu indicated that food stopped being served at six. She looked at Joe again.

Nope, she thought, you aren't going to be able to convince him to open the kitchen for you, lightweight.

While Clair was debating whether or not to finish the drink and stick around until her buzz wore off, the door opened, and a buxom brunette walked in, dragging a very drunk boy into a seat at the bar. He wobbled a bit and then steadied himself.

"Joe!" the girl shouted, pointing at the boy. "I believe this is yours?"

Joe shook his head and looked the boy straight in the eye.

"Mike, what's wrong with you?"

"I'm drunk!" Mike answered, misunderstanding the rhetorical question, a big grin on his face. "Emily says I'm a no good cea . . . cree . . ."

"Cretin!" Emily shrilled. "You're a no-good cretin, and I am *so* done cleaning up your messes." She stomped toward the bathroom on the other side of the bar. When she passed Clair, she stopped dead, eyes popping.

"Clair Douglas?" she said, eyeing Clair up and down.

"Emily Sanchez?" Clair answered, getting a good look at the girl up close for the first time. Clair hadn't recognized her. They had been friends early in high school, before Clair joined the Christian club. She was one of the people Clair left behind when she started hanging out with only the group members.

"Thought it was you," Emily said, and continued walking to the bathroom.

Clair felt her face flush.

Great, she thought, I'm in town for half a day, and already my past has decided to eat me alive.

Clair decided she didn't want to stay any longer and signaled Joe for the check. As she was signing the bill, she heard a plop in the seat next to her, and looked up. Emily was sitting on the barstool, elbow on the counter, ordering a lemon drop.

"Looked good," she said, taking a long draw from her drink as she watched Joe hoist Mike out of the chair and back through a door behind the bar.

Clair stared at her drink and tried to find the right words. She felt like she should apologize for just dropping their friendship, but she didn't know this Emily anymore. The Emily she remembered was a quiet, slightly plump academic who loved Disney movies more than anything in the world. The person sitting next to her was an exotic beauty with a heated temper.

"So"—Emily turned to her before she could decide—"what happened with you all those years ago?"

Clair's mouth dropped. No one had ever asked her what had happened. Most of the people she knew from before had either moved out of town or had forgotten she existed. Clair shut her lips, took a hard look at the woman sitting next to her, and decided to tell the truth.

Clair told Emily her story. She left out the part about the bathtub. It was weird enough telling her sob story to a girl she barely knew, without implying that she was suicidal at one point in her life.

When she was done, Emily finished her lemon drop and turned to face Clair.

"Wow, I never knew. No one did actually," she looked at Clair, face crumpled in thought.

"What?" Clair asked.

"I guess I just thought that you got pregnant or something, not that you were so destroyed by that club that you left."

Ouch. Clair gulped down the rest of her drink. She had never thought of herself as a quitter, but that time in her life had been the worst, and she only remembered wanting out.

"I mean, I would have done the same thing," Emily said, with a smile, "but I would have killed someone first."

Clair laughed, and Emily joined in while Joe brought them both water.

"Yeah," Emily said, taking a sip, "I understand. You don't have to worry about them, though. They aren't around anymore."

Clair looked up at Emily, her breath hitching in her chest. It was stupid, really, after all this time, to feel anxiety just thinking about those people.

"Why did they leave?" she found herself asking.

"Low interest," Emily chuckled. "Eventually the company stopped funding the division, and the club ceased forming."

Clair couldn't decide how she felt about that. It had been a few years, the sting wasn't as bad anymore, and if they had left when Clair was in high school, she would have been thrilled. But now it just made her sad that they never figured out a way to fix the organization.

"So," Emily said, "where'd you go to college?"

They chatted for a while about classes. Clair learned that Emily had left for Stanford and then returned home prior to graduating to get a job in order to help her parents with money when their restaurant closed. She was still going to the junior college in town, though, majoring in psychology.

"No wonder you were so cool about hearing my sob story," Clair said, nudging Emily.

"Oh, no, it's not my major that makes me a good listener." Emily put her hand to her heart, mock sincerity in her voice. "It's my desire to heal the world, one delinquent at a time."

Clair laughed, feeling nearly sober.

"So, who was that Mike guy?"

"Oh, well"—Emily rolled her eyes, disdain and confusion passing across her face—"he's my latest attempt at a relationship."

"Oh," Clair said. "How long have you been dating?"

"About a year," she said, pushing the ice in her water around with the straw. "Things are going well, as you saw." She sighed and let go of the straw. "Sometimes I just don't know if it's worth it. His parents sent him to reform school a few years ago, before we met, and when he screwed things up there, they sent him to Joe. He is doing as good a job as he can—Joe, not Mike. Mike just keeps screwing things up for himself. But I started liking the bad boys when I learned that princesses and princes are only in the fairy tales."

Clair didn't know what had taught Emily that lesson but thought it would be best not to ask right away. Instead, she said the first thing that came to her mind. "Well, I know that a year feels like a long time, but after a year of—I'm guessing—nights like tonight, can you really see a life with him?"

"Nope," Emily said, signing her bill and getting up from her seat, "but we might have to hang out again before you are able to convince me to dump him."

Later that night as Clair was lying in her old bed, feeling uncomfortable, she replayed her night with Emily, and felt like things might not be as bad as she had imagined, living back home.

As she stared around at the pink walls, the posters of old boy bands, and even worse, all the stuffed animals, she sighed. This was not the environment for building a new life. The bookshelves were dusty, and there were clothes leftover in her closet that no longer fit. This room no longer fit.

Clair decided that tomorrow she would move into the guest bedroom. Too much of the same old things made her feel like she never left, and she wanted a new start.

After she and Emily had exchanged numbers at the bar, they said their goodbyes for the evening. Clair insisted that Emily send her a text when she got home, to which Emily looked so shocked Clair laughed before explaining that it was a tradition she had kept with her friends in college. Emily reluctantly agreed, saying that in a town like Healdsburg it would be a good thing if she got abducted, because the local news would finally have an interesting story.

Emily texted just as Clair was about to fall asleep: "Made it home. Meet me tomorrow at the college."

Maybe it was because Clair didn't have a job, or because she didn't want to organize the things in her room, or because it was something to do. Whatever the reason, she agreed to audit one of Emily's classes.

At least it was art history.

Currently, the professor was discussing a painting by Giovanni Baglione, called *Sacred and Profane Love.*

The image depicted what looked like a beautiful male angel poised above another less masculine and slightly overweight angel, his right arm reaching up behind him toward heaven as if to evoke a lightning bolt. Behind the avenging angel, in the bottom left-hand corner of the frame, was a demon-like creature painted a defused red, with horns and the face of a human in shock.

The image was startling. Emily, however, couldn't be bothered.

Instead, she was furiously beginning a text over and over, deleting each failed attempt in a manner that reminded Clair of a cartoon she had once seen.

"Em," Clair whispered, trying not to draw any attention, "whatcha doing?"

Emily glanced sideways at Clair for a fraction of a second in a way that said, "You should know this already," and went back to scribbling. Resigning from her duty as newly established friend, and assuming the letter had something to do with Mike and last night, Clair sighed and leaned back in the chair to reevaluate the painting.

The angel on the bottom must have done something to receive this type of reaction from the avenger, but there was something wrong with the attacker's face: it was serene, lacking any sign of anger, or any emotion at all. If the avenging angel was angry, the artist would have painted some hint of anger, right?

No, she thought, the angel is just doing his job—his duty. Like a trained soldier, he is just snuffing out an obvious loose end.

But even then, the voice continued, *why not attack the demonic creature in the corner? Why attack one of its own kind?*

"Also known as Clair-obscura, a process artists would use to stress the differences between light and dark . . ."

Thinking she heard her name, Clair decided to pay more attention, but the class was already packing to leave.

"I look forward to reading your essays on the evaluation of light and dark within the pieces we have been reviewing. Including this one!" was the professor's last attempt at holding the students' attention before he too began to leave the room.

"What was that called again?" Emily had resumed the world of the living and was frantically writing down notes.

"Clair-obscura," said Clair.

"No," Emily sighed, "that was just the description. He said another name before that I didn't get."

"Oh, sorry," Clair shrugged. "Maybe it's online?"

Emily got up from the chair, telling Clair to hurry up because she only had fifteen minutes until her calculus class and she wanted to brainstorm the positive and negative effects of homicide.

Clair spent the rest of the afternoon following Emily, attending her classes and feeling a whole lot better about graduating. For one thing, she liked not having homework anymore. Unfortunately, she didn't like her lack of income.

When she got home that night, Clair made dinner for Dotty and herself—simple stir fry with a loaf of sourdough—and ate her meal in the spare bedroom, finally unpacking the boxes.

Clair moved the old books off the bookshelf in the spare room into a box, placing them by the side entrance to the antique shop that connected through the kitchen into the house. She wasn't sure what her grandmother—who was currently running numbers in the shop with her own dinner—would want to do with them, but she needed the space. She threw her clothes into the four-drawer mahogany chest in the corner of the room and placed her face wash, bath gel, and general toiletry supplies in the adjoining bathroom.

Once everything was relatively set up, she surveyed her work.

Clair had decided to keep the lace curtains on the window that stretched to the floor, and she brought the desk in from her old room, but left the television. She was glad this room was larger than her old one, because she had enough space to fit her queen-size bed from college and her two wooden bookshelves.

Satisfied, she fell onto the bed and thought about the positives in her life. She had made a friend and was in a new room. This, she decided, wasn't a bad start for her first few days home.

Flipping onto her stomach, she leaned over to grab the postcards from Zelda and Nastran off the wooden side table. They had even sent a few pictures of them sipping piña coladas on the beach, and a spicy photo of them with a hot surfer dude they named Alex. (However, on the back, Nastran wrote that they weren't quite sure that was his name.) Overall they were having a great time, and encouraged Clair to find a job and get her explicit body part out to join them.

Clair decided that tomorrow she would begin her job search.

EMILY

Emily had to admit that a text probably wasn't going to solve her relationship problems.

Even though she wasn't ready to give up on Mike, Clair had a point: he needed to shape up or ship out. Emily tried typing out how she felt in class today, while Clair watched with concern written all over her face, but it was no good.

She just couldn't figure out her boyfriend.

On the one hand, she loved him. Emily knew she loved him, but *liked* him? His personality was prickly at the best of times, but he was smart. He just didn't show it.

She walked in the front door of her parents' house and was met with the smell of carnitas and fresh tortillas.

"Hola, Mija," her mother's voice rang through the house like a bell.

She turned the corner to find her mother, Laura, stirring a pot of beans with one hand and adding spices with the other. Emily thought her mother was the most beautiful woman in the world. She had long, muscular legs attached to a wide waist that led to full breasts and puckered lips. Right now her hair was up in a messy bun, with bits of black curls falling around her face as she cooked.

Even though her parents had enforced English in their house—either to give Emily a head start in school or to just keep her up with the other students, she wasn't sure—Emily still understood enough Spanish to converse with anyone fluidly.

"Hola, Mom."

"How were your classes today?" Laura turned to face her daughter, eyes bright.

"They were alright."

Ever since she had returned from Stanford, she didn't have the heart to tell her parents that the junior college classes were not academically challenging. Emily never mentioned it because they would insist she go back to Stanford, and even though they would never admit it, she knew that they needed her rent.

Emily worked part-time as a hairdresser for the local salon. She enjoyed the science and chemistry involved with the dyes, and loved it when her clients walked out feeling like new. Who wouldn't want to have a place where they could sit in a chair for a few hours and stand up new again?

In fact, since she had come back to town, the salon received more patrons than ever. Even some of the older men, who believed pampering to be a female affair, would come into the shop and enjoy a wash and cut.

Plus, the salon never lacked gossip.

Just the other day a woman came in and was talking with Trisha, one of the other part-timers, about seeing the mayor at the local fast-food restaurant with an unidentified male that was not her husband.

When Trisha asked her client if they were doing the deed, the client looked confused and said she hadn't seen anything but would keep her eyes open.

Emily had tried not to laugh.

Eavesdropping wasn't something she liked doing in the shop, but sometimes it was just too interesting to overhear all the stories.

Speaking of stories.

"Mom, you'll never guess who is back in town," Emily said, watching Laura turn back toward her.

"Who?"

"Clair Douglas. Do you remember her?"

"Oh, yes," Laura said with a smile, "the little girl you would play princess games with when you were in middle school?"

"Yep, that's the one." Emily grabbed an apple off the kitchen table and took a bite. "In high school, she joined that club and went AWOL for a bit. But I guess she's back now, recently graduated."

"You are going to graduate soon too, right?" her mother said, moving the beans off the burner and heating corn tortillas over the open flame.

"Yeah."

She would get her associates degree within the year, but after that, there was nothing else she could accomplish at the college. She decided to lie to her parents about being done with school and just continue taking random classes and working at the salon until her dad could find a better job. "But it might take me longer than I thought."

"These things take time." Laura gave Emily an encouraging smile. Neither of her parents had gone to college, so they didn't understand the degree process.

Before the recession, their restaurant made enough money to support their mortgage and Emily's tuition payments. Now, they were living off her rent money and her father's job working for the recycling center.

Emily hoped one day the restaurant would reopen, but now was not the time.

Her dad came home just in time for dinner, ate quickly, and went to bed. Emily knew he was upset with her because she was providing for the family, but times were hard, and she wished he would just get over it so they could go back to being happy.

The three of them had always been close, even when the restaurant was booming and her parents were busy. Emily remembered sitting in the restaurant's kitchen, talking to the additional chefs while her mom cooked and her dad supervised, and both of them running the books at night. As soon as the shop would close, the three of them would go home and play board games, talk about their day, and laugh for hours. There used to be so much laughing. Emily could remember her parents smiling at each other, and the loving way they moved around each other—like the sun around the earth. Now they barely spoke, and she knew their relationship was strained.

After her mom went to sleep, Emily trudged into her room and was getting ready for bed, when she got a text from Mike: "hey ther seewet thang."

Emily let out a frustrated sigh and texted him back. "Are you drunk again?"

A few minutes later she received his reply, "mayyybeeeee vom join me."

Emily got into bed, sent a reply of "No," and turned her phone off. She knew in the morning there would be about ten texts from him saying random things, but she didn't care. Tonight he was on his own.

Right before she dozed off, Emily had a vision of Mike falling into a ditch. She leaned over and turned her phone back on.

Just in case, she thought.

Clair

The next day Clair woke up early, put on her hiking boots, grabbed her camera bag, and headed out the back door and into the woods.

As a kid she would explore the closer trails, pretending she was on an adventure in Medieval times or that she was a Native American making paints and eating bugs. She only ever ate one bug, and it wasn't that big of a deal.

The morning was brisk, and she could feel the light fog pressing in around her. She followed the worn trail uphill for a while, but where it began to loop back down toward the town, she pushed off the trail and further up the mountain, enjoying the strain in her muscles as gravity tried to hold her down. Her breath became more and more labored as she worked her muscles, and after a few weeks of not exercising, she could feel the strain in her legs painfully toying with her willpower to keep going. Clair was surprised, considering the way she was eating lately, that she was able to hike as far as she was without stopping.

Hearing the sound of a nearby creek, Clair stopped going up and horizontally pursued the sound. It was about three feet wide, flowing freely through stones and moss as it zigzagged along down the hill. She could see water skaters and small fish fighting against the current, clinging to the plant life. A few maple trees were growing near the water's edge, and Clair sat, leaning against the rough bark while she stretched her legs.

She must have been about halfway up the mountain. At least, *she* called them mountains.

It wasn't that the hills were small, but they weren't that high either. They were clustered together, some beginning halfway up another, and it was fun to try to see where they led. Once, when Clair was younger, she had seen a cave that she was sure had to have belonged to a local mountain lion, but wasn't brave enough to check.

Pulling out her camera, Clair dialed up the manual settings and snapped a few photos. She loved the way the shutter sounded when it opened and closed, like the world was being sucked into the camera and then released, leaving an image behind. Photography wasn't considered valuable enough to be a major at her college, but she loved it all the same. It was like painting: she looked at the world, framed it, and then captured it in a meaningful way.

She just wanted some time to think. There was something about the forest that spoke to her heart, and while the last few days at home hadn't been as difficult a transition as she had originally thought, it was still a big life change.

Here the forest felt alive, and so did she.

As she was relaxing, her mind began to nag at her about finding a job. While she was going through college, she had one goal: to be the best she could at her major and graduate on time. Now that the goal was completed, Clair realized she had never considered a direct career path.

She decided that whatever the outcome of her search today, she would be okay. If anything, she could always take over the antique shop when Dotty retired. It wasn't her ideal job, but it was the family business.

Finally relaxed, Clair got up and began shooting pictures of the stream and water life. She liked taking macro shots by leaning over the water and putting her lens as close as she dared. She never looked at the images until she was downloading them to her computer, preferring the surprise of seeing her pictures on a larger screen as if they were being developed like original film in a darkroom.

Satisfied with her work, she walked over to her bag, put the camera away, and began the trek back down the hill. She never knew if she was going directly toward home, but walking downward would always take her to town, and on this particular hill, Clair knew she would hit the trail before popping into someone's backyard. It had happened once when she was younger, but the family had accepted her apology rather easily. However, it wouldn't be the same situation if it happened now, so she decided to try to follow the path she had made on her ascent.

The morning birds were all singing by the time Clair made it down the hill, the fog burned off and crisp warm sunlight pouring through the trees.

She walked up to the house, quietly entered through the sliding door, and walked upstairs to her new room. She took a shower, massaging her calves and taking the time to wash her hair thoroughly. She would need to be her most professional self today to impress potential employers.

After drying and straightening her hair, she picked out a black pencil skirt, with a light pink button-up blouse and short tan heels. She liked the way the clothes fit her figure, accenting her small curves and making her chest look more substantial (she mentally thanked the push-up bra from Zelda). She walked over to her small mirror on the wall and picked off a long silver necklace, and finished the outfit with a pair of pearl earrings Dotty had given her as a present for graduating.

As Clair was toasting her breakfast tart, Dotty came downstairs, grabbed some coffee, and wished her luck, before walking into the antique shop.

A few minutes later, Clair was in her car, strawberry tart in one hand, wheel in the other, driving the two short miles to downtown. She parked next to the sidewalk right before Main Street, the road that boasted fewer than thirty businesses and shops.

She passed a hardware store, a doughnut shop, and a gym, before entering the first boutique. It was a small shop that had custom jeans on display as well as a few designer handbags and jewelry. The woman behind the counter was middle-aged, reading the latest copy of *In Style*.

"Hello," Clair said, her best smile in place. "I was wondering if you were hiring?"

"No," the woman said without looking at her. "Sorry."

Deciding that it was only stop one, Clair kept her positive attitude and continued her journey downtown. The rest of her attempts were not as nerve-racking as the first: the butcher took her resume and smiled at her, but she doubted there would be a call back for her in that profession, and she left her information with an administrative assistant at the city council building, who listened to her skills and promised to give the information to her boss.

As she was crossing the intersection to head back down the other side of Main Street, Clair noticed a small flower shop in the corner, whose sign read "Forever Flowers." Even though she couldn't keep plants alive for long, Clair figured they might be in need of a secretary.

Entering the shop was like walking into a wall of scent: lilac, jasmine, vanilla. There were birds of paradise, daisies, roses, calla lilies, carnations, and more—as well as the biggest selection of flora that Clair had ever seen. She was examining a hybrid of orchid when a portly woman, a little younger than her grandmother, walked around the corner and nearly dropped the fern she was carrying.

"Oh!" she said, collecting herself and placing the fern on the counter. "Sorry, you gave me a fright! Wasn't expecting anyone to be in so early. What can I help you with?"

She had a kind face and an easy smile. Her nametag, which was covered in flower stickers, said her name was Jean. Even though Clair didn't think she would find any work here, she introduced herself and asked Jean if she was hiring.

"I'm sorry, dear," Jean said, frowning. "There is barely enough work here for me! Did you already try the city council office? They usually hire young people like yourself."

"Yes, thank you," Clair said, trying not to show the disappointment on her face. She was starting to feel like this was a hopeless venture. "I'll just keep looking."

"You look familiar," Jean said, studying her. "Where do your parents live?"

Since this woman had already said she wouldn't hire her, Clair decided it wouldn't hurt to explain how she had moved back in with her grandmother, who owned the antique shop.

You know, Clair thought, the one everyone thinks is crazy.

"Oh!" said Jean, her face lighting up. "You're Dotty's granddaughter. How good!"

That threw her. Clair had never heard a positive response from any townsperson when Dotty was mentioned. Even in grade school Clair's friends' parents rarely let their children go to her house for sleepovers.

"How do you know my grandmother?" she asked, curious.

"She used to sell me some of her flowers. I always made a profit when I had her stock in my store," Jean said wistfully. "Will you tell her I said hello? I see her walking downtown sometimes when I get here early enough, but she is always in such a hurry!"

"Yes, of course," Clair said, liking this woman more by the minute. She made a mental note to invite Jean over for dinner sometime. If Clair could make friends, then Dotty could at least have *one* ally in town. "I'll be sure to let her know."

Jean smiled, and Clair left the flower shop feeling a lot better. Maybe there was still hope for them in this town.

As she walked, the wind picked up and brought with it the smell of fresh coffee. Dotty didn't like to keep coffee in the house because she considered it a legalized drug. Clair, however, wouldn't have made it through school without the elixir.

She headed for the smell and found the small shop, aptly named Awake, near the middle of Main Street. There were three people in line and a few more sitting at the tables reading, working on laptops, or chatting with friends.

Clair patiently waited in line while the other customers were helped.

Looking around, she saw a small bookshelf sporting Awake mugs, some packaged coffee, and other caffeine-related products.

She decided it would be easier on her budget if she made coffee at home each day. Clair checked to make sure no one was getting into line behind her, jumped out to grab one of the coffee bags, and bounced back into her spot. When it was her turn, she asked the barista for a dark roast drip with two pumps of hazelnut. She also held up the coffee beans she had grabbed from the shelf.

"That's a good one," the barista said, pointing at the bag. Melody, Clair read on her nametag, was a slight woman, about Clair's age, with short red hair and a pierced eyebrow.

"Good," Clair breathed. "I'm going to need it."

A man came out of the back door, smiling and holding a large box. He glanced at Melody, and then at Clair, his eyes lingering on her for a few seconds, before turning and placing the box on a shelf. He was hot—tall and muscular, with dark skin and brown eyes. He started unloading the box, and Clair admired the way his T-shirt bunched up around his biceps.

"Why's that?"

Clair forced her attention back to Melody, trying to remember what she had said. "What?"

"You said you needed the coffee. Why did you say it that way?"

Clair sighed. "I must have dropped my resume off at about fifteen places this morning, and I don't think I'm any closer to being employed." Clair wasn't sure why she was telling this girl her story, but she shrugged it off.

Melody pointed to the front window. A sign read, Now Hiring.

"Oh!" Clair turned back to Melody, who was giggling. "I don't have any barista experience."

"That's okay," she said. "I didn't either. Andrew!"

Andrew was the hot boy standing right behind her still unloading the box. He turned around, glancing between Clair and Melody.

"Clair here is looking for a job," Melody said, gesturing to Clair.

Andrew looked over at Clair again.

"What hours can you work?" he said, with a genuine smile, the kind of smile that made a girl's stomach feel like melting butter.

"Well," Clair said, "I don't really have a life right now, so whenever you need me."

"Perfect," he said. "You start tomorrow morning. Leave a copy of your resume with Melody."

"Wow, thanks!" Clair shouted, feeling on top of the world.

Andrew threw her a blank name tag and apron.

"Don't thank him yet," Melody said, casting a sly glance at Andrew. "He will have you working the earliest shifts we have."

But Clair didn't care—she had a job! And a hot boss. What could be wrong with that?

Clair made it home in time for lunch. Dotty had cooked meatloaf and was slicing it as Clair walked in the door.

"Well don't you look professional," she said, smiling. "Glad you're using those earrings."

"Thanks, Grandma," Clair said, feeling elated as she sat at the small wooden table in the kitchen. It was made of a dark redwood and only large enough for two chairs. Clair preferred to use it as an island for cutting and preparing food, but didn't feel the need to bother Dotty about getting a bigger table, when it was always just the two of them.

"Did you have any luck downtown today?" Dotty asked, dishing out carrots and slices of the loaf.

"Well, not at first," Clair said, taking a large bite, "but then I stopped at the coffee shop, and they offered me a chance. I start tomorrow."

"Coffee shop, huh?" Dotty sat down and started cutting her meat into smaller pieces, a wry smile on her face. "A legalized drug. Good job, dear."

She was a tea person.

She knew her grandmother was happy for her despite what she said, mostly because Dotty was worried Clair would get bored moving back home. Having a job would keep her busy.

"How's the antique shop today?"

"It's never really busy until the weekend when the wineries are open," Dotty said, "so the morning was slow, and I suspect the rest of the day will be a little slow too. But I put those books from the spare bedroom in the shop, so maybe they will sell sometime this century."

Clair didn't know what Dotty did on slow days. It must be boring to be alone all day with no one entering the shop.

That reminded her. “Grandma,” she said, “I ran into a woman named Jean today, she runs the flower shop downtown.”

“Yes?” Dotty was focused on cutting her meat.

“Well, she said you used to sell her the best flowers in town. She seemed nice.” Clair let the idea hang there. She knew Dotty didn’t like to socialize anymore, but couldn’t help but feel it would be good for both of them to have some friends in town.

“Yes, I did, and she is nice,” Dotty said, glancing up at Clair, the question in her eyes if not on her lips.

“I think I might invite her over for dinner some time,” Clair said, looking down at her plate and taking a particularly large bite of meatloaf. There were a few seconds of silence before Dotty finally spoke.

“Fine,” she sighed.

Clair looked up and smiled.

“Just give me some notice. The antique shop keeps things pretty messy around here.”

“No problemo,” Clair said, feeling proud of her grandmother. It took courage for her to have agreed, considering the people in town were so negative about her.

After lunch, Dotty went back to the store, and Clair went up to her room to fiddle around on the Internet, looking up information on coffee shops and being a barista. Most of the blogs were just about coffee in general or people fighting about the best mochaccino. After an hour, Clair gave up and was reading a book when Emily texted, “It’s Friday, you need a social life. Meet at bowling at 8.”

DORTHEA

Her return has been normal, Dotty thought, putting away the leftovers from dinner. She was worried when she came home to find Clair ripping down the shrubbery around the house, but it hadn't affected the enchantments that protected them.

Clair was so impulsive.

Dotty smiled, remembering how Clair looked in her pink tank top and jean shorts, wearing her old gardening gloves and looking so determined. She really was just like Dorthea in her youth. The thought brought a larger smile to her face.

After she finished washing, Dotty walked over to the little door that separated the antique shop from the rest of the house, placing a hand on the handle. Warm.

Good, she thought, turning the knob and walking into the shop. Dotty had a system: everything was okay when the door knob was slightly warm, but when something went wrong, it would be ice cold.

Clair had almost discovered this trick when she was about twelve, but Dotty blamed it on the air conditioning, and Clair let it go.

She walked into the shop, the cold night air bringing goose bumps to the bare skin on her arms. It would heat up, though, come morning, the sun hitting the roof throughout the day, casting rays of light across the treasures.

Clair had gone out bowling, of all things, so she had some time to herself.

The antique shop never failed to take her breath away. Walls upon walls of items, big and small, zigzagging through the space, creating a magical land where one random piece had a relationship with another totally unrelated artifact. There was a dialog that no writer could ever create. It was the best kind of magic.

Dotty passed the section devoted to glass, admiring once again the beautiful antiquities of Italian glassware she and James had found in that little shop off the canal. The owner had been an older woman, who only spoke Italian. But that hadn't mattered to James, who could speak any language, and he talked with her for over an hour, making her smile the entire time. James had to have the whole set. It cost them a fortune, but he said they were too beautiful to leave without. She also knew that the owner needed the money, and James was always liberal with his finances.

Sighing, she turned another corner and found her desk, situated in the middle of the shop. It was just out of the way enough that people could walk past it and not be distracted by the multitude of papers she had strewn all over. She always had more room to think here, surrounded by her past life, than she ever felt anywhere else.

She sat down in the mahogany high-back chair James had bought her in Southern Africa, the handles hand-cut to look like rivers flowing over, and began shifting through her papers.

They had enough money to keep them going for a long while yet. Even if the savings ran out, there were enough non-magical artifacts of gold or silver to pawn away. Thinking of money reminded Dotty of Clair's new job.

"Clair a barista?" Dotty snickered thinking about it. She loved her dearly, and knew Clair could do anything she put her mind to, but Dotty had always hoped she would find a career away from Healdsburg.

The thought worried her.

So far everything had been fine. Clair had found a friend in Emily, who seemed normal. There was that one moment years ago when something happened in that club in high school, but she had pulled herself together and moved on.

Dotty was proud of her.

So long as Clair remains a secret to the realm, she thought, I can keep her safe.

It wasn't a question, but still, she waited for the feeling that everything would be alright, that her small plea had been heard by the unknown, and accepted.

That feeling didn't come.

CLAIR

Clair arrived at the bowling alley a little before eight. It was situated near the edge of town and was large enough to hold half of Healdsburg. Twenty-five lanes, each boasting live television scoreboards, adorned with a large picture that ran down the entire wall above the lanes depicting a ball crashing into pins.

Clair sat down at one of the round tables that separated the food area from the lanes, and watched other people bowl.

She liked being early to events, but it only just occurred to her that this might have been one of those times she should have been fashionably late.

A few minutes later Emily walked in with three people in tow: a blonde girl who was being escorted by a boy with his hand around her waist, and behind them, Andrew.

Clair felt the heat rush to her face and was immediately thankful that she had a tan.

Emily waved at Clair and walked over, introducing the tall blonde as Tiffany; the boy with his hand around her waist as her boyfriend, Alex; and Andrew.

Clair waved at Andrew, feeling a little awkward. Emily noticed the familiarity.

"How do you two know each other?"

"Remember when I texted saying I got a job?" Clair said, gesturing to Andrew.

Emily laughed and just smiled at Andrew, who also smiled but seemed just as uncomfortable as Clair.

Clair asked how they all knew each other, and Emily said that they had met in an economics class a few semesters prior.

"Oh," Clair said, looking at Andrew. "I didn't know you were going to the college."

"I'm not majoring in managing a coffee shop, if that's what you are asking," Andrew said with a laugh. Clair liked the way he laughed; it was infectious. He was just one of those people you instantly liked.

"Sorry," she said, feeling stupid. "I didn't mean it like that."

"It's okay," he said. "It's better than taking out student loans. It's just going to take me longer to graduate."

"Yeah," Clair said, sighing. "I feel you on that one."

He grabbed a blue ball, and she grabbed a pink one, following Emily and the others to a lane in the middle of the ally.

"Why's that?" Andrew said, watching Clair practice inserting her fingers into the ball, judging its weight.

"What?" she said, mentally kicking herself for the second time for not paying attention.

Andrew laughed again. "Why do you 'feel me on that'?"

Clair tried to ignore the way he had just said to feel him, and focused on answering the question.

"Well, that's why I needed that job you gave me," Clair said. "Student loan bills will be coming in the mail soon, and I need some type of income to pay them off."

"I didn't *give* you anything, Clair," Andrew laughed, leaning playfully into her space. "You will earn it tomorrow."

Clair felt her face grow hot, and turned to watch Emily throw her first shot.

Strike.

Clair wished she had bowled more in college. Andrew must have seen the worry on her face.

"Don't worry," he said. "Emily has been bowling for a few years now. I think she imagines the pins as Mike's face."

Clair laughed. Emily's relationship problems were well known.

When it was her turn, Clair knocked down five pins and considered that a good start. Emily smiled and gave her some pointers while Alex and Tiffany went off to grab some pitchers of beer. When they came back, they poured Clair a cup, which she accepted gratefully, sipping the tart-smelling liquid and trying not to make a face.

They bowled three games. Emily won two, and Andrew won the final round. Clair came in last all three games, but her score did get above seventy during the last round.

However, by scoring the lowest game in the bowling alley's history during the first round, she earned a pat on the back from the elderly owner. Andrew said she did a good job and would get better with time.

All in all, the night was exactly what Clair needed—some fun with a group of people just like her, stuck in Healdsburg trying to figure out their lives.

As she was walking to her car, Emily ran up to Clair, eyes locked on Andrew as he unlocked his car across the parking lot. "Have a good day at work tomorrow," she said, with a wink.

Chris

hy isn't it moving?"

Chris stood a few feet from where he could sense The Gate. Usually it would have moved on by now, but it hadn't.

"Why is it still here?"

As Chris was pacing around the outer levels of the barrier, he started to hum. It was just something he did to relieve stress when he was overburdened with thought. He didn't know the tune. It wasn't a popular radio song or any other known song, but he hummed it anyway.

Something must be wrong, he thought for the millionth time.

If The Gate didn't move, it would attract the wrong attention. He was sure of it. He wasn't sure how he knew, but he just did. Like almost everything else in his new life, it was instinctual.

Chris kicked the nearest tree, shaking it to the roots.

"Just move already!" he shouted.

But The Gate remained silent, only a breath of a presence amongst the still trees.

No wildlife would live here; the animals knew better. Some would flit in and past when The Gate was gone, but plants were the only things that could live near the barrier and not feel uncomfortable.

Chris realized that waiting for The Gate to move was like watching paint dry. He let out a long, heated breath through his nostrils and decided to go for a walk.

Even though he didn't need to exercise, he loved feeling alive. His muscles stretched as his legs pushed him up the hill, through the forest, and out of the bowl where The Gate still sat. He reached the top of the hill, admiring the beauty of Healdsburg in the early morning, before walking down through the woods toward the town.

Before he knew it, he had reached the path onto Main Street.

Chris didn't feel like talking with anyone today, so he shielded himself. One of the best parts of being what he was: the ability to become unseen. It wasn't that he was invisible. If someone concentrated hard enough, and if he wasn't moving, they could see him. But people were always so preoccupied that it never happened.

And so he walked, and thought, and hoped that The Gate would move.

It was early, and there weren't many people out yet in the town. He liked walking in the morning when he didn't have to talk to anyone. It wasn't that he was unsocial, but acting human made him weary. For the most part, when he had to interact with the townspeople, they believed his story and found other things to gossip about, but it could still become a problem in a small town; there were only so many interesting stories, and Chris didn't want to become one of them.

A car came speeding up the road.

As the driver passed, she locked eyes with him.

Chris stopped dead in his tracks.

CLAIR

She was going to be late. She hated being late.

Clair kicked herself inwardly for staying and drinking wine with Emily last night at her parents' house, and then unceremoniously passing out on her couch.

She smiled.

They had so much fun staying up until the early morning talking about nothing in particular. Clair loved having a close friend again, especially since she had feared coming home to be alone.

But now she was going to be late to her first day of work.

Clair jammed the keys into her car and apologized for not letting it warm up as she slammed into reverse. The car jerked as she backed out of the spot, but when she pulled out of the court, it stopped being angry, and purred like usual.

I love you, car, Clair thought as she sped into town.

It was about five in the morning, the summer sun just beginning to hit the streets through the fog. Clair decided that at this hour the quickest way to get home to change would be directly through Main Street.

She turned off the small road that led down from where Emily lived, and onto a main road.

She had so much to do today.

Her shift at Awake would last eight hours, and her bank account thanked her. After the night out bowling, Clair was worried that working with Andrew would be difficult. But the first few days of training with him hadn't been as bad as they could have been. She only messed one thing up—putting the decaf coffee in the regular coffee machine—to which Andrew laughed and said most people wouldn't notice. He was fun to work with and preferred an encouraging approach to teaching, unlike Melody, who liked to scream "Hussle!" at Clair every chance she got, laughing like a villain the entire time.

The next phase of training would be the most intense part of the day, where Clair would learn how to make the fancy drinks with steamed milk and syrups, followed by a few hours of supervised customer interaction. Clair was looking forward to working with people.

She was about to make the right-hand turn onto Main Street, for a straight shot home, when the light turned red.

Damn, she thought while she waited for the light to turn green again.

There was no one on the road, but the lights in Healdsburg were all timed, and this light was the longest in existence. When it finally turned green, she raced down the road past all the little closed shops that made the street look like a ghost town.

Halfway home, she noticed a person walking. Thinking it might be her grandmother, she stared. As she passed, he looked up into her eyes.

Clair felt a shiver go down her spine before she passed him.

Weird, she thought, blaming her lack of male interaction for the last six months. Maybe she should start dating again.

Shaking her head to clear that thought, she sped up the hill, slammed the car into park, and sprinted into the house. Deciding there would be no time for a shower, she washed her face, brushed her teeth, and pulled her hair into a very barista-like bun, pausing in her hurry to put on some liquid eyeliner and mascara.

Clair looked at her features in the mirror. She didn't dislike her hair pulled back, but it accented her heart-shaped face and made her look younger. In fact, there had been a few times after a workout that she and her friends had gone for drinks and the bouncers had looked at her ID like it was a very good fake. She always hated it when that happened.

Oh well, no time, she thought as she grabbed her new red apron and nametag. She had smartly adorned it with a gold star sticker from her old room. It made her name stand out, and she hoped it gave her boss the impression that she was a keeper.

In many ways, the voice spoke, the suggestion palpable.

Clair inwardly narrowed her eyes at it before shaking her head for the second time that morning and running downstairs into the kitchen to grab a sugary pastry she would have to hike off later, when she almost crashed into Dotty.

"Oh!" Clair said, steadying herself. "Morning Grandma—sorry running late—back for dinner!"

"Good morning, Clair," Dotty laughed. She was wearing her walking shoes and sporting a bright pink beanie.

"Love the beanie, Grandma," Clair laughed as she plundered the pastry basket, grateful she had thought to go to the store yesterday. She didn't know why her grandmother only kept healthy food in the house. It was nice but also extremely inconvenient when she was running late.

"I stole it from your old room. I hope you don't mind," Dotty said, watching as Clair poured filtered water into a purple plastic bottle. "Is something wrong with that room?" she added, face crumpled with concern.

"Oh." Clair had forgotten to explain why she moved into the guest room. "Nothing's wrong with the room, Grandma. I just wanted a change."

"Okay." Dorthea smiled at Clair. "Just checking, dear."

Clair smiled back, wished her a good walk, and flew out the door.

As soon as she parked—on a street directly off Main, in a spot almost too small for her four-door Toyota—she flung open her car door and ran into the coffee shop just as the clock reached six.

Andrew was laughing behind the counter, but Melody looked pissed.

"Pay up," he said, hand extended toward Melody.

"Damn it, Clair," Melody said, passing Andrew a five-dollar bill and walking into the storage closet.

"You had a bet going?" Clair laughed, pulling on her apron and fastening it behind her back.

"She should have known better than to bet against you," Andrew said, with a heartbreaking smile.

Clair felt her stomach flutter as she turned to fill the half-and-half and milk dispensers. This was definitely going to be a problem.

Clair learned that it would be her responsibility, as the only barista with a college degree, to go through the mail. Most of the letters were solicitations, product promotional flyers, and local business deals. Andrew told Clair to put the coupons out on the table where the creamer and sugar were set, because the customers appreciated it and would grab them throughout the week.

As Andrew was opening the windows and starting the coffee machines, Clair noticed an inventory list and boxes that had shipped from the company where they bought their goods. There weren't any customers in the shop yet, and she wanted to make herself useful, so she started unpacking boxes and checking to make sure everything that was ordered had arrived. There was one missing paper towel roll.

"Hey, Andrew," she said, looking from the order slip to the stuff she had piled around the shop, and back again. "I think we are missing a paper towel roll."

She was still looking at the piles when, all of a sudden, he was behind her, glancing at the list.

Their bodies weren't touching, but she could feel his warm breath near her ear, and noticed he smelled like coffee and vanilla. She looked up at him, their faces inches apart, and his eyes met hers.

"Um, it's okay," he said, looking from the list to the inventory on the floor. "It's only one roll."

"Okay," she said, moving away from him and trying to breathe normally again.

What's wrong with me? she thought. He was her boss for gosh sake.

The rest of the day passed in silence. Andrew, Melody, and Clair worked side by side without any more incidents on Clair's part. She stayed as far away from him as possible without being too obvious.

She couldn't afford a boyfriend right now any more than she could afford to lose her job.

And in this case, they were one in the same.

After work, Clair went home to find Dotty busy with customers. Instead of joining her in the shop, she decided to change into her hiking clothes, grab her camera, and head up the mountain. It had been a few days since her last hike, and she still had a few hours until sunset.

After she passed the creek she stopped at last time, Clair went further up the mountain until she reached the top, and looked down.

The forest spread out all around her. She could see most of the hills from this height. Only a few were higher than the one she just climbed. It almost created a bowl, with all the trees sloping inward and down toward the center.

Turning around, she could see the entire town of Healdsburg spread out below, and it really was small. Main Street was only as long as her pinky from where Clair stood. The tiny houses and streets were dotting the land like toys, until they reached the vineyards that went on and on into the distance, their expansive green fields soon to be overrun with grapes.

Judging by the sun, she still had a couple of hours, and she had never been past this hill.

The forest grew denser as she descended into the bowl, and about a half mile down she spotted a deer amongst the trees. Quietly, she took out her camera and was able to snap a few pictures before it pranced away. Clair liked it here; the forest was thick, untouched, and wild. As she traveled deeper, the sounds got quieter. It wasn't until she was nearing the bottom of the bowl that she stopped to listen. Usually a creek would make noise, or the birds and smaller animals would produce some rustling sound.

Here there was nothing. It was too still.

Straining her ears, Clair realized there was something, a faint buzzing coming from somewhere in front of her . . .

Clair heard a branch crack, and turned around. There was a man standing in the forest behind her.

She felt the terror seize her, but pushed it down deep.

"Sorry," he said, holding up his hands in front of him, "I didn't realize anyone else was hiking around here."

Clair took a few deep breaths to clear the adrenaline that was coursing through her veins while she examined him. He was tall, at least a foot taller than Clair, with a decent build and short brown hair that fell in disarray around his eyes. He was wearing walking shoes, not hiking shoes, with jeans and a white T-shirt. Clair was pretty sure if he tried to attack her she could outrun him.

"It's okay," she said, relaxing a little. "Why are you out here?"

He walked slowly toward her, still keeping a healthy distance. She remained tensed and ready to run if needed.

"I live over those hills," he said, pointing behind him.

"You live in the forest?" She didn't remember seeing a house, but it wasn't impossible with all of the trees. As he got closer, Clair noticed that he had the grayest eyes she had ever seen—like storm clouds on an overcast day before the rain.

She recognized him.

"I remember you," she said, cocking her head to the side as she recalled the moment. "You were walking downtown this morning."

Clair was sure now that he was the same guy she had seen.

"Yes . . ." he said, eyes never leaving her. The way he was looking at her made Clair feel uncomfortable. It wasn't the way she had seen murderers look at prey in horror films; it was more like she was some rare creature in a sci-fi movie. "I haven't seen you in town before. Are you new here?"

"Not really," she said, slowly putting her camera away but never taking her eyes off him. "I live with my grandmother down the hill. I just moved back."

"Oh," he said. Clair could see his body visibly relax, and he stopped staring at her long enough to scratch the back of his head. "Sorry, I'm just not used to seeing new people around here, especially ones who hike this far into the forest."

"Yeah," Clair relaxed a little. "I'm Clair, by the way."

"Chris."

Even though they were close enough to shake hands with a small reach, Clair didn't offer, and he didn't seem to mind.

After a few seconds of awkward silence, Clair started backing up the hill.

"See you later."

He remained as still as the trees around him.

Clair continued to look over her shoulder as she sprinted up the hill, making sure he wasn't following her, only stopping at the top for a quick look back down at the bowl. She scanned the tree line, looking for the house, but couldn't find it.

Weird, she thought.

It was getting dark, a chill creeping into the air. Clair shivered as she jogged the rest of the way home.

SAM

The Karnak Temple in Luxor, Egypt, allowed visitors into the Temple of Amun only after walking the two-mile Avenue of the Sphinxes—also known as the Sacred Way—that traveled from Karnak to Luxor.

Sam almost forgot about the woman from the photo when he saw all of the artifacts in the temple: porcelain bottles of the Egyptian gods cast with accents of gold, containing the organs of the powerful; scrolls of medical achievements from the Early Dynastic Period when upper and lower Egypt were first unified under Menes, rumored to have been the first crowned pharaoh.

Sam crossed the circular room to inspect a drawing on papyrus that was decorated with gold stitching. The art depicted a glass vial amulet, held by a coiled snake with red rubies for eyes, sewn onto the papyrus. The caption next to the work told the story of the lost snake amulet, said to hold the blood of the last great pharaoh, Amuntek. It was found missing from his neck the same night as his untimely and unexplainable death. Historians, according to the caption, had thought the amulet would eventually resurface on the black market, sold to the highest bidder, but it seemed to have simply disappeared from the earth. The most disturbing part of the artwork was what appeared to be real blood, probably from the artist himself, staining the vial.

Sam turned and saw the reason for his trip.

In the center of the room, on a large marble pillar, was the Mau. While he was studying the vase, Sam thought about how interesting it was that the ancient Egyptians worshiped cats. Sam was allergic to cats, but every religion has problems.

The Mau still had a slight glow to it, reflecting its magical properties, if not necessarily angelic, a fact he would not be able to test unless he could hold it. But that didn't matter. Any magical artifact could be found by a human, but not always used, and the woman from the photo had clearly been exposed to the magic within this Mau. Sam decided that she was either a very lucky human or knew something about the hierarchy of angels.

Whatever the case, Sam got on a plane to seek her out.

And now he was sitting in a coffee shop located in a small town called Healdsburg in the early afternoon, waiting for a chance to see this woman named Dorthea.

He had asked the boy working behind the counter, Andrew, what he knew about Dorthea, but didn't get much information. Neither did he hear anything useful from the boy's coworker, Melody.

The coffee shop was starting to fill up with people, taking seats by the window and blocking his view. If this woman was close to an angelic presence, even with the photo he had of her being fifty years old, he would still be able to spot her without knowing exactly what she looked like.

Sam had tried to find a current picture of her on the Internet, or anything describing her appearance or whereabouts, but the only thing he could find was a last-known address in this small town. Yet even with the address, he couldn't find her house, and Sam thought that was just a bit too suspicious.

A tall girl with deep-brown hair and silver eyes was eyeing him while waiting for her cappuccino.

Sam didn't consider himself ugly.

In fact, despite his numerical age, he didn't look over thirty years old. With his buzzed light brown hair and blue eyes, in conjunction with his medium build, Sam had been approached a few times in this new life by women.

Usually they enjoyed his British accent, but as soon as he started talking to them, he usually convinced the girls to find something better to do with their time. His preferred sidestepping subject was the inclusion of African-American soldiers in the Civil War and how their addition to the Northern battalion was the sole reason the North won. There had been a few history buffs he had to distract with talk about his collection of fur coats or whatever else it took for them to get angry or distracted and walk away.

Being an angel had its upsides, but in his opinion, it also tended to attract too much unwanted female attention. It wasn't that being an angel kept Sam from being a man—not in the slightest. He was still prone to physical stimulus and even enjoyed a good lager, but the angelic life—this redemptive, second life—was only his for a purpose, and when that purpose was met, Sam knew his time would end.

As he was thinking about the best way to question people about Dorthea without raising an alarm, a girl walked into the coffee shop wearing a red work apron, and retreated behind the counter. Her hair was straight, falling just past her shoulders, with a light brownish tint. She seemed flustered as she started making the coffee orders, but gradually relaxed, conversing easily with the other employees and customers.

If she hadn't said anything, he might not have caught her. But there it was in her voice—something that shouldn't be there. A slight pitch that was barely noticeable, except to anyone like him.

He was sure of it.

Angel.

What was an angel doing working at a coffee shop? Sam had to admit he had taken some odd jobs in the last few hundred years, but he had only worked long enough to amass enough money to continue the search for his purpose.

The way this girl moved and talked, in conjunction with the mysterious woman from the photograph—Sam couldn't help but wonder what was going on in this small town.

He watched her for a few more minutes, trying to see if she made any attempt to catch his eye. Angels could usually sense each other. The newer ones had less defined senses, but most could instinctually use their skills to locate fellow travelers. This girl was acting like she didn't know what she was, because she never once even glanced at Sam.

In fact, Sam was almost certain she *couldn't* see him.

The door opened, bringing with it a scent Sam had not smelled in a long time—The Gate.

And another angel. "What the hell is going on here?"

He watched the boy walk up to the counter and order a tea. The girl knew him.

"Hey, Chris," she said, taking his order and smiling at him.

"Hello, Clair," he said, tentatively pulling out his wallet and handing her a few ones. "I didn't know you worked here."

"Yep," she said, pouring the hot tea into a paper cup. "I just started about a week ago."

The boy behind the counter, Andrew, was watching their conversation out of the corner of his eye, apparent dislike on his face.

"That's cool," Chris said, moving around the corner to stand at the bar next to where the drinks were served. "Do you like it?"

"You are asking me, while I am working, whether or not I like my job?" Clair laughed. Her smile was infectious, with just a hint of flirtation. She handed Chris his tea.

"Yeah," Chris chuckled. "Oops. Not my best plan."

His back was turned to Sam, but he must have been smiling because Clair kept glancing over at Chris while she made other drinks. He was so focused on the girl that he didn't sense Sam either. Sam was starting to feel offended.

"Thanks," Chris said after a bit, and walked out the door.

Sam sat there for a minute after Chris left the shop, and then quietly walked out, following his scent.

It was strong on him—stronger than it should have been if Sam guessed his purpose correctly. He was definitely a new minor angel, because he hadn't glanced at Sam once in the coffee shop.

Sam watched as Chris walked along Main Street until he hit the end, making a right-angle stride and heading straight up into the forest.

Success, Sam thought, walking quickly after him.

The forest was thick even at its starting point right off the road, but Sam was sure he could sense the boy somewhere ahead of him as he loped through the trees.

About halfway through, he heard something and stopped.

"Why are you following me?"

An arm was wrapped around his throat, and the scent told him it was the boy he had been following.

"You are good," Sam said, quickly dislocating the arm from his neck and pinning the boy to the ground with a knee to his throat, "but not *that* good."

It took a little convincing, but eventually Sam got the boy, Chris, to use his senses to determine whether or not Sam was an enemy—which he wasn't.

After he gave Chris a hand up from the ground, Sam asked the question that was bothering him the most.

"Who was the girl?"

"I don't know." Chris looked at him, concern on his face. "I saw her a few days ago, and could sense something was different about her . . . but I couldn't tell what. So I went to investigate."

New minor angels, Sam thought, sighing, so impetuous.

"Why are you here?" Chris asked. "I haven't seen another minor angel before."

Sam explained the glowing woman from the picture and the Mau in Cairo. Then, when he saw the confusion on the kid's face, he explained his age—and the search for his purpose.

Sam gave Chris a minute to take all the information in. Chris couldn't have been more than a few years old, even though he looked to be about twenty human years.

"Now tell me," Sam said when his patience gave out, "what are you doing here, smelling like The Gate?"

Chris was shocked for only a second before the guarded expression returned to his eyes.

Doesn't trust me yet, Sam thought. This was a good trait for a young minor angel.

"I woke up here about two years ago," Chris began, putting his hands in his pockets. Sam knew it was a hard tale, especially for the new ones. It was all so fresh. "The Gate was here when I first woke, and then it moved, and I knew—I just knew I was supposed to guard it when it decided to stop."

Sam felt a pang of jealousy. This kid didn't even have to go *looking* for his purpose; he was placed next to it.

"I understand," Sam said, explaining his run-ins with other minor angels and their purposes. "I ran into The Gate once, centuries ago, and it wasn't my purpose—but it smelled just like you."

"Yes," Chris said, sniffing his shirt. Maybe he couldn't smell it anymore since he was around it so much. "About four weeks ago The Gate stopped moving."

There were a few seconds of silence.

"*What?*" Sam said.

"I know!" Chris put his hands up in the air, defensive. "I don't know what happened. But it hasn't moved, and things are . . . seeping."

Sam could see the worry in his eyes. This was not a good situation at all, but there was another question on his mind.

"The girl was around The Gate?"

"Yes, that's weird, right?" Chris asked, his brow furrowed. "Normally people don't get within a mile of it, but she was right there."

"It is not normal," Sam said, "but neither is she."

Chris was holding onto each of his words, and Sam felt a moment of purpose.

Am I supposed to guide him? He had never seen that type of function before, but something inside him resonated with this boy.

"You were right to inspect her further. She seems angelic," Sam said, looking around the forest. "Though how much I am not sure. We need to test her."

"Test her?" Chris said, concern on his face.

He doesn't like that idea, Sam thought. Interesting.

"Yes," he said. "You said things were seeping. Seeping how?"

CLAIR

They spent most of the afternoon talking about Mike and whether or not Emily should kill him or give him a billionth chance. She knew Emily loved Mike, but Clair had a feeling he was more trouble than he was worth.

"Em," Clair said, putting the car into park in front of her house, "I know you love Mike. I mean you must love him to put up with him and all the stuff you've been telling me he's done, but he's blowing it, and sounds like he's been blowing it for a long time."

Emily got out of the car and walked up to Clair's mailbox, grabbing the day's post as well as a flower that was hooked into the flag. Clair was about to ask about the flower, but Emily started talking.

"Yeah," she said, with a sarcastic smile and a wink, "but I go for the bad guys."

Clair sighed, letting the subject drop, and started walking up the front steps, forgetting the flower while she tried to think of what to say to Emily.

"He just sounds like he's an a-hole to you all of the time," she said, inserting the key into the wooden front door.

"Why do you always say it like that?" Emily was facing Clair, leaning against the door with her arms crossed around the mail, and her head cocked to one side.

Clair stopped fiddling with the keys and looked over at her. This was her friend, her only real friend in town, and she liked Emily. It was time to tell her the truth.

"I just don't want to see you get hurt," Clair said. Emily started to protest, but Clair continued. "I know you have been hurt before, I mean, what you said about learning that fairytales aren't real and there are no princesses and princes, but one day it might be different, worse, and—it might rip a hole right through your heart, and I don't want you to sell yourself short."

For a second Emily stared into her eyes, face a mask of confusion, and then she was laughing, holding her sides as she gasped for air.

Clair was so stunned her mouth fell open.

"Oh, no, no!" Emily said, in between laughs. "Don't look so shocked. I'm not laughing at what you said, though I appreciate every word."

"Then what?" Clair said, smiling as she watched Emily wipe the tears from her eyes.

"I meant," she said, "why do you always pronounce 'ass hole' as 'a-hole.'"

"Oh!" Clair laughed. "I have no idea."

"It's appreciated, though, by the way," she tilted her head, smiling at Clair before looking back toward the desolate front yard. "I hope, one day, to find a guy who loves me enough to buy me a garden like this." She spread out her arms as if to encompass the entire dead space.

Clair playfully punched her in the arm.

"Well at the rate you're going, get used to this luxury."

Both girls were still laughing when they finally entered the house, Emily moving to the kitchen to make snacks while Clair dropped her bag into a slot near the door. The afternoon light was pouring through the windows, casting white beams across the floor and the random antiques that had become a part of their house collection.

There was something else too—a faint smell like vanilla.

"Do you smell that?" Clair asked, walking toward the kitchen. Every step brought on new waves of flavor—cinnamon, curry, vanilla, spices she couldn't identify exactly. It was as if the scent was continually changing. When she walked through the kitchen door, the air was thicker somehow, as if it were literally filling the room.

But there was no food.

Instead, Emily had placed a single white lily in a vase on the wooden cutting table.

"It's pretty," Emily said, barely glancing at the flower as she moved to the fridge to gather snacks.

Clair, however, was mesmerized.

The lily was larger than a table plate, its five petals spotted with an intricate pattern of pink dots. The stamen was filled with thick pollen, and the light coming through the window was bathing the flower in the brightest white, making the thick stem a deep forest green and the petals ghostlike.

Why hadn't Clair noticed it outside? And why was Emily not interested in it? The flower was the only thing in the kitchen that was new; everything else was where it had been before they'd gone out—fridge with barely any food, dishes cleaned, and the pantry almost empty.

"'Bout time she has a real flower in here. I wonder who left it? With all the flower-painted antiques, you'd think she'd keep a garden."

"She did," Clair said, barely paying attention as she gingerly touched one of the large white petals. It felt like silk, thin enough that the light streaming through the windows made it glow.

"She did?" Emily asked, grabbing bread from the meager pantry. "Why did she stop?"

"Long story," Clair said, though she was pretty sure everyone in town, including Emily, had their own ideas.

Most of the stories were elaborated, but the principle was the same: Dotty and her brother James went all over the world together living in multiple countries, collecting antiques, and looking for art. They had been two of the happiest and most contagious people in town—and they always had the rarest, most interesting artifacts in the antique shop.

Everyone said that James had just died suddenly. No one really knew how it happened, Dotty never talked with Clair about it. Someone in elementary school once told her that on the night of his funeral, Dotty took all his clothes and every picture of him out into the woods and lit the whole pile on fire while she danced around it under the moon like a regular witch out of Salem.

After that, she pretty much kept to herself, and the townspeople who knew about her kept away from the shop.

"You really don't smell this?" Clair turned to find Emily dishing out mini peanut butter and jelly sandwiches along with a lot of other finger foods.

"Nope," she said, licking peanut butter off her fingers. "But I do smell jelly!"

CHRIS

Chris and Sam were in the woods, watching the girls through the kitchen window.

After their first meeting, Chris brought Sam back to his house in the forest, a small one-story building with a large vegetable garden out back. He liked to grow his own food, preferring the lack of pesticides and that he didn't have to pay for groceries as often. He also liked that his house was close to The Gate, should trouble arise. He had been at home, a couple of miles away, when he heard Clair blundering through the forest, and stopped her as she stood so close to the treasure he guarded with his life.

After Chris had made some tea and pulled together salads for the two of them, Sam asked again about the seeping problem and they devised the lily plan together.

There was a border around Clair's house that kept them from getting too close. Luckily, the girl Emily had grabbed the flower with the mail. If she hadn't, they wouldn't be witnessing what they were now.

"This could prove angelic blood," Sam said, watching Clair stroke the lily. "But it doesn't explain why she doesn't know what she is, or that she couldn't see or smell the lily until it was in the house."

Chris was standing very still, watching the girls. It had been his idea to bring the flower from the boundary where it had slipped through The Gate, but he still felt uneasy about what they were doing. They were basically stalking the girl.

Even though he had only spent a short amount of time with Sam, talking about what it meant to be a minor angel, what Sam had found in his research, and about The Gate, Chris learned to trust him, but didn't like the idea of messing with Clair. There was just something about her, and the thought of her in trouble unnerved him.

"I don't know," Chris said, turning to face Sam. "If she was a minor angel, she would have woken up with that knowledge, right?"

"Of course," Sam nodded. "All the angels I have met said just that."

"So maybe she isn't a minor angel," Chris said, thinking out loud. "Maybe she's something else."

Sam's brow furrowed in thought, and his face turned dark. He didn't like that idea at all, apparently.

"But she can't be evil," Chris continued, assuming that was what was worrying Sam. He turned back to watch the girls laugh and interact. "She wouldn't be able to keep human friends."

They had decided early on that Emily was pure human, after following her for a day and studying her character. Emily had been crucial for the plan to work.

"What about researching the woman in the picture?" Chris said, trying to steer the subject away from Clair. He didn't know why he felt so protective of this girl.

"What about her?" Sam said, turning his attention back to Chris.

"Well, don't you think it's more important to find out who *she* is, since the connection could be closer to a higher-ranking angel?"

There was a quiet scraping noise coming up the road, and Sam and Chris froze, listening.

"Human?" Chris said, sensing the air.

"Yes, definitely," Sam said.

They both stared down the road past the house to where the path wound, waiting to see what came around the bend.

An older woman, with a pink beanie and walking shoes, was huffing up the path carrying bags of groceries. The girls in the house must have heard her coming because Clair opened the front door and ran to help the woman with the bags.

"Grandma!" Clair yelled, laughing at the woman. "Why didn't you just let me get the groceries with my car?"

"It's okay. It was a slow today in the shop, so I closed up," she said, her voice coming in jagged breaths. "Besides, I obviously need the extra cardio."

"Grandma," Clair said, concerned, "you exercise every morning. Don't strain yourself."

"Hey, Ms. Dotty," Emily shouted from the door.

"Hello, Emily, glad to see you." Dotty smiled at the girl; then her face fell, and her eyes went cloudy. "Girls, get inside."

Emily and Clair exchanged puzzled glances.

"What?" Clair said, a nervous laugh escaping her. "What's wrong, Grandma?"

"Get inside, *now*!"

Clair walked slowly to the door, gave Emily a puzzled glance, and whispered, "Having a moment."

"It's okay," Emily whispered back before entering the house, leaving Dorthea standing in the front yard, still as stone.

Chris and Sam watched her, barely breathing.

"I know you are there," she said to the emptiness around her. "Leave."

Only his eyes moved, but Sam clearly told Chris not to say a word and not to move.

After a minute of standing in the street, Dotty shook her head and muttered something that sounded an awful lot like "maybe am having a moment," before she walked into the house.

Chris knew nothing good would happen next.

He was right.

A few seconds later Dotty came running out of the house, carrying the lily high above her head in a fist, to the border of the property, where she threw it to the ground and began jumping on it repeatedly.

Clair ran outside and was yelling frantically at Dotty, telling her to calm down and not strain herself. Emily was gripping the doorframe, her mouth hanging open while she watched Clair wrestle Dorthea into submission before leading her back to the house.

When Clair passed Emily, she said, "I think I feel like grabbing some popcorn . . . Want to go to the store with me?"

Emily shut her mouth and nodded, obviously not wanting to go into the house with the crazy woman.

"Okay," Clair said, trying to keep her voice calm. "Just stay here. I'm going to make her some tea, and then I'll drive us into town."

"Sorry," Emily whispered as Clair walked into the house. Clair gave a half-smile and disappeared.

"Well," Sam said, turning to Chris, "I think we have some answers."

CLAIR

Clair walked outside and picked up the broken flower. Three of the five petals were bent, creating brown bruises where they had been harshly folded. The once gold-dusted stamen was now devoid of pollen, and the stem had skid-like abrasions along the side from when it had been kicked against the cement. Considering the beating Dotty had delivered, Clair was surprised the flower wasn't worse for wear.

"I didn't realize she was *that* against plants," Emily said, obviously still a little shaken. "Has she always been like that?"

"No," Clair said, gently touching each of the ruined petals. She was on the verge of tears but didn't know why. "Sometimes she just has a hard time, I guess. I'm sorry about that, Em."

"It's okay," Emily said, smiling. "I'm good at handling drama."

Clair smiled a bit but was still feeling depressed. The flower had been so beautiful. Why had Dotty flipped out?

"Hey," Emily said, drawing Clair's attention, "I think it's definitely a night for chocolate, popcorn, and a rom-com."

Clair couldn't help but laugh. "Yes, please!"

They drove to the supermarket, talking about the newest romantic comedies available at the rent-a-box and discussing the movies they had both seen recently. The only movies Clair refused to watch were horror films, and Emily said that was okay because she only went to scary movies with boys.

"Why is that?" Clair asked, shuffling through the DVDs for rent in the box.

"Because then when you get scared, it's an excuse to lean in closer," she smiled evilly. Clair laughed.

They had found the perfect movie, *Love Actually*, grabbed a few chocolate bars and a box of microwavable popcorn, and started heading back down Main Street toward home, when Clair had a thought.

"Hey, Em, mind if we stop for a minute?"

"Nope," she said, "I'll wait in the car." It was a warm summer day, the windows were down, and Emily had her chair reclined in the passenger seat, sunglasses taking in the bright sunlight.

Clair parked the car near the flower shop and watched Jean hefting large bags of soil from around the corner into the store. Clair waved, and Jean smiled back.

Clair grabbed the flower from the backseat, left Emily to tan, and wandered into the shop. She watched as Jean lugged the bag to the back, where she dropped it in a pile with others and returned to Clair.

"Hey there," Jean said, catching her breath. "I didn't think you were working today."

"Nope." Clair had developed the habit of saying hello to Jean before her shifts. "I worked this morning, but only a half shift because Melody said she needed the hours for some heavy-metal band's concert tickets."

Jean smiled, her eyes drifting to the broken flower Clair had cradled in her left hand. "What do you have there?"

"I was hoping you could tell me." Clair gently placed the flower on the counter, stretching it out and attempting to straighten the ripped petals.

Jean examined the stamen and the pollen, what was left of it, gently prodding here and there.

"Well," she said eventually, "it's a phylum of lily, but what type I can't tell exactly." She looked a little miffed.

"Is something wrong?" Clair asked.

"I usually can tell," Jean said with a small laugh. "Hurts my pride when I get a tough case like this one."

Clair thought that if Dotty hadn't jumped on it, Jean probably would have been able to give her more information about the flower.

"Well, I appreciate any info, so thank you," Clair said, gently picking it up.

"Wait, leave it here. I'd like to study it more, if that's alright."

"Do you smell it?" Clair felt her adrenaline spike. Emily hadn't smelled it and didn't have any interest in it, but maybe Jean could sense something.

"Smell what?" Jean looked over at Clair, one eyebrow raised. "Lilies don't typically have a scent, except to flies, and even then it's a foul smell like dung."

"Oh." Clair felt her body deflate. "Okay, sure. If you find anything more about it, will you let me know?"

"Of course," she said with a smile.

Clair helped Jean carry the rest of the bags of soil into the store and returned to find Emily asleep in the front seat. Clair honked the horn, and Emily woke with a start, blaming her nap on the wonderful weather and her fight with Mike over the phone the previous night.

The next day Clair woke up for work feeling a lot better. Her shift was only for a few hours today, and she was ready to get back into the woods after all of the junk food from the night before.

She got ready in a hurry and ran down the stairs. It was a cool summer morning, and she decided to ride her bike to work. Dotty was already awake and in the kitchen making some scrambled eggs and sausage.

"Good morning, dear," she said. "Want some breakfast?"

Clair's stomach made a large gurgling sound, and both of them laughed.

They talked a bit about their plans for the day, the idle chatter helping to ease some of the tension in the room from the day before. Clair still didn't know whether or not to ask her about why the flower had wigged her out. As it turned out, she didn't have to.

"I wanted to apologize," Dotty began, clearing her plate in the sink and turning to Clair, "for yesterday." Her gray hair was tangled from sleep, and her eyes were crinkled with concern. "Sometimes I have to relive moments from my past, and they are . . . difficult to face."

"Don't worry about it." Clair smiled at her. Dotty returned the expression and cleaned Clair's plate when she finished. Clair wished her a good day and flew out the door, grabbing her old bike from the garage. She had smartly filled the tires with air the night before, making sure there were no holes.

She headed into town, settling the bike at a slow pace as she enjoyed the morning. There was still some fog in the air, the wetness hitting her face as she pedaled through town, rounding the corner onto Main Street and coming to a halt in front of Awake.

Andrew arrived just as Clair was locking her tire around a fire hydrant. He parked his yellow Camaro, with its large black pinstripe down the hood of the car, right in front of the shop and walked up to Clair.

"Good morning." His smile was infectious. He opened the shop, flicking on the lights.

"Hey, Andrew." Clair smiled and walked in after him. As he was fishing his red apron out from one of the cabinets below the register, Clair noticed that his already tan skin looked a little sunburnt.

"Do anything fun on your day off yesterday?" she asked.

"Went to the coast," he said, eyes lighting up. "Do you surf?"

Clair laughed. Coordination had never been her thing, and neither had sports, for that matter. The only exercise Clair got was hiking, or jogging, which she did infrequently.

"No, I don't have the balance." She shrugged.

Andrew laughed and gently hit her shoulder with his hand. He had been doing little nudges like that a lot lately, Clair thought, but she didn't mind. Andrew was part of her new friend group with Emily, and she liked hanging out with him.

The morning passed by uneventfully. People came in, got their coffee, and continued with their day. The few regulars set up their laptops, fingers typing away, or read books, sitting at the tables or in the leather armchairs near the windows, absorbing the warm summer light. Clair made conversation with everyone, asking them about their lives and trying to make them smile when possible.

Sam, a new regular Clair had met a few days ago, came in and ordered a soy latte, asking her for the time. Sam had light brown hair above bright blue eyes and looked to be in his late twenties. Clair laughed and pointed to the clock behind her.

"Oh, sorry," he said, a slight smile on his face. Something about the way he was looking at her said he wasn't sorry, and that he didn't care about the time. Clair shrugged and handed him his coffee. She watched him sit at his usual table in the corner near the window and pull a book from his bag.

A few minutes later, Clair saw Chris walk in the shop, but Andrew beat her to the register.

"Hello, how can I help you?"

"I'd like an iced tea please," Chris said, handing Andrew the money and sending a small smile in Clair's direction.

"Hey, Chris," Clair said, prepping the tea and placing it on the bar for him to grab.

"Hey," he said, sitting in one of the chairs located near the serving station. He never stayed to drink his tea, yet there he was, sitting. Clair stared as she watched his gray eyes scan the room before landing back on her. They were so light today, almost as if the sun was about to peek from behind them. Clair realized she was staring, and he must have sensed her embarrassment because he smiled and asked, "How was your weekend?"

"It was good," she said, glancing at the door to make sure a line wasn't forming. Andrew could handle the customers, but currently he was hovering to her right, organizing the coffee cups. "I watched a movie with a friend and worked."

His smile widened, displaying a spectacular set of dimples, and Clair felt her blood flow a little faster. It might have been her imagination, but she was sure his eyes got lighter when he smiled, like the joy couldn't be contained in his body.

"Nice," he said, his eyes never leaving hers. "Didn't go hiking?"

Clair had to think about it. She usually tried to go every few days, but she hadn't gone at all last weekend.

"Nope," she said, "didn't get a chance to. I'm going today after work."

"Clair, there's a small line," Andrew said from behind her. Clair grabbed the cups with the orders written on them and began making drinks.

"Mind if I join you?" Chris said, and Clair almost dropped one of the cups she had been filling with steamed milk. She looked over at Chris, and he continued. "I've been meaning to workout but haven't had the time or the willpower." He laughed, the white T-shirt stretching around his biceps as he crossed his arms on the counter. His eyes were so bright, and he exuded a type of positivity that was infectious.

"Sure," she said, a small nervous laugh escaping her lips. She quickly covered it with a cough. "My shift ends in a few hours . . . meet me here?"

"Sounds good," he said, getting up and walking toward the door. "See you later."

The rest of the day went by extremely fast after that. Clair found herself thinking about what Chris would be like to hike with, or even talk to, and worried about conversation topics. They had only made idle chitchat at Awake.

Chris arrived just as she was walking out the door. He was wearing jeans and a white T-shirt. Clair wondered if he owned any other color shirts besides white.

"Hey," she said, unlocking her bike.

"Hey," he said, smiling.

Oh, God, Clair thought. This is awkward. Why am I being so awkward? She decided that if she just kept talking, then there would be less awkwardness.

"I need to go home to get some hiking attire on, and then we can head up the path that's near my house," she said, looking at his attire. "You can hike in jeans?"

"Yep, not a problem," he said, shrugging his shoulders. She wasn't sure if Chris knew how to hike. Who hiked in jeans? Maybe he just wanted to hang out with her, but then she remembered that he had been in a similar outfit that day she stumbled upon him in the woods.

He seemed genuinely excited for the hike, and Clair hoped he didn't tire easily.

Not wanting to be rude, Clair walked with Chris toward her house, the bike in between them creating a comfortable amount of space. They talked a little about Healdsburg and its crazy inhabitants, about his house in the hills, and what it was like for Clair working at the coffee shop. He was tall, and she had to take about three steps for every one of his. Clair learned that he kept a small garden with vegetables and some fruit trees in his backyard, and Clair told him that it sounded like a lot of work.

"It's well worth it."

"More power to you." Clair smiled, and Chris sent her a smile with a raised eyebrow.

"What?" she said, her eyebrows knitting together.

"Nothing." He laughed. She felt like she had missed some inside joke.

As they got closer to her house, Clair began to worry about letting him inside while she changed. She didn't know him that well, and even though he seemed nice, she wasn't sure if it would be wise. She also didn't know how to introduce Chris if Dotty was home. Did this make them friends?

But it didn't end up being an issue.

When they were yards from her house, Chris said he was going to wait near the entrance to the trail, to stretch, and walked away. Clair let out a breath of air as she watched him walk to the bottom of the hill, bending his legs and reaching up with those muscled arms. She wondered how he got those arms, and realized she was being ridiculous. She was not some high schooler ogling after a hot boy. She had plenty of boyfriends in college and considered herself very attractive.

Clair shook her head and rode the bike the short distance home. She left it in the garage and ran upstairs to throw on shorts and a tank top.

When she came back outside and around to the pedestrian trail, Chris was stretched and waiting. As they trekked up the trail, he asked her questions about her life, and Clair began talking about Emily, college, and moving back home. When she realized she had been monopolizing the conversation, she asked Chris about his vegetable garden and whether or not he had any pets.

"Wouldn't be a good idea." He laughed.

"Not a pet person?" Clair teased, surprising herself. She didn't usually feel comfortable this quickly with someone she barely knew.

Chris laughed. "Not really."

When they reached the part where the trail wound back down toward town, Clair looked at Chris with a challenging smile and pushed ahead, into the thick of the forest.

She was breathing heavily, her lungs straining for enough oxygen to feed her working legs. She loved the way her muscles would create their own heat, and the coolness that came from the air rushing past her sweaty skin. Clair lost herself in the moment before she remembered Chris was next to her.

She felt awkward for letting the conversation lapse but also surprised at how easy it was to just *be* with him. When she looked over at him, Clair noticed he was beginning to grow tense, face wrinkled with concern. It wasn't from the uphill stress, because his breathing wasn't nearly as labored as her own, so she decided to keep him talking.

"Where do your parents live now?" she asked, remembering he had said he owned the house he lived in.

"I don't know," he said, slightly hesitant. "I was adopted, and my foster parents died a while ago."

"I'm sorry," Clair said, wishing she hadn't asked. Her parents had died, but at least she had Dotty. It sounded like Chris didn't have anyone. "My parents died in a car crash, right after I was born."

Chris looked over at her, concern washing out of those dark gray eyes. "I'm sorry, Clair," he said, and Clair had never seen anyone look so sincere. It was intimidating to have someone look at her that intensely.

"It was a long time ago." She looked away and waved her hand to dismiss the subject and the tension. "I didn't know either of them. Plus, I have Dotty."

Chris asked a few questions about her grandmother, and Clair was surprised to find that he didn't know the witch story. Then she remembered that Chris had said he moved to town a couple of years ago.

He asked to stop a little way up the hill, and rolled up his jeans to just below his knees, exposing white skin. Clair laughed.

"Going to try to get tan?" she said, smile in place.

"Couldn't hurt," he said, eyes bright.

They continued walking.

He was ahead of her up the hill by a few feet, legs easily taking the rocks and branches, his breath even and without labor. She didn't mind her view either, the way his jeans hugged his legs and butt. She almost tripped, and reminded herself to pay attention to where she was walking.

All of a sudden Clair heard breaking wood and looked up to see a branch the size of a small car coming at her.

She flung herself sideways to the ground, scraping her arm and feeling blood rush to the cut, but watched as the branch was blown toward her. She extended her left hand up to shield her face, and felt like someone kicked her in the stomach as she watched the branch float past her head and land with a thud a few feet away.

She had a hard time getting air as she quickly pushed herself to her feet, clasping her bleeding right arm.

"You saw that, right?!" she yelled for Chris, feeling queasy and looking around for him.

But he was no longer alone.

Standing next to him was a man, and he was staring at Clair like she was some type of rare animal. She recognized him.

"Sam," she said as she backed away, putting distance between the two men and herself. Chris raised his hands in front of him, trying to placate her like a wild animal.

"Clair," he said, holding her eyes. "This is my friend Sam, who you already know."

"Hello," Sam said, his face like stone.

Clair was so confused she couldn't think straight.

"How . . ." she said. "I don't remember seeing you anywhere. How did you get here? Did you both see that?"

She looked at Chris, heart pounding. Her head was screaming that she was stupid to have trusted him so quickly, and even more idiotic for not telling anyone where she was going. She set her feet to run.

"Clair, it's okay," Chris said, taking a step toward her. She took one in the opposite direction, and he immediately froze. "Clair, we're here to help you. What you just did . . ."

"What you just did," interjected Sam, "is proof that you are not all human."

Wait . . . what? Clair thought.

Chris glared at Sam and then looked back at Clair, his eyes pleading. "I'm sorry we tested you this way Clair, but if you give us a chance to explain . . ."

"Tested me?" she said, still confused. She saw his eyes dart to the branch and back, and the pieces connected. "*You* made the branch fall?"

Chris winced, but Sam seemed impatient.

"Clair, you are angelic," he said. "Your blood just saved you from death."

She stood there for a minute, glancing between the two of them. They are both insane, she thought. This was an accident. This is some sort of joke.

She looked at the distance between her and them—about eight feet—and debated running. She could probably outrun Sam, but not Chris. He was too good at hiking, she had noticed, and could easily overtake her.

Clair took another step backward. They didn't move.

"I don't know what's wrong with the two of you," she said, continuing her slow retreat, "but I don't want anything to do with this."

Chris sighed, and she could see his body deflate. He looked defeated. Sam put his hands in his back pockets.

"Well," Sam said, watching Clair slowly retreat, "when you are ready to face the truth, we'll be waiting."

Clair took that as an opportunity to run.

She sprinted down the hill, her arm dripping blood and her muscles aching with the effort.

Once she reached the main trail, she practically flew the rest of the way home, wrenching open the back door just as the sun went down.

"Clair?" Dotty said from somewhere in the house. Clair leaned against the sliding back door, taking deep breaths, her body shaking with fear. Dotty came around the corner, eyes bulging.

"Clair! What happened?" She rushed over and began examining Clair's arm, turning it between her hands. "It's not too bad. It was shallow. Let's get you into the kitchen. Now."

After Dotty had washed the wound, she brought out gauze and began wrapping Clair's forearm while she sat on the counter in the kitchen.

"So," she said, eyes sliding up to Clair as she wound the gauze around and around. "What happened?"

Clair didn't know what to say. She couldn't blow this bit of insanity off as a simple voice in her head. The branch had fallen, and she had stopped it—somehow. Maybe it had just been fate, a gust of wind through the forest.

She looked down at Dotty.

For some reason, she didn't want to tell her what had happened.

"I thought I heard a rattlesnake," she said, putting her best effort into the lie, innocent smile in place, "and panicked."

"You?" Dotty said, eyebrow raised. "Never seen you panic before. Did you hit a tree?"

The lie came too easily. "Kind of."

That night Clair went to bed feeling tense.

She checked to make sure the door was locked three times before finally shutting off all the lights in the house, and even then she wasn't able to turn off her computer until past midnight.

Sam had said they would be *waiting* for her.

What did that mean? Were they watching her even now, waiting for her to exit the house? The thought wasn't comforting. Clair had always liked that their house was located on the edge of the forest, away from town. It gave them space. But tonight it left too much room for fear.

Reaching over to the side table, Clair opened the small drawer and checked to see that her knife was still there. It was pathetic, she knew, to think that a knife would stop the two men from attacking her or Dotty, but it was something.

Better to be prepared, the voice said, comforting her.

An hour later she drifted off, but sleep didn't bring relief.

She was walking through the forest, but the trees were purple—the light coming through them a washed-out gray. There was a small creek nearby, the water flowing and creating music so sweet she could taste it in her mouth like a decadent honeyed wine.

She was looking for something.

All of a sudden she came upon a man in the forest. He had large white wings, his face blurred by the feathers that were coming loose from them and flying around the forest. He barely fit in the clearing, each wingtip touching the abnormally large fir trees that encircled the space.

When she reached out to touch one of the wings, she saw her hand. In its place were feathers, bright white. She ran to the creek and looked at her reflection.

Wings the size of elephants sprang from her back, and her face was covered in feathers, her feet long black demonic talons.

Clair got up and ran to the feathered man, and called a name—she didn't know what. Her mind was struggling to drown out the music from the water, to make sense of everything around her, but the feathers were closing in around her face, blurring her vision.

The man turned, his face familiar but strange all at the same time.

"Accept what you are, Clair." His voice was filling the air with the sound of clanging bells, beautiful and overbearing.

"No!" she shouted, the feathers on her body growing closer around her face, suffocating her. "Don't do this to me!"

"It is already done."

Clair woke early the next morning. She stretched under the warm white sheets, feeling the strain in her muscles contract and relax deliciously.

Dotty must have been out walking, because Clair couldn't hear her bustling around downstairs in the house. The sun was barely peeking through the trees outside her window as she contemplated her choice.

Last night, after the dream, she had decided to talk with the crazy boys—on her terms and within sight of safety.

She took as much time as possible to get ready, making a breakfast bagel with cheese, eggs, and salsa, eating it slowly while watching the forest through the kitchen window.

She couldn't see them, but she knew they were there.

Having prolonged the situation as long as she could, Clair grabbed the long kitchen knife from her room and placed it in her back pocket, ensuring the hilt was easily accessible, while making a mental note not to fall backward.

She walked out the front door and headed into the forest to the right of the house.

"I know you're there!" she shouted at the trees, waiting.

A few seconds later Chris wandered into view, hands up in front of him. There were dark circles under his eyes.

"Were you there the whole night?" Clair asked, and almost kicked herself for feeling bad for him.

"Yes," he said. "I wanted to make sure you were . . . okay."

"Sure you did," she said, crossing her arms and cocking her head to the side. "That *friend* of yours, Sam, told you to stand guard, didn't he?"

Chris smiled shyly and lowered his arms.

Clair shook her head and looked at him. He was the same person she went into the forest with yesterday—blue jeans, white T-shirt, gray clouded eyes. The only thing that had changed was his messy hair.

"So," she said, breaking the short silence, "you lied to me."

Chris winced, surprising her.

"I'm sorry," he said, smile gone. "But this is important. How important, I don't even know yet."

He was worried, but she didn't have time to care about his feelings when she couldn't even process her own.

"Okay . . ." she said, not knowing what to think of that statement, or what was going to happen next. "Where's Sam?" she asked, scanning the tree line and trying to find him lurking.

"He isn't here." There was a note of something strange in his voice. Clair got the feeling that Chris and Sam had different opinions about her. "He told me to call him when you came around."

Chris was still standing there looking at her.

"Was there something else you wanted to say without Sam here?"

"Yes," he said, and walked toward her until they were only a foot apart. Her breath hitched in her chest. She could smell the fresh pine on his shirt and see little dark spots in his gray eyes. Even though he was a foot away, she could feel the heat radiating from him, and it unnerved her that she liked it so much.

"Whatever this means," Chris continued, his voice deep and raspy from lack of sleep, "whatever type of angel you are," he paused, his eyes searching the depths of her own, "it makes you special, powerful."

Clair looked into his deep eyes and felt something inside her hum. As she watched him turn around and head into the forest, she realized she hadn't been breathing.

"Are you going to use some angelic power to *call* Sam?" Clair yelled sarcastically after him.

He turned around, pulling a shiny black cell phone from his pocket. Clair thought his smile was a bit too smug.

Sam arrived a few minutes later, so silent Clair almost jumped out of her skin when she saw him.

"So," Clair said, collecting herself and looking between the two of them, "prove to me that I'm an angel."

"Is there a way to do that?" Chris looked at Sam, eyebrows raised.

Sam looked past Clair to her house.

"I need you to bring that table outside," Sam said, pointing to the wooden coffee table through the kitchen window.

Clair looked toward the kitchen.

"Why?"

"I think it was made from a certain special tree," Sam said, glaring at her.

"Fine," she said, growing impatient and wondering what the hell his problem was. Clair looked back at the table. It had to weigh at least fifty pounds. "I'm going to need help."

Chris stepped forward, but Sam blocked him with an outstretched arm.

"No," he said, looking at Clair. "We can't get past the edge of your property. There's a barrier. You have to do it alone. Make sure you bring it to this exact spot in the forest."

There was a second of silence while Clair processed.

"Let me get this straight," she said, eyeing the two of them. "You are both going to watch me drag that table out here into the forest, by *myself*?"

"Clair," Sam sighed, looking frustrated, "you want answers, and we can give you some. It's obvious that woman knows something, but at the moment, I would rather deal with you first."

"*That woman*? She's my grandmother," Clair said. She wanted to punch him in the face. "And her name is Dorthea—or Dotty. But never call her *that woman*."

With that, she turned on her heel and stomped to the house. The table was heavy. Getting it through the door was a nightmare. She had to tilt the damn thing on its side and push it through by the long wooden legs, where it landed like a drunk bridesmaid on its face in the dirt. She managed to get it halfway to the forest's edge, stopping only once to catch her breath, and glared at the men watching her struggle.

As soon as she crossed the line into the thicker part of the forest, Sam and Chris each grabbed a side and brought it deeper into the woods, placing it in a patch of sunlight. Chris stepped away and looked to Sam for instruction.

"Take the knife out of your pocket," Sam told Clair.

She had forgotten it was there, which could have been extremely inconvenient had she fallen while she was dragging the chair through the woods. Clair grabbed the blade by the hilt and held it steadily in her right hand. She wasn't going to give this man a weapon.

"Now," Sam said, not reaching for it, "squeeze some of your blood onto the wood."

Some part of her knew that was coming. It happened in all the movies. Spells required blood sacrifice—either a full human, a chicken, sometimes a dove in that epic movie with Sandra Bullock, *Practical Magic*. And since they said she was an angel, she suspected something like this would happen, considering the Old Testament and how often people would kill lambs. She didn't like feeling like the lamb, though.

It took a few seconds for her to muster the courage (she didn't like blood), but she pricked her finger with the knife, wincing as the blood spilled, bright and red, onto the dark wood.

The wood, which had never had water damage in the entirety of Clair's life, drank her blood like a fine wine, the color changing from deep crimson to bright gold.

There was a slight pause where Sam inhaled, exhaled, and repeated this task. Clair didn't know him very well, but she knew enough about people that it wasn't a good sign.

"She has seraph blood in her." Sam planted both hands on the table, eyes fixed on the blood, her blood, the color dimming from golden to a normal reddish brown.

"That doesn't make any sense!" Chris pounded his fist into the nearest tree, shaking green leaves from the branches.

"The table doesn't lie," Sam said, staring at the spot.

"It's impossible." Chris was staring off into the trees. "No seraph has ever left the eternal realm."

Clair didn't understand. Seraph? Like highest-ranking angel, seraph? She was pretty sure the Old Testament mentioned they were multi-eyed alien-looking creatures that sat next to God's throne like guard dogs. She was so confused. They were angels, they said they were angels (Clair made a mental note to make them prove that somehow), and so it wouldn't be weird for her to be another type of angel.

Suddenly, Chris grew rigid, his eyes very wide.

"There was one," said Sam.

Chris turned to face Clair, eyes blank and empty.

"One what?" Clair asked. She was trying to follow the strange conversation.

Sam turned to her, his brow furrowed above sad eyes. "One seraph who left the realm. You might know him as Satan."

Clair felt as if all the air had been sucked from her lungs.

She knew she was standing in the forest, but somewhere in her mind, she could hear screaming, a piercing sound that spoke of death, of destruction, of an eternal battle that raged between evil and good.

And here she was, standing between angels, a draft pick for the devil.

"I can't be." She was looking between the two of them, her breath coming fast and shallow. They were crazy. She wasn't some Satanic being, or derived from Satan, or anything of the sort.

"You are part seraph, Clair." Sam was facing her, hands fisted at his sides. "This table was made from the wood of a *Cercis siliquastrum*, or Judas tree, the same tree Judas hung from after betraying Christ . . . The table can't lie."

Chris walked over to her and touched her shoulder. She winced, but he didn't remove his hand. Clair felt the warmth through her shirt.

"I know this is a lot to process," he began, "but you need to acknowledge the truth. Go deep within yourself, ask the question, and see how you feel."

Clair moved away from him and leaned against the nearest tree.

Taking a deep breath, she closed her eyes and tried to slow her heartbeat, focusing on her core. Once she felt calm, she asked—in her heart—"Am I an angel?"

Yes.

Clair's eyes flew open. The voice had answered.

"The voice is my angel blood?"

Sam and Chris glanced at each other.

"The voice?" asked Chris.

Clair decided it wouldn't be a good idea to admit that she might be even crazier than an angel from hell.

"Never mind." She paced around the table. Chris had his eyebrows knit together, and Sam had crossed his arms over his chest.

"I don't understand." Clair stared into Sam's blue eyes. "How come you *just* found me? Why couldn't you find me before?"

"Well honestly," Sam said, "I wasn't looking for you, and neither was Chris. I was looking for your grandmother."

Clair felt her mouth drop open, but she snapped it back into place, her muscles tense. "What did you want with my grandmother?"

"We think," said Chris, stepping between Sam and Clair, drawing her attention, "that she was exposed to a high level of angelic energy when she was younger . . . an energy that could have something to do with your birth."

Clair couldn't believe it. But it had to be true, because she was born. She had the baby pictures to prove it.

"Why would she keep this information from me?" Clair said to no one in particular.

A few moments of silence passed before Sam answered. "We don't know," he said. "There are a lot of things we don't know, but we would like to. Dorthea—"

"Dotty," Clair corrected automatically.

Sam glared at her, obviously annoyed at being interrupted.

"You should call her Dotty. I know I said her name was Dorthea, but that sounds way too formal right now, and I never call her that, and since she doesn't have any friends in town, I haven't heard anyone else call her that, so call her Dotty."

"Dotty . . ." he said, watching Clair pace. "We need to talk with Dotty."

Clair thought about this for a minute then decided that she too wanted to have a few words with her grandmother.

"Okay, I'll allow that," she said, moving around the table again. "But first, what are you two? I know you aren't like me, aren't a seraph, or whatever, because of the way you just freaked out."

"No," said Chris. "We're minor angels, but mostly we're like humans."

"We have been sent here to atone for what we did, not live another life." Sam was upset, and Chris looked like a kicked puppy.

"Atone . . ." Clair said. The word was too deep and meaningful to mean something good. Clair was smart enough to tell by their expressions that they were sent here to atone for something bad.

"Were you murderers?" she asked, not really wanting to know the answer. These two were her only link to a life she never knew existed, besides her grandmother, who had kept this from her, or didn't know, or something. If they were evil, then she might never be able to trust them, or learn about what all of this meant for her future.

"Not exactly." Chris was looking at the trees, his eyes far away and clouded.

"Truth is," said Sam, "we don't really know exactly who we were. We only wake with the understanding of our existence and that we have been given a second chance."

Clair was processing.

She took a few heavy breaths and willed her mind to focus. She was an angel. They were angels. She might be the daughter of the devil, she might not. Somehow she wasn't freaking out. That was a good sign.

"Okay," she said, shaking her hands out at her side. She did that sometimes when she needed to get her blood flowing. "What are the basics?"

Sam and Chris exchanged another glance.

"Stop doing that," said Clair. "I want answers, and I don't know if you two can communicate with each other just by looking. Give me straight answers."

"Well," said Sam, leaning against the table. "It's been a few hundred years since I became a minor angel . . ." He looked to Chris, who was still staring off into the distance.

"It was a couple of years ago," Chris began, putting his hands in his pockets as he turned to Clair. "All I remember is light and a feeling of peace. We wake up in a new place, with an identity and no idea who we were before we died."

He was watching Clair's expression, testing to see how much she could handle. She made sure to keep her face a mask.

He continued.

"When we wake up, we know that we have been given an opportunity—I don't know how we know this, we just do"—he glanced at Sam, who nodded—"to atone for our actions . . . for the life we took."

Clair stopped breathing. "So . . . you are murderers."

"No," said Chris. "We took our own lives."

Clair glanced from Sam to Chris as understanding washed over her like a waterfall. "You killed yourselves?"

"Yes," said Sam. "Minor angels, as my studies have found, are created by the Eternal Good—God, you might understand him as—to give us a second chance at redemption . . . a second chance at eternal life."

Clair immediately thought of that night, all those years ago, in the bathtub.

The first night she had heard the voice.

CHRIS

Chris thought the meeting in the forest yesterday went well—all things considered.

After the table test, Sam told Clair that she would be taking lessons with the two of them in the woods as often as she could until Sam figured out the best way to approach Dorthea. It took a while for Clair to feel comfortable with the idea, and she only agreed to the meetings if Chris was a part of the training. She was also forbidden from telling anyone what she was or what they were doing.

Clair protested, saying Dotty needed to know what was happening, but Sam was adamant—going so far as to threaten to curse her if she didn't comply. Clair reluctantly agreed, and Chris thought it was only because she didn't know anything about angel powers and couldn't tell if Sam was lying.

Chris couldn't even tell.

Sam decided to stay with Chris at his house in the woods, and was currently sitting at the kitchen table reading the local newspaper that Chris had brought back from his trip to Awake earlier that morning.

He had just wanted to make sure Clair was still emotionally stable after finding everything out the day before, but it turned out she was more than okay, she was excited.

"Hey, Chris!" she had shouted, a bit too loud when he walked in the door to the coffee shop.

"Hey," he had said, the smile coming easily to his face. She was bustling about like normal, making drinks and chatting with people as if nothing was amiss. It had given him hope; she was strong.

"See you later today!" was the last thing she had said to him before devoting all her attention to the many Awake customers. It had only been then that Chris realized that Clair would be coming over to *his* place.

Chris sat down across from Sam and scrutinized his house.

If it wasn't for the modern windows, it would look more like a cabin than a house: two bedrooms, one bathroom, a small kitchen with a plain white fridge, and an even smaller living room. It did have a wonderful stone fireplace, though.

He looked up at Sam, who was sipping his tea. Chris had made them a breakfast of eggs and toast, and situated Sam in the spare bedroom. Sam seemed comfortable enough, and Chris was happy for the company after two years alone.

"So," Chris said, taking a bite of toast. "What will we be teaching Clair today?"

Chris felt just as new to this whole thing as Clair and was excited to be learning the techniques. Sam didn't even look up from the paper.

"Nothing yet," he said, flipping a page. "Today I want to get a feel for her physical capabilities and begin her nutrition regimen."

"Nutrition what?" Chris repeated, curious.

Sam folded the paper and leaned back in his chair.

"We will need to evaluate her stamina and muscle to fat ratio in order to determine how much work she needs to do."

When Sam saw the confusion on Chris's face, he continued. "Having a high-ranking angel's blood doesn't mean that Clair can continue living her life the way she has been and still be able to accomplish the skills she will need to know in order to survive.

"Based on what I can tell so far, the barrier Dorthea no doubt created around her house, and the general proximity of this town, have kept her hidden from evil. But now that she has awakened the power in her blood, it is more likely to find her."

"But," Chris said, staring at Sam, "we were the ones who awakened her blood by performing that test."

"Yes," Sam arched an eyebrow. "So?"

"So," Chris said, appalled, "we cursed her! If we hadn't forced the branch to fall, she might never have—"

"Never have what?" Sam interjected, leaning into the table, arms folded. "Never have realized what she was? Never have had the chance to play a significant part in the eternal struggle between evil and good? No, Chris . . . maybe she wouldn't. But you're letting your personal feelings for this girl impair your judgment."

Chris felt like he had been slapped in the face. Feelings?

Sam leaned back in the chair again and studied him. "Look at it this way. As far as we know, there has never been a seraph in the earthly realm. The only one ever mentioned was in the Christian New Testament as Satan, but all religions know the Ultimate Good and Ultimate Evil by different names. That is to say, what they are called is not as important as what they *represent* and the roles they play in the earthly realm. So based on this information, what do you think it means that Clair has seraph blood?"

Chris leaned back in his own chair, hands in his lap, and considered.

"Well," he said, processing. "Maybe that something is changing . . . for good *or* evil?"

Sam smiled. "Exactly."

Later that afternoon Chris walked back to Awake to escort Clair to his house for the first training session. Clair said she would keep their meetings secret to her friends and Dotty by excusing her disappearances on the pretense of going for a hike.

She was sitting outside the shop waiting for him when he arrived.

"Hey, Chris," she said, standing.

"Hey," he said, picking up her small bag and hefting it over his shoulder. She smiled oddly at him when he picked up the bag, but shrugged and followed him in the direction of the forest.

They talked about her day, and Clair asked him what they would be learning in the first session, to which he admitted that Sam had everything planned.

"He is the ringleader in this operation, isn't he?"

They were nearing his house, the thick tops of the trees casting rays of light on their faces.

"Yes." He laughed, and Clair seemed to loosen up a bit. He knew she was putting up a confident attitude, but the whole situation must have unnerved her at least a little bit.

When they reached his house, he suddenly felt self-conscious, and immediately dismissed the feeling as ridiculous. It was a much smaller house than she lived in, barely equaling the size of the antique shop, but things like that were not supposed to be important—at least not to someone like him.

"It's wonderful," Clair said, a little breathless. She looked up at him, her brown eyes reflecting the light of the sun. He felt his heart flip over in his chest. She broke the eye contact and walked up the porch steps. "It's like something out of a fairy tale."

"Thanks." Chris felt his chest swell with pride and shook his head to clear his reaction to her presence. It was like Sam said; it wasn't his purpose to feel anything for this girl. He was a minor angel, he had a job to do.

Sam was already in the living room when they walked in, some strange metal tools next to him. Clair paused, and Chris heard her heartbeat accelerate.

"It's okay," he whispered, gently touching her elbow and feeling a strange pulse of heat that he tried to ignore. "Those are just medical tools. No more blood," he added for good measure.

Clair nodded. Sam was laying out the last of the tools, an oddly shaped metal device that looked like two dull scythes clamped together.

"Hello, Clair," Sam said. Clair just stared at him. It was obvious she still didn't like him much. "Please stand in the middle of the room."

Clair glanced at Chris for encouragement. He nodded and smiled. He was glad that she was looking to him for support, and again mentally slapped himself.

Once Clair was in the center of the room, Sam pulled out a measuring tape and began. It was a quiet affair, none of them speaking while Sam measured every possible part of Clair—the inches on her arms, hands and neck. She blushed a bit when Sam measured her chest and thighs, and Chris politely looked away.

After he was done with measurements, Sam picked up the scythe object, and Clair took a step backward.

"What is that?" she said, eyeing it.

"It's going to measure your body fat percentage," Sam said, placing the object under Clair's bicep and grabbing the loose skin with his hand, pinching.

"Ow," she said, glaring at Sam. He ignored her and placed the tool over the place he had been squeezing. Sam sighed and removed the tool.

"Why did you just huff?" she asked him, rubbing her arm to ease the red mark.

"Well, if you must know," he said, placing the object down and turning to face her, hands on his hips, "we have a lot of work to do."

"Of course we do!" Clair yelled, hands in fists at her sides. "I agreed to get trained, and all you have done is take measurements!"

Sam's eyes narrowed. "I can't teach you anything until we get you into shape."

Even Chris knew that was not the right thing to say.

Clair's mouth fell open, her eyes popping. "What the hell does *that* mean?"

"It means," Sam said, his own voice rising, "that you have too much body fat. What do you eat all the time, junk food?"

Clair had just raised her fist when Chris stepped between the two of them, trying not to laugh at the ridiculous way Sam had handled the situation and the anger in Clair's eyes.

"Whoa, whoa guys," he said, placing a hand out on either side of him to calm them down. "This isn't going to be easy, getting along with each other, but it needs to be done, right?"

Chris looked from Sam to Clair. Sam nodded, but Clair was still glaring at him, eyes narrowed. "I am not fat."

"I'm sure," Chris said before Sam could speak, "that what Sam *meant* to say was that the type of food you eat needs to change because it has been affecting your blood . . . right, Sam?" Chris hoped Sam could see the plea in his eyes.

"Sure," Sam said, folding his arms over his chest and staring down at Clair.

"Alright then," Chris said, lowering his hands. "I think we have had enough training for one day . . ."

Getting these two angels to work together in peace was going to be the most difficult task in the world.

Chris smiled inwardly at the irony.

"Sure," Sam said, walking toward the spare room and shutting the door behind him.

Clair turned to Chris. "He is such a jerk!"

"No, he isn't," Chris said, continuing before Clair could protest. "He just doesn't always say things politely. But Sam really does care about this—about training you."

Clair just looked at him and shook her head. "This is going to be more difficult than I thought, and not for the reasons I thought either."

Chris laughed. Clair turned to look around the house, her eyes lingering on the fireplace. "This is beautiful," she said, walking over to the mantle and touching the rough rock. "Did you put this in?"

"No," Chris said, walking over next to her. "It was already a part of the house . . ."

Clair must have sensed his change of mood, because she looked up at him.

"What do you remember . . . about waking up as an angel?"

Chris had to think about it. There wasn't much he could remember from that time, and nothing from his past life.

"It was like waking up from a dream, into another dream," he said, his eyes unfocused. "I woke up here, actually, in this very house. No one lived here, and I knew it was mine because of the envelope." Clair opened her mouth to say something, but Chris continued. "And I felt the pull of the forest . . . and I just knew, I knew I was supposed to be here."

Clair nodded, then asked her question. "What envelope?"

"Sam said the same thing happened to him, except it was a scroll," he laughed, thinking about how funny it all sounded. Clair looked confused. "Sam is over eight hundred years old."

Clair's eyes popped, but Chris continued.

"But anyways," he said. "We wake up with a new identity, some money, and in my case, the deed to this house."

"But who leaves the envelope?"

"I don't know," Chris said, looking toward Sam's door. Somehow Chris knew Sam was listening, and had the feeling Sam might know more about being a minor angel than he was telling Clair or Chris.

"Well," Clair sighed, "I don't know what I would do without you to protect me from killing Sam."

"Yeah," Chris laughed. "I'm sure these sessions will be very interesting, to say the least."

Clair rolled her eyes and continued scanning the house. It should have felt awkward, he thought, standing there not speaking, but it didn't.

"Want to see my garden? It's just out back."

Clair nodded, and he led her through his bedroom to the sliding back door and out into the yard. Even in the summer, he was able to keep an impressive amount of plant life.

Rows upon rows of bright green vegetation were growing in huddled areas, stretching from the front of the yard to the back wooden fence on the other side. Seasonings like basil, thyme, dill, mint, parsley, mustard seeds, and cilantro, along with vegetables and fruit: tomatoes, carrots, squash, zucchini, lettuce, cucumbers, avocados, along with trees of apples and oranges and cherries, and a small hutch where he grew mushrooms.

But some of his plants were just for fun, like the mini-palm trees he had discovered and some of the other flowers he used to accent the vegetables.

"Chris," Clair said, walking over to a row of green cherry tomatoes and caressing one round, unripe fruit. "This is amazing!"

"Thanks," he said, feeling as if the sun had just gotten a little hotter. "Do you like vegetables?" Did he really just ask her if she like vegetables? What was wrong with him.

"I'm not an enthusiast." She laughed and looked over at him, completely missing the geeky question. "Why do you keep so many? You can't possibly eat all of these on your own."

"Actually, I do eat almost everything that grows," Chris said, watching Clair's eyes grow wide. "Don't get me wrong, I leave little baskets at some of the townspeople's houses sometimes . . . but I only eat what I grow."

Clair's mouth fell open. "What?"

"Yeah," he laughed, rubbing the back of his neck with his hand. "I have a chicken coop on the other side of the yard, where I keep a few hens—for the eggs, of course. There are some ducks too."

"Do you eat the ducks?" Clair asked, cocking her head to the side.

"Of course not," he said, liking the way her hair fell over her shoulders. It was catching the light just the right way. "The ducks are free to come and go as they please, but I think they like the seed I give the chickens."

Clair smiled. "Can I see them?"

"Sure," he said, shrugging. They were just birds. Clair walked quickly to the side of the house and gasped, letting a small giggle escape her lips while she watched the hens cluck and peck around the pen.

"They're so cute!" she said, grabbing some feed from their bowl and holding it out to them. One of the ducks wobbled over and began eating. Clair looked so happy Chris felt a balloon of joy fill his stomach. She was so beautiful, leaning into the pen, her hair pulled over one shoulder with a few strands falling and framing her face.

She looked back up at him and smiled. She was beautiful.

"I think I made a friend." She gestured to the duck, completely unaware that his heart felt as if it had stopped beating.

"I think you did."

CLAIR

Sam gave Clair a strict diet and a list of food she could eat, mostly fruits and vegetables, which she had been following for a week straight. But today he would be teaching her basic breathing techniques. She wasn't fat, and she didn't consider herself out of shape. Sure she wasn't super muscular, and she had already lost a pound on his diet, but she didn't eat all *that* badly, at least not as bad as Sam made her feel.

Sam also wanted Clair to start looking for information in the antique shop whenever Dotty was out of the house, but she had only managed to get into the shop without Dotty home once and was unable to find anything. She had been going into the shop with Dotty since she was a child, hiding amongst the tapestries, gingerly touching the glass and English tea sets. She felt too at home there to notice something unordinary. All of it was magical to Clair; the shop itself was another world.

"Clair," Sam said, "will you ever learn to breathe through your nose without sounding like some snoring animal?"

Sam sat cross-legged on a tree trunk in front of her, arms resting on his knees and palms facing up to take in the light. His eyes were still closed, thank goodness, or else she was sure they would be glaring down at her and the look of death she was shooting at him.

Clair wasn't sure what she had been expecting from her first actual lesson about being an angel, but this was a serious disappointment. Sam spent the first hour taking more health specs—"How much do you eat?" "What is your resting heart rate?" "How much water do you drink?" "What are your sleeping patterns?"—after which he watched Clair breathe in and out of her nose for twenty minutes, giving her instructions on proper intake and release.

Suffice it to say, Clair was sick of Sam.

"I'm breathing like you told me!" Clair shouted into the quiet forest.

Chris was somewhere nearby looking for herbs, as was his new personal pastime. She was sure it was just because he didn't want to get in between the two of them again.

Sam opened his eyes, his breath even and almost unnoticeable. The swift movement sent a spike of adrenaline through her body, as if it recognized the threat he posed even if her mind did not. He reminded her of a deadly snake, a reptile sunning itself before striking an unsuspecting mouse. Clair would be damned if she was that mouse.

"How do you do that?" she sighed, resigned to the truth that he was, in fact, very good at controlling himself. "I can't even *see* that you are breathing, let alone hear you."

Sam closed his eyes again, and Clair could almost visibly see his anger and frustration with her disappear.

"Patience, Clair," he said, opening and closing his fingers, "and diligence. Your breathing is irate and loud because your mind is clouded. What are you stressed about? What are you allowing to permeate your thoughts besides a sense of calm?"

Clair thought about it for a minute. She had been thinking about Emily, and how she was supposed to go bowling tonight. She was also thinking about Chris and his ability to grow his own food in his backyard, how hard that must be, and how he looked in the green T-shirt he was wearing today instead of the usual white one. It definitely set off his gray eyes, and she hoped she would actually get to see him in gray some time, but thought that might make him too hot to look at. She was also thinking about how his green shirt reminded her that the forest looked extra green today because of the fog that had stayed later into the morning, and about how green reminded her of all the salad she had been eating lately on Sam's diet, and that she hated salad but couldn't figure out a way to make it more interesting. Could salad be healthy and interesting?

Thinking about what she was thinking about showed Clair that, yes, she was overthinking thought. This made her head hurt.

"Okay," she said, sighing and returning to Yoda position, closing her eyes and listening to the silence around her. "How do I clear my mind?"

"You need to relax," he said. "When your eyes are closed it allows your other senses to take over . . . listen closely, touch the air around you, taste the oxygen on your tongue. Begin by tensing all of your muscles, until you feel so tight you might burst, and then relax until you feel so loose you might fall apart."

Clair tensed, feeling her muscles tighten, her breath ceasing, allowing the tension to press her body until, finally, she released it, relaxing her shoulders, neck, abs, and legs until they felt free once more. Her limbs felt smooth, fluid, all of her muscles relaxed. And for a single moment in time, it was just the air floating silently into her lungs, the slight wind running past her face, and the silence.

She could feel the breeze through her fingers.

It felt wonderful.

Until Chris came crashing through the forest talking about plants and she lost her focus, her breath becoming more erratic.

Clair opened her eyes to see Sam staring at her, mouth in an almost wry smile of slight approval before he yelled at Chris.

After those first lessons, she learned that Sam wouldn't begin tapping into her powers until she had been on his diet for a couple of weeks, and that Chris was assigned to hike with Clair through the woods to get her into shape.

And so, every day Chris would hike with Clair. She led the way, him mostly loping by her side and answering as many questions as he could. He said he didn't have all the information, but she didn't care. She just wanted a glimpse into this world, *her world*, one she had never known.

Clair wasn't sure if Chris liked hiking or not. Either way, he didn't get on her nerves like Sam, so she didn't mind his company.

One day, on a particularly strenuous morning hike, they paused to talk about a specific plant. Clair learned, after a few days of hiking with Chris, that he really did love plants—all plants. The man wasn't picky. They were his thing: he knew almost every type in the forest and even kept a list of which ones were medically helpful. Clair found it all interesting, but mostly she just enjoyed the way his face would transform with excitement when they found particularly rare ones.

"This," said Chris, eyes light as he leaned over a green leafy bush on the ground, "is a fern. Dismissible. But this," he pointed to the bottom of the plant where a small bulbous bloom was growing, "is something much more special."

As Chris was reaching to pick the bulb, Clair saw a ball of fur flying toward them, and screamed.

Chris was on his feet so fast he was a blur, extending his right hand and shouting something in a foreign language. The bobcat stopped dead, biting at the air shield surrounding Chris as he shielded Clair. The cat grew tired of the unwanted blowout and growled, stalking back into the cave. Before the rest of her mind could process what had happened, she realized it was the same cave she used to avoid as a child.

"I'm so sorry," he said, lowering his hand and muttering cursing before turning to her. "I shouldn't have let my guard down."

He was breathing heavily, his normally light eyes storm clouds and lightening, a small sheen of sweat on his brow.

Clair felt her own heartbeat slow to a normal speed before her brain clicked into gear. "You just cast a spell!"

"Of course I cast a spell," he said, matter-of-factly, rubbing his forehead to clear the perspiration. "I don't want to die."

That threw her.

There were so many questions in her head she shouldn't have been surprised that they made their way into her eyes.

"We can die, Clair." Chris was staring straight into her soul, trying to decide just how much she could take without breaking.

"But," she finally managed, "why? Why would you die?"

Chris stared off into the dense forest around them, the morning light casting floating rays through the trees.

"What a hell that would be," he started walking down the hill, "to live forever, to never rest. I don't know how Sam has survived all these centuries, *waiting*. I can guess that the higher up angels around the Ultimate Good live the longest." He glanced at Clair before shrugging. "I imagine it has something to do with being in its presence. It must be constantly regenerating, to be eternal . . . but all angels eventually die. It's a gift the Good allows everyone."

They found a nice spot next to the creek and sat down on a fallen tree. Clair stretched her legs out, taking in a ray of sunlight and thinking about the idea that there may be no God, just Good and Evil.

Chris picked a small flower from the ground, twirling it by the stem. He plucked one of its petals, small and white, turning it over and over, gently rubbing it between his forefinger and thumb.

"What would you consider magic Clair?" he asked, eyes focused as he bent over the petal.

"Well," she said, "magic is mysterious, and absolute."

"What do you mean by absolute?"

"I mean, from what I have learned from sci-fi, it can be drawn upon at any time and it's infinite power. Unless you're the bad guy." She made a point to look away from Chris and up at a chirping bird when she said that, because even though she trusted Chris and they were friends, she wasn't sure if Sam and Chris thought *she* might be evil, depending on her parentage. "The bad guy never seems to have enough power."

"Look at this," he said, standing and placing the petal in her hand. The middle was now clear, the outer edges still white and intact.

"How did you do that?" she breathed, touching the fibers and testing their strength. It was still fully complete, but she could see the ground through it.

"You could do it too, even without your angelic blood. Humans could do it," he said, staring at the petal. "I merely removed the outer color. The inner is all the same, reflecting the world around it. The fibers are the most important part because they hold the plant together; it's an invisible strength."

He was trying to tell her something without saying it, but she didn't want to hear it. They began walking again, and Chris changed the subject.

"So tomorrow we are going to do something a little different."

"What do you mean by different?"

"I want to start testing your blood—the angelic part," he said with a smile, stepping easily over a large stone. "Sam gave me permission," he added with a wink.

They were near the bottom of the bowl in the forest, where it was so unusually quiet. Chris always seemed to want to hike near this spot, but Clair liked it as well. It was oddly peaceful here, the smells of the forest mixing with something else, oddly familiar.

"Okay," she said, thinking of blood and needles. She never gave blood, because the nurses could never find her veins. Now she knew there was a reason. "I don't think you can get it from my veins, though. They move."

"Don't worry," he said, smiling. "I don't need to remove your blood to test it."

Clair knew that all too well, thinking bitterly of the test Sam and Chris had devised and her scabbed arm. Still, it was a relief. She was slightly tense standing so close to Chris when it was just the two of them, surrounded by quiet forest. Whenever she was with him, she could feel this pull, like her bones wanted to jump out of her skin and mesh with his. It was a creepy visual, but that's how it felt. She knew she was becoming too attached, knew that these feelings she was having for him were happening too soon and were completely off track, for both of them. So she tried to ignore it.

She realized she had been staring, and asked what he wanted to test.

"Starting this morning, after our hike, I want you to fast until tomorrow morning."

Clair just stared at him. "*What?*"

Chris walked a bit ahead of her and turned, his eyebrows knit together. "You know, *fast*—don't eat for a day."

"I know what fasting *is*, Chris," she said angrily. "But why do you want me to do it?"

"I'll show you tomorrow. Don't worry," he added with a smile.

Clair let her face fall. No food?

Chris was staring at her.

"What?"

"Have you ever skipped a meal before Clair?" She could tell he was trying hard not to laugh.

She had to think about it.

"I don't think so," she said. "Maybe once."

"Trust me—" Chris laughed and shook his head "—it'll be worth it. No food. Twenty-four hours."

"Fine," she said, turning on her heel and back up the hill toward home.

"Where are you going?" he shouted after her.

"Home," she shouted over her shoulder. "If I can't eat, I sure as hell am not working out anymore. You think I have a temper now, you don't know me when I'm hungry."

Clair was sure she could still hear him laughing when she reached the top of the bowl.

EMILY

Ever since Clair went on that hike with that Chris guy, she has been acting weird."

Emily was leaning against the wall of the Brown Bear, facing the small parking lot and watching Mike toss a tennis ball against it. He was supposed to be prepping the tables for the lunch crowd but told Emily he was on a break. That was fifteen minutes ago.

Still, Emily wanted to talk with him. They had been spending less and less time together, and even though he said everything was fine, she knew he was using with those ex-jocks he had been hanging out with recently.

"Maybe they're doing it," Mike said with a wicked smile and a wink in her direction, carelessly flinging the ball closer and closer to her head.

"I doubt it." Emily narrowed her eyes. "And watch where you are throwing that ball. It hits me, and you are so dead."

His smile only widened as he flung a shot two inches from her face, catching the rebound with ease. Emily had to remind herself this was one of the reasons she had fallen in love with him. He was quick to push the boundaries, and that devilish smile made her blood heat with just one look. Mike was your typical white-boy—dirty-blond hair, brown eyes, not too tall, with a medium build. But Mike was still hot, smoking hot, and Emily enjoyed remembering the way her tan skin meshed with his lighter tone.

She wasn't sure why the question came to mind, but she said it before she could reconsider. "Have you heard from your parents at all lately?"

Nothing about his posture changed, but Emily saw the veins in his neck pop.

"No." He caught the ball and walked over to lean against the wall next to her. "Why do you ask?"

Emily wasn't sure exactly.

Mike hadn't spoken to his parents since they had been dating, which was over a year and a half. She knew Joe was in contact with them, but they never once wanted to speak with their son. And even though Mike was a strong person, headstrong to be sure, Emily knew it was difficult for him.

She looked over into his brown eyes, sliding her hand down the wall and entwining her fingers with his warm ones. She always thought he had painter's hands, long and thin but not like skin stretched over bone.

"Just asking," she said with a smile.

He smiled at her, exposing white, straight teeth. She was close enough to smell the cinnamon of his gum—and something else.

"Mike!" she said, moving closer and sniffing his mouth. "Did you have a drink already?"

His eyes clouded, and he moved away from the wall, his back facing her. Emily felt her blood heat.

"It's not even noon yet! And you're working! If Joe finds out . . ."

"He won't find out!" He cut into her sentence, spinning to face her. "It's not that big of a deal, Em. Stop being such a prude."

Emily was *not* a prude.

She was just trying to help. Instead, they were growing further and further apart. He was changing, and even though she considered herself a tolerant person, she would not follow him down this path.

What happened to the boy she had fallen in love with? Maybe that was the problem. Maybe she had fallen in love with a boy and not a person even slightly interested in becoming a man.

Even a year ago he was a wild child, sneaking her into movies, climbing in her window at night (even though he didn't need to), where they would actually stay up talking about what they wanted from life, their hopes and dreams. Emily had been living her own little fairy tale, and now the ending was turning into a dark romance.

Just then Joe walked out and grunted for Mike to get back to work.

"See you later, Em," he said, letting the ball fall to the ground, where it bounced, bounced, bounced before slowly rolling away.

"Bowling tonight?"

It was a sad attempt, but worth trying.

"Sure," he said, pausing to kiss her on the cheek. "See you later."

Emily arrived at work a few minutes before her first client was due into the salon.

Rita, the receptionist, a slight blonde girl with short hair and a love of fashion, was already categorizing client files and writing up the schedules.

"Hey, Rita," Emily said. "I know I have Mrs. Doppler today, and then it's Mr. Kingston from the mayor's office, right?"

"Yep, sounds right." Rita was clicking away on the computer. "You also scheduled Tina for a bang cut at the end of the day."

Emily forgot about that. She liked to offer free bang trims to her customers in between full and partial highlights or styles. It helped them out but also kept them coming to her regularly.

When Emily had first moved back to town, she started working for Ray's Hair Salon, one of the only salons in Healdsburg (unless you wanted a quick fix at the barber shop off Main Street), and she only had the customers none of the other stylists had time for. Now she had over thirty personal clients, which, in a town this size, was impressive.

Emily walked over to her station and started cleaning her tools. She liked working with hair, and in a small way the conversations she had with her clients were a lot like being a psychologist, with the artistic flair of styling hair at the same time. She had always been the one to cut her friends' hair in high school, and while every little girl had at some point or another cut their dolls' hair, Emily took pride in the fashionable bobs and layers her dolls still had after all these years.

A small smile came to her lips at the thought. Her mother had been so encouraging, and her father wanted nothing less for her than whatever she could dream. Now her income was helping to support both of them, and even though she wasn't Catholic anymore, Emily felt blessed that she was able to enjoy her work.

She had enough clients to rent her station back from the owner after only a few months. She was no longer a salaried employee, and she secretly called her spot Emily's Hair Heaven. It was corny, but she liked it well enough.

Mrs. Doppler walked into the salon, a portly woman with just as big a heart, who greeted Emily with a large smile.

"Hello, dear! Have you heard about the new bakery renovations? Apparently . . ."

And from that moment on, Emily listened to the gossip of the town. Mrs. Doppler was the local veterinarian, occasionally working with the ranch owners on prize race horses, but most often on house pets. Today must have been a regular day.

While Emily shampooed and conditioned, Mrs. Doppler told her all about how Henry, Mr. Fleetenburg's cat, accidently swallowed his hearing aid. Unfortunately, the only thing she could do for the cat was give him laxatives and hope that nature took its course.

There was never a lack of gossip in such a small town, but most people stuck to their own lives, talking about their children, wives, or work experiences.

It wasn't until the end of the day when Tina came in for her bang trim that Emily got a taste of some real gossip.

"Oh, that's so much better!" Tina was admiring the cut in the floor-length mirror. "They were being dreadfully unruly."

"Anytime," Emily said, sweeping up the hair around her station. She was five minutes late to bowling, but she had texted Andrew asking him to save her a spot and get her shoes, and if Mike was there yet. He wasn't.

"Did you know Clair Douglas is back in town?" Tina asked, adjusting the shorter bangs.

"Yes, actually," Emily said, keeping her voice even. "I ran into her at the Brown Bear a few weeks ago."

"Oh!" Tina said, eyes widening with curiosity. "Well she doesn't *appear* to have been pregnant or harmed in some way like most people thought when she disappeared all those years ago." When

Emily only nodded, Tina continued, probing for information. "I saw her at the coffee shop a few days ago, working for Andrew."

"Yes," Emily said, folding the black hair guard and placing it back in the drawer. "She finished college a couple of months ago and couldn't find a job, so she moved back."

"Awe, poor thing, been happening to a lot of people nowadays."

Emily knew that too well.

"I see Dorthea walking around town in the early mornings every once in a while as well," Tina continued. "Still as odd as ever. You heard that story about her in the forest, right?"

Emily nodded and insisted she *had* heard the gossip on Dotty, hundreds of times. But Dorthea had always been kind to Emily, albeit a little strange about flowers, and people in town tended to overexaggerate things.

"Alright, dear"—she waved—"til next time."

Emily cleaned the rest of her tools, grabbed her tips with a quick goodbye to Rita, and drove straight to bowling. She hoped to see Mike's car in the parking lot, but that was wishful thinking. Sighing, she walked into the alley. It was crowded, their little group stuck at the last lane.

Even from a few feet away, Emily could tell that Andrew was flirting with Clair, who looked more tired than usual. She had bags under her eyes that kept drooping while she tried to pay attention to Andrew.

"Long hike?" Emily said, walking over to the two of them and grabbing her shoes from Andrew.

"Yeah," Clair yawned.

Andrew laughed, and so did Clair, but Emily was tired of seeing her friend so, well, *tired*. She also didn't like the feeling that Clair was keeping things from her. She had been going on hikes with Chris almost every day and never once said anything about it.

"You should skip hiking one day and have Chris join us for bowing." Emily watched Clair narrow her eyes in suspicion. She had heard the *real* question, but Andrew hadn't noticed. He did not, however, look happy about Chris joining the bowling group.

"He doesn't like bowling," Clair said, eyeing Emily more intently. "Plus, he's just a hiking friend."

"Who could hate bowling?" Andrew said, with a little too much enthusiasm.

Emily huffed and sat down, unlacing the red and blue bowling shoes while Andrew and Clair continued their previous conversation, something about a video game. Emily wondered when he was going to ask Clair out—and what Clair would say. Emily decided she needed some girl time with Clair to talk about Chris and Andrew, but also to get some advice about Mike.

They played two games before Mike showed up, drunk, two low-lives in tow. Andrew did his best to buffer the conversation, but Mike was overboard, loud, and drawing the attention of the owner. The two thugs with him went outside, probably to get high, and Mike grabbed Emily's arm and pulled her away from the group.

"Let's get out of here." His breath was sour, eyes clouded and unfocused.

"Mike," Emily sighed, pulling her arm away, "you're drunk."

"So?" he said with a drawl. "C'mon, baby, you know you want me."

Emily was both sad and furious, tired of his behavior.

"Go home, Mike," she said, turning to head back to the group. But he grabbed her arm, hard, his nails digging painfully into her skin as he pulled her back toward him.

"What if I don't want to?"

Andrew was there in a heartbeat, pushing Mike away and steering him outside without a word. Clair walked over to Emily, gently inspecting the spot on her arm where Mike had gripped her. It stung a bit, but as Clair touched it, it started tingling like it was asleep, and a warm sensation filled the area.

"I'm okay," Emily said, pulling her arm away and stretching the muscle. "It actually doesn't feel that bad. Just my pride is wounded." Emily was trying to smile but knew Clair wasn't convinced that *just* her pride was wounded.

Andrew walked back in.

"I put him in a cab," he said, a little out of breath. Andrew was a lot bigger than Mike, but that didn't matter when Mike was drunk. "I'm sorry, Em."

"Thanks, Andrew," she said.

"Want me to drive you home?" Clair was smiling at her other side, concern in her tired eyes. She was so glad to have them both in her life.

"No. Actually," Emily said, looking at Clair, "I need some girl time."

Andrew laughed, the tension easing from his body. Emily knew that he was fine with Clair hanging out with another girl, especially when that girl had his best interests at heart.

Clair smiled. "Lead the way."

Clair had offered to drive, but Emily wanted to keep it a surprise.

Her mother's old Accord puttered down the twisty streets, Clair in the passenger seat. Emily was sure that something was going on with her, and thought that with a little trip down memory lane, she could get it out of her.

They pulled up in front of the old high school, the colors faded by the sun. Emily parked.

"What?" Clair laughed, looking at the statue of the badger in the middle of the entryway. "We are having girl time *here*?"

"Yep." Emily got out of the car and began walking toward the center of the school.

There were so many memories flooding back to her as they walked together in silence.

She passed the plastic lunch tables and remembered sitting there with her first love, Steven Romero. Everyone called him Steven Romeo because he was the hottest guy in drama. When Emily looked back, Clair seemed far away, lost in her own memories.

They stopped in the center of the school, an open pavilion with an expansive lawn and a large cement mural that was about ten feet high. They walked around to the back of the mural and climbed up the shorter ledge, walking over and sitting down on the highest edge of the block that overlooked the campus. Emily pulled out two root beers she had thrown into her purse at the bowling alley, and handed one to Clair, who looked at it curiously.

"If we get caught drinking real alcohol in public, especially at a high school, we are busted," Emily said, popping the bottle of soda. "Plus, they taste better anyways, and it's the same amount of calories, we both know it."

Clair laughed and set the root beer down next to her.

"Thanks, Em, but I'm not thirsty."

"Do you like him? Chris?" Emily enjoyed being a forward person. It wouldn't be right for Clair to let Andrew think he had a chance if she had feelings for this Chris guy—that is, if Andrew ever made a move.

Emily watched Clair stare off across the high school grounds. She looked twice her age tonight—the fluorescent light from the lamps deepening the bags under her eyes. She took a calculated sip of water from a bottle she had tucked into her purse.

"Well," Clair began, lost in thought, "I don't know. He's just so . . . different." She looked up into Emily's eyes. "But, no . . . I don't think we will get past friendship."

"Well," Emily said, glancing back across the field, "there's always Andrew."

Clair laughed. Andrew couldn't be more obvious about his affection, which was just how he was, Emily knew.

"Yeah, but he's my boss. Plus, I don't want a boyfriend right now. I'm barely figuring out what I want to do for a career . . ."

"Who said anything about a boyfriend?" Emily took a big sip of the soda. "Just date a bit. It could be fun," she finished with a wink, dropping the root beer into a recycling bin below. It crashed with a loud cracking sound.

Clair laughed and shrugged her shoulders, wincing. Emily looked down at her.

"Just a peril of hiking." Clair dismissed the issue with a wave of her hand.

"Mm-hmm." Emily decided that Clair still wasn't telling her everything, but vowed to try again when she wasn't tired. They sat for a while and stared at the stars. It was nice to have someone like Clair to sit with, without needing to fill the space with talking. It was like a balm to her stinging heart.

When would Mike ever learn?

"Well," Emily said, standing and stretching, "ready to go home?"

"Sure." Clair dropped the empty water bottle down into the trash. "Thanks again, Em. I missed *us* time."

"Anytime," Emily said. "And by anytime, I mean again, soon."

CLAIR

The next day Clair woke up to an empty stomach.

She had to adjust her whole day in order to break her fast this morning at exactly twenty-four hours. So, instead of driving to work Clair was hiking through the forest with Chris, who was yards ahead of her.

"I'm pretty sure I'm going to die of starvation."

Clair was struggling to keep up with him as they trudged through the forest, his long legs easily outrunning her empty stomach.

She wanted food *now*.

"I doubt that," he said, a smile in his voice. "It's only been," he looked at his watch, "Twenty-three hours and thirty-five minutes since you ate."

Chris stopped near the creek halfway into the bowl. He liked to come here a lot, Clair noticed, but she had yet to ask him why. He dropped his backpack and looked around—scanning for mountain lions most likely. Everything must have been safe, because he told Clair to take a sip of water.

It was only then that she remembered the bruises on Emily's arm, and the tingling feeling in her fingers when she had touched them.

"Chris," Clair said, looking up at him, "last night Emily got bruises, and when I touched them, I felt a tingling sensation in my fingers, and she texted this morning that they were gone."

Chris smiled and sat down, cross-legged.

"Is this a question Clair?"

She looked at his smiling face. It was so easy to get along with him, unlike Sam. Chris never stopped her from asking questions, and even found the positives in her failed attempts at breathing correctly.

"I guess not," she said with a smile.

After that she sat down across from him, legs crossed, and continued the breathing techniques Sam insisted she learn. She just could never quite get as calm as she needed to be. It was like her heart was racing beyond her mind.

So far being an angel in training hadn't been what she thought. For one thing, she wasn't using any super powers and didn't feel like anything different was happening in her body. She had been on the nutrition schedule almost a week, apart from the last twenty-four hours, and it didn't make her feel any more in tune with her blood or powers, or whatever.

"Okay," Chris said after a few minutes had passed. Clair opened her eyes and felt relaxed, watching him pull a carrot from his backpack.

"*Really?*" she said, exasperated. "All I get is a carrot?"

Chris walked past her to the creek and washed the plant, gently scrubbing it until the dirt was gone.

"I grew this, so it has the most nutrients and no chemicals."

Clair felt her stomach rumble at the sight of the orange sustenance and decided she didn't care what he gave her as long as she ate something. Chris kneeled down in front of her and handed her the carrot. She took a bite.

It was *sweet*, abnormally sweet like candy. She looked at Chris, who was watching her with curiosity.

"It tastes really sweet," she said, taking another bite.

By the third bite, Clair noticed something happening: all around her the plants were beginning to glow, radiant with multicolored auras. She turned and looked at the creek, the normally blue water foggy white as if it was taken with a camera whose shutter was left open over time. Clair was so excited she turned back to Chris—and almost dropped the carrot.

His skin was bright white, his eyes like lightning.

She gasped.

Chris laughed, and it sounded like thunder, like a storm that covered the sky.

"Stand up," he said, grabbing her hand. His touch was like fire, the warmth keeping her sane. She thought this must be what hallucinating on some type of drug would feel like.

"Look around at the air," Chris said, his hand a blur of energy. "Do you see them?"

Clair looked. Throughout the forest, filling almost every inch of space were swirling dots of rainbow colors, moving like spirits through the trees. "What are they?"

"They are influences," Chris said, eyes watching Clair with renewed excitement. "Depending on the person, they can be negative or positive energy. When people make a choice, these influences react and energize that choice: for better or worse."

She sighed and watched the energies float around her hand like otters swim the sea. She could almost imagine little cooing noises coming from them.

"What was in that carrot?" she said, half accusatory, half amazed as she gazed at the wonders of the forest.

"Nothing," he said. "This is your blood, Clair, partly clean because of the fast. This is how you could see the world with pure nutrients."

Clair watched a bird float through the clear blue sky. When she focused, she could see its feathers, tipped with brown, its beak orange but fading to yellow as it got closer to its black eyes. The hawk must have been hundreds of feet in the air, but she could *see* it.

"Clair."

She turned back to Chris. His eyes were deep pools of gray as they gazed into hers. She felt more than alive, more than human for the first time since forever.

In that moment, Clair felt like an angel.

Needless to say, Clair went to work an hour later, feeling on top of the world.

It was like her whole body was humming, pulsing with the power of her blood. Most of the effects had worn off by the time she reached Awake, but she couldn't help smiling at everyone she passed.

She was greeted with a large smile from Andrew, who had a cup of coffee ready for her as soon as she walked in the door.

"Thanks, Andrew," she said, smiling at him. He was always so nice to her, and so *normal.*

It was a relief to be around him and listen to his stories about his classes and family. Andrew was one of those great guys: good family, good moral standing, gentlemanly, had goals for his life—and a job.

The bell above the door rang, and Clair watched as a family of three walked into the shop. The woman was portly, with curly hair and a genuinely happy disposition, while the man was thin with graying hair and laugh lines around his eyes. But their son, who looked to be about twelve, was a gawky boy with bright blond, almost white hair and deep gray eyes, wearing a gray T-shirt and blue jeans.

"Hello," Clair said brightly to the adults. "What would you like?"

The question was directed at the parents, but it was the boy who answered.

"Large cappuccino with an extra shot of espresso and a biscotti."

Clair felt her eyes snap to the boy.

"Jude," his mother crooned, "what did you forget to say?"

The boy, Jude, rolled his eyes. "Please."

Clair nodded and asked what else they wanted, to which the parents replied that it was only Jude who drank coffee. Once she was done making the drink, Jude grabbed it and walked out the door, his parents on his heels.

Clair thought the boy was weird, but eventually became busy with other customers and forgot about him.

About halfway through the day, Melody called in sick, and Andrew and Clair ended up working side-by-side, talking and laughing about nothing in particular. They had been discussing an essay he needed to write for an anthropology class when he said, "By the way, have you seen that new movie, *Love in Strange Times?*"

"No, I haven't." Clair rinsed a coffee filter and was having a hard time getting it back into the machine. "It looks cute, though."

She was just about to shove the filter when Andrew came up next to her, gently grabbed the filter, and gently put it away. Clair looked up at him and felt her adrenaline pick up. He was close enough that she could smell the mint on his breath from his favorite gum.

"Well," he said, keeping the small space between them. "I was wondering if you wanted to go with me tonight, to see it."

Clair didn't know what to say. She liked Andrew, and she was attracted to him. But she just didn't know whether or not she wanted to be in a relationship with him.

"I mean," he continued after her short pause, "we could make it a group thing if you want."

He was so sweet, thinking she was concerned about being alone with him. Clair had dated a few guys in her lifetime, and she knew how to handle a date, but Andrew was special. He was one of the good guys.

"No, that's okay," she said, putting a smile on her face. "It sounds fun."

His smile widened as they made the plans. Andrew said he would pick her up around six, which would give them both enough time to go home and get ready after work. When the date was set, Andrew loosened up and told her about this Mongolian barbeque place he was going to take her to for dinner. It sounded great.

After they closed the shop, Clair went home and showered, blow-drying her hair and running a straightener over it. Dotty was in the kitchen making dinner when Clair walked downstairs, makeup done with a little more effort than usual.

"Don't you look nice!" Dotty walked over, appraising. "Where are you off to?"

"Um, a date, actually," Clair said, feeling the heat rise to her cheeks. "With Andrew."

Dotty smiled and handed Clair a twenty. "Have fun."

Andrew picked her up right at six and drove them to a small restaurant off of Main Street in town.

The barbecue was amazing.

They were each given a bowl and then got to choose from a multitude of ingredients. Clair filled her bowl to the top with foods she wasn't supposed to eat: chicken, beef, broccoli, sprouts, and spices. In the middle of the restaurant was a large round stove that the chef used to cook their ingredients, spraying teriyaki sauce over each bowl and dumping it onto the stove, turning the ingredients over and over until they were steaming.

Andrew paid, getting them both a beer, and led Clair over to a table near the window. It was beginning to get dark outside, the sky a warm orange.

Together they ate and laughed, talking about their college experiences, politics, and even Clair's parents, which Andrew handled well, insisting that she had a great upbringing with Dotty.

In her time with Andrew, Clair forgot about evil and good, forgot about the fact that she was an angel or even about what the future could hold. Andrew had a bright smile and a warm laugh, and he made Clair feel normal.

After they ate, they went to see the movie—a sappy love story about a man who gets sent back to the Stone Age and meets his love.

When the credits were playing, Clair got a text from Sam. She could almost hear the frustration in his voice. Sam hated the cell phone Chris had insisted he buy in order for them to communicate more easily. "Hiking with Chris tomorrow morning and night. You need to push yourself."

Andrew saw the stress on her face and asked her about it, but Clair brushed it off as nothing. He drove her home, the two of them laughing about how ridiculous the movie was, and when he parked, he walked around to her side to open her door and escorted her up the front steps to her house.

She thanked him for the movie and dinner, smiling. He had his hands in his pockets, and she could almost see what he might have looked like as a little kid, with his hair ruffled and his smile mischievous.

As she turned to head into the house, Andrew grabbed her wrist. She spun around to meet him and found herself plunged into a long kiss.

He tasted like mint and beer, two things Clair found particularly tasty, his lips warm against hers. She kissed him back, running her hand up his neck and feeling his pulse quicken.

When he pulled back, she could see the light in his eyes, and her skin felt warm and electrified.

"So," he said, tucking a lock of hair behind her ear, "more than friends now, please?" He was smiling, and she wondered how long he had been waiting to kiss her.

She laughed. "More than friends."

Clair watched Andrew drive away, and walked straight into the house. Dotty was sitting on the sofa watching the news, which she never did.

"How was your date?" she said, flicking off the television and walking up to Clair.

"It was . . . nice, actually." Clair couldn't keep the blush from her cheeks, and she knew she must look pretty keyed up.

But Dotty looked thrilled.

"Good!" she said with a knowing grin. "This boy Andrew has my approval already."

DORTHEA

It had been years since James had died, and still Dotty couldn't forgive him.

The day was brisk—or morning, as it was just past dawn—fog covering the sky and floating through the quiet town. This was the time she liked to walk, before everyone was up and about.

She used to walk during the afternoon, before.

But that was a long time ago.

The fog would burn off shortly, the light turning the now faded green, yellow, and brown houses a warm sugar and lime. It always amazed Dorthea how fast time changed things and how slow it felt passing—at least for her. She never noticed until she looked in the mirror and saw the old lady staring back out of a younger woman's eyes.

That was heartbreak though—snaps you back to reality, leaves the body warm but growing colder by the day, waiting for the light that was once burning inside.

And, oh, what a light they had!

Africa, Asia, India, South America, and then North to settle down. What an adventure life used to be, so many priceless moments and even more precious secrets shared. It was a time in her life when an unhappy moment was rare, where days were long and nights, well, they were hot.

Very hot.

She laughed to herself at her bluntness.

"You hear that? Very hot nights," she said, glancing up toward the sky with a wicked smile.

She was passing the church now, a small white building with a bell, and stained glass windows depicting Biblical scenes.

What timing, she thought a bit sarcastically, holding back another laugh. Ever the opportunist.

She rolled her eyes, glad that there was nobody around to see her making faces to no one in particular. That would be just what she needed—more fuel for the rumor fire.

For the most part, the people in town all knew each other, coming together for outings and parties, but in her case, they just stayed away altogether. The spirited stories of her moonlit outing all those years ago kept children from walking into the antique shop on Halloween, afraid that the town witch might burn them up in a bonfire. Dotty always felt that Halloween was a great night to have a fire lit in her fireplace, and every once in a while, she would toss a pinecone into it, sending green sparks up and out the chimney—just for her own personal enjoyment, of course.

Being known as a witch had its benefits: passersby would hear the stories, and the brave ones would come by to see what an antique shop owned by a well-known witch might hold. Usually they ended up buying something from the exotic wares, making mild comments on the copious amounts of flower-covered items, and be on their way with only a slightly curious glance at Dorthea.

Small towns breed small-town anxieties, she thought. Little wonder why Salem was such a mess.

But suburban life had not been her original choice, not her destiny. It had been relieving, that night in the woods.

She turned a corner and almost smacked straight into Chris, the boy from town Clair had pointed to once in the distance before skipping off with him for a hike. He put his hands in the air and was apologizing until he recognized who she was and his eyes went wide.

Great, thought Dotty, the town already won him over. No wonder he never comes close to the house. Best play nice.

"Hello, Chris," she said. "Great morning for a walk."

His eyes relaxed, but his body remained rigid; she could scarcely tell he was breathing.

"Yes," he said, looking around the street. "You're up early."

"I prefer the solitude of the morning," she said, trying to find a way out of the conversation so she could go back home before people started milling around.

She had to keep her cooped-up witch reputation, of course.

Just then a car drove by, too fast to be a local—a lost tourist looking for Napa—and as they both turned to watch, startled by the sudden break in silence, Dotty smelled something.

When she turned to look back at Chris, he was already headed down the other side of the street, waving his hand and shouting, "See you later!"

Dotty was frozen.

Somewhere in the back of her mind she could hear the low rumble of starting cars, people moving, the coffee shop brewing up drugs.

It was like the blood had been thawed in her veins, her head cleared for the first time in years. All her memories came flooding back to her.

Chris had just made a very big mistake.

The Airport

She looked up at the screen in front of her: Delayed.

The invention of airplanes should have made this process easier, but imperfection still flawed humanity. She turned and scanned the room. There were enough humans here that no one would notice if someone disappeared.

Her energy had been low ever since the incident in New York. She was still angry with herself for letting The Gate get away but was sure that it wouldn't matter. She had enough energy left to sense where it was currently stopped, the pendant at her neck warm with life.

She turned back to the screen and scanned the flight list again. As she was deciding whether or not to exchange her tickets, she felt eyes on her. She turned to see a man staring at her in a not-so-polite way. She didn't have to ask him what he was thinking.

If vanity had been his only vice, he might have escaped, but greed was there, along with lust. She turned to him and smiled, enjoying the way his essence started floating faster through his body.

"Hello," he said, approaching her with a smile. "Is there anything I can help you with?"

He was attractive for his age, a businessman in a suit, with salty hair. She noticed the band on his finger.

"Yes, actually," she said, biting her lower lip and watching his eyes follow her hand as she adjusted her low-cut shirt to expose a little more skin. He got the memo. The gold amulet was pulsing at the thought of his life energy.

"I am looking for terminal six."

"It's this way," he said, hand pressing into the small of her back as he walked her toward the terminal. On the way she asked him where he was headed, to which he replied something about a business trip. She used her best seductive smile as she gestured to a small alcove off the main lane.

"Shall we?"

It didn't take much to convince him to follow her into the corner closet. At first things were going just as he wanted them to—clothes coming off, his breathing fast—until his heart was exposed, and she fed off his lust, vanity, and deceit, pulling the invisible life force from his body until he was nothing but blood, flesh, and bone.

But no life.

When she was done, she felt new again, watching the ebony skin on her arms shine with the warmth of the new energy that filled her body. The amulet around her neck was appeased once more.

She left him in the closet.

As the plane was boarding, she reached out for The Gate, feeling the pulse exit from the amulet and then return, bringing with it the location. It hadn't moved.

"Have a good flight," the attendant said, smile intact.

"Thanks," she said. This time, she thought. This time.

DORTHEA

ow could he have been so stupid?

Maybe he just stumbled upon a spot, Dotty thought. Maybe it was just an accident and the scent lingered.

No.

Chris had definitely been there, and he knew. He wouldn't have acted so squirrely around Dotty if he didn't at least suspect something. But to walk around with the smell all over him—it was just too close, too foolish.

She wondered what Clair knew, if anything.

How did he even find her? Maybe he didn't know about Clair. Dotty shook her head. Of course he couldn't know. But he might suspect her. Maybe that was why he met her in town. Maybe he grew suspicious of Dorthea based on his time with Clair, but he couldn't *know*—or they'd be in a much more dangerous situation right now, all three of them.

The back door opened and closed.

"Clair?"

Dotty was standing in the kitchen, her hand gently poised on top of a rather large kitchen knife.

Like that'd do any good, a small voice in the back of her head mocked her.

"Yep!" Clair shouted back. Shuffling alerted Dotty that shoes were coming off, and a camera bag was being set down, which meant that they were muddy, which meant she had been in the woods again.

A few seconds later, Clair was standing before her in the kitchen, face red from the hike.

"How was your day?" Dotty held out a glass of orange juice, freshly squeezed. Clair looked at it like it was a foreign object. They didn't keep a lot of fresh food in the house, but thirst won out.

"It was okay," she said, taking a long swig. "Not much happened. How about you?"

"Usual," Dotty replied, cutting the carrots for the stew. "Dusted, walked, and ran into Chris."

"Oh?" nothing in her tone or expression gave the slightest hint of secrecy.

"Nice boy, a bit on the unusual side but very polite, smells good," she said, hoping to get an emotional response to gauge the severity of the situation.

It was all in a blush.

Clair didn't blush.

Damn.

"Yes, well," Clair said, a small laugh escaping her lips, "he is interesting."

"You said that before," Dotty sighed. She didn't want to show her cards without being more certain about the game. "What makes you say that exactly?"

Like an alert dog, Clair picked up on the odd vibe in her voice. She looked up sideways from her glass.

"Like you said, he smells good."

So I'm not the only one testing the waters, she thought.

Dotty laughed, moving from the small wooden table that was just a little out of place, to the fridge, pretending to grab more ingredients. That was one of the best things about making soup: it could always take more, even if it didn't need it.

"Well, scent is one of the six senses, so a one-of-six *is* interesting."

Clair laughed and loosened up after that, changing the subject to Emily and Andrew and her horrible skills at bowling.

There was no way to push the Chris subject more tonight. Dotty decided he knew something and Clair could be in danger, but as it was, all she seemed to be was infatuated.

This, in their case, could destroy them all.

Dotty made a plan.

Clair

lair woke up feeling horrible.

Her dreams kept her up most of the night, but she never could remember them in the morning, and her training sessions were beginning to take a toll on her body.

Sam took over her lessons. All of them were about focusing her mind while she was in the state of sight after fasting. Which meant Clair was fasting every other day. He also tried to teach her what to look for in the antique shop. She had tried looking through the books for anything out of place, but all she found were encyclopedias—she just wasn't trained to look for the right words or meanings.

Clair wanted to talk with Dotty about everything: Chris, Sam, her angel abilities. She wanted to run to her grandmother and hold her and ask the question that was killing her inside every day: Who am I?

But she couldn't. She knew she couldn't.

It was also difficult keeping it from Emily, who was noticing a change in Clair's attitude, and Andrew, who was always so nice and considerate even though Clair had to blow off a few of their dates. She knew Andrew wanted to be her boyfriend, but even though she liked him, she wasn't sure it was a good idea with everything that was happening. They were definitely more than friends, but Clair was fine with dating. It was easier. She just had too much going on.

Clair knew eventually Emily would figure it out, though, and she missed being able to talk to her friend. She liked Chris, and even Sam, at times. They were important in the development of her powers, and she was constantly thinking of new questions to ask them, but she *missed* Emily and hated lying to Dotty.

Last night had been close.

She had been watching Dotty put away the leftovers while Clair pretended to look at non-existent pictures through her camera display from a hike she hadn't actually taken.

"Get any good ones?" Dotty smiled, the glasses positioned on her head making her gray hair stand up at odd angles.

"Yep," Clair lied, smiling and looking down at the display again. She had been on the verge of spilling everything. How could this woman not be her grandmother? Clair loved her, and Dotty loved Clair, she knew it. Maybe that was all they needed to be a family after the truth came out.

Even if Clair was stolen, or was the daughter of the greatest evil in the universe, maybe they could still be grandmother and granddaughter. But Clair knew Dotty was growing more suspicious. If Chris and Sam didn't figure out a way of approaching her soon, Dotty would figure everything out, and who knew what could happen if she did.

Clair still couldn't get them past the boundary around the house.

Either Dotty knew more than she appeared to, or someone or *something* else had placed the barrier of strong magic around the house, preventing anything abnormal from entering.

As Clair was trying to get the morning waves out of her hair with her straightener, she got a text from Emily: "Been two weeks since girl time. Picking you up from work today. Wine tasting, my treat."

Clair laughed, sending a quick, excited reply.

It had been a while since she spent time with Emily. Recently, Clair was so tired, she had been skipping out on bowling, and Andrew remarked a few times that he would cover her shifts if she needed more sleep. But in truth, Clair loved her chances to be in the coffee shop. It was a great way to relax her mind from all the sessions with Sam.

Now there was only one person she needed to text.

Clair sent Sam a text telling him she was canceling their training session tonight, using the excuse that her muscles and mind needed the break.

Clair wondered briefly if Sam would say no. He was very strict about the whole thing. What would she say if he forbade her from skipping practice? What would she choose?

She was still trying to master the effects of fasting, to focus her mind on certain colors and aspects of the light within each living thing in order to identify strengths and weaknesses. Sam had Clair fasting every other day, so on the days she was allowed to eat, Clair ate hundreds of calories. Then Sam would have her hike them off with Chris.

But she liked those hikes.

Chris was quickly becoming more to Clair, in ways she couldn't really describe. He was always so encouraging and helpful, Clair wished he was the one training her. When she told him that, he had laughed, insisting that Sam was the better teacher and much more qualified, considering his over eight-hundred years of experience.

Just then Clair got a jumbled text back from Sam that she was sure was supposed to say "Fine." She stuffed her phone into her pocket, a huge smile on her face. She finished her makeup and decided to walk to work. If Emily was going to pick her up at the end of the day, it would be better to leave her car at home and not on Main Street. She grabbed a muffin from the counter in the kitchen and, in case her grandmother was still in bed, she quietly shut and locked the front door.

While she walked, Clair decided the day was shaping up to be considerably better than the last few. Not only did she get out of training, but it was sunny with a nice cool breeze. And she would get to spend some time with Emily. Clair had never been to the wineries. When she left for college, she left for good, with the intention of never coming back. That backfired. But still, Clair thought it would be interesting to see Healdsburg through the eyes of the tourists.

Halfway to work, Clair heard her phone beep and die. She had forgotten to charge it last night. She stopped in her tracks, pulled out the hunk of machinery, and tried to restart it. *Dead.* Clair looked behind her and decided she was too far from home to walk back for her charger and make it to work on time. Sighing and hoping Emily had a charger, Clair continued toward work.

She beat Andrew to the shop and waited outside. He had yet to give her a key. About five minutes later he came flying down the road.

"Hey!" he shouted from his car, throwing the yellow Camaro into park, and jumped out and walked past her to open the door to the coffee shop. He was about to put the key in the lock, when he stopped, turned to Clair, and kissed her. Clair was so shocked she forgot to breathe. They had agreed not to show affection at work. Andrew was the manager, and Clair didn't want people thinking that she was getting special treatment, or starting any other type of gossip that could spread from this town.

She did note that he tasted like mint toothpaste and smelled like some type of spicy cologne right before he pulled away.

"Sorry," he said, his eyes betraying just how *not* sorry he was, "couldn't have done that if I opened the shop."

He winked and walked inside.

Andrew made Clair feel winded, like the earth was moving so fast around him and everything he did, that she had to constantly be running to keep up.

"How was your night?" Clair asked while she went to grab her apron from the cabinet behind the counter.

"Good. Dinner with the fam, nothing special." He was pouring coffee beans into one of the big machines. "How about you?"

"Good," she said, starting on the decaf. "Well, better now. Emily is taking me wine tasting tonight."

Clair made sure to unleash her best smile when she told Andrew this bit of information. She knew he didn't like her spending time with Chris, even though she had told him countless times that he was only a friend, and, after all, Clair was dating Andrew. That should have told him something right there.

Andrew's smile widened.

"That's great!"

The rest of the day went by quickly. Andrew, Melody, and Clair shared a short lunch break of sandwiches, talking about the most recent video game Andrew was obsessed with, while Clair asked him about his opinion on the local wineries. He said he wasn't a big fan of wine but that Emily knew her stuff and not to be worried. Melody said all wine was terrible and to go to an actual bar. They all laughed.

Emily picked Clair up a little before her shift ended, Andrew waving them off and telling her to have a good time. They got into her Accord and drove out of town, passing fields with rows and rows of grapevines organized into straight lines. Clair liked to stare out the window when she wasn't driving and watch for the gap in between each row to come into view and then disappear as quickly as it came.

Soon Emily slowed, and they entered a driveway with an overhead sign that read "Sun Valley Wines." They drove down the driveway for a quarter of a mile before coming to a small open parking lot in front of the largest wooden building Clair had ever seen. If she didn't know any better, she would have thought it was a very large house, the walls built with whole logs reaching over fifteen feet high.

They got out of the car and walked up to the entrance. Two large wooden doors the color of a burnt red sunset made Clair think of an entrance to a castle, not a winery. Emily laughed as she watched Clair stare open-mouthed at the structure.

"How have you never been here?" she said, reaching out and pulling open the door.

"I don't know," Clair said, entering the building.

It was breathtaking.

In the center of the room was a round bar, shelves of wine and liquor reaching up to the ceiling. On the inside of the bar, three bartenders were moving about, serving the many customers. It was crowded, and Clair was reminded that it was a Saturday. Working at the coffee shop meant that she worked weekends, and with all of the training, it was no wonder she had forgotten what day it was. But the best part of the tasting room was the artwork

All around the room were different forms of art: Sculptures neatly placed at random intervals, intermixing with the standing tables lit with candles and napkins for customers to set their drinks on and have conversation. The walls held multitudes of paintings, embroidery, photography, and other mixed media she was dying to go and inspect.

Emily led her toward the bar and sat down on one of the plush leather stools. She was wearing a red, low-cut top, her thick black hair in natural ringlets falling neatly past her shoulders. It was only then that Clair looked at her own outfit: purple spaghetti strap tank top and blue jeans, her hair in a sloppy bun, makeup most likely needing to be retouched.

Clair envied Emily's natural beauty. Her tan skin and full lips, curvy waist, and easy-going laugh always had people flocking to her. Thinking about it, Clair considered herself lucky to have such a friend. Emily had welcomed her back almost instantly, even after all of the past issues with their relationship.

"What will you have?"

A bartender came over and smiled seductively at Emily. He was wearing a button-up white shirt, with a black cord necklace displaying a shark's tooth, and had short brown hair that fell just to his dark brown eyes.

"Two wine tastings please," Emily said, pulling out her wallet. Clair stopped her with a hand.

"Nope, Em, this is on me." Clair pulled out her wallet and handed the bartender her cash before Emily could protest. He looked over at her and unleashed one of the most dashing smiles she had ever seen.

"Girls' night?" he said, turning back to Emily.

"You bet," Emily said with a small smile.

The bartender asked for their identification cards and spent extra time reviewing Emily's, most likely to find out where she lived. Emily looked over at Clair and rolled her eyes. The bartender seemed to get the hint, quitting his attempts and moving away to get them their first tasting of a light chardonnay. Emily said that they should walk around and look at the art, so they went separate ways.

Clair had been dying to check out some of the sculpture, and the first piece she walked up to was a convincing replica of a Rodin. The male was hunched over, his eyes marbled out of a coppery clay. It was beautiful, the reflection of pain and humanity portrayed in one swift capture of human movement.

This was what Clair loved about art.

She could never make a sculpture, struggling through those classes in college. It was amazing to her how someone could visualize something as wonderful as the statue before her and then create it from a slab of stone.

Clair moved along to the walls.

Each artwork was labeled with a title and artist, most of them from Healdsburg. She walked through landscapes created from fabric stitching, watercolors of home interiors, and fantasy, all interwoven next to each other just like the multi-dimensional townspeople they represented.

By the sixth piece and third tasting, Clair could feel the wine taking effect on her senses, dulling the chatter of the people in the room behind her and blurring the edges of her vision. It was a nice sensation, being able to relax and look at the work for as long as she wanted without worrying about the time she was taking to process each piece. The wine was also easing the stiffness in her muscles and the tension in her mind from all the training.

Chris and Sam had insisted that it was important she learn to use her gifts, and Clair didn't protest. She loved feeling like she was a part of something special, something beyond anything she thought possible for her life, but it was becoming more and more difficult as each day passed. Whenever Clair wasn't training, she was working, and when she had the chance to relax, she could never silence her mind—she wasn't sleeping well.

Clair moved down the wall to her right, coming upon a painting of what looked like a green forest surrounding a large maple tree. The artist had created brilliant shades of orange and red that were coming together within the leaves like a sunset, the branches leaning as if bent by an invisible wind. It was a tree stuck in the middle of fall, surrounded by a forest in summer.

The interpretation was beautiful, and Clair empathized with the tree. It was behind the times, not on board with the rest of the world as it clung to fall while summer pressed on.

She imagined Chris amongst the pines in the background, walking with his easy gait through the forest, speaking of magic. As her eyes roamed the deep greens of the shrubs around the tree, Clair came across a bush in the bottom right corner and almost screamed.

Two yellow eyes were staring at her.

She blinked and took a deep breath. This was a painting; they weren't really eyes. In fact, as she looked more closely, they could have just been out of place yellow leaves.

But something in Clair's mind knew this wasn't true. They were eyes, yellow as the sun, staring intently at her like some predatory animal was hiding in the bush.

Clair looked at the cue card next to the painting: Anonymous, No Title.

Emily joined her then, taking Clair's glass and replacing it with another one filled with red wine. Clair had forgotten to go back for the next part of the tasting.

"Beautiful," Emily said, staring at the painting.

"It is." Clair was staring into those bright yellow eyes. "Who do you think painted it?"

"No idea." Emily moved on down the wall to a watercolor. "Don't know why someone wouldn't want to put their name on that piece. It's definitely not bad. If I did art, I wouldn't put my name on it, just because I wouldn't want anyone knowing how horrible I am."

Clair laughed and looked back at the painting. Those eyes . . . they were so haunting.

They tasted the last two wines, which were wonderful, before heading back to Emily's house for some food. It was a later dinner than Clair had had in a while, and by the time Emily was done microwaving the leftover tamales, she was starving.

Emily said they had to be a bit quiet because her parents were probably both asleep already. Clair knew her dad worked at the local electric factory and Emily's mother was making jewelry, but Emily supplied most of the income for her family with her job at the salon. Even though Clair knew they had their problems, she was jealous of the family feeling that erupted from Emily's home.

There were pictures all over her walls of distant relatives and previous family members who had long since passed, and even portraits of Emily with her mother and father at various stages in her life. Clair thought back to her house with Dotty and couldn't recall a single family photograph on the walls. The antique shop boasted a wide arrange of images of random people, collected and categorized by year. But none of them were people she should know, should feel some connection to because of heritage.

Emily handed her a second plate with two tamales on it, and her stomach rumbled loudly in delight when she took the first bite.

"You need to eat more," Emily said, laughing.

Clair laughed as well, thinking about what Sam would say about her eating such a high-calorie food, and dug in deeper, even taking thirds when Emily offered.

It was getting late, and Clair hadn't been up past nine o'clock since she and Emily went to the high school to have girl time weeks ago. It was nice getting to talk with her friend, hear about how Mike was doing but also get grilled about Andrew.

Clair told Emily all about dating Andrew. She hadn't had a chance to since she had been skipping out on bowling, and made sure to include all the heated details about their first kiss, and all the kisses since then. She also talked about how Andrew was a perfect gentleman at work, only sending her cute smiles and keeping their relationship professional. She talked with Emily about her concerns in regard to the fact that he was her boss, and how everyone in town would talk.

Emily said Clair was overthinking things, which was true, and told her to just let things ride and see where they went. Emily was right of course—Clair always tended to put the cart before the horse, trying to predict all outcomes for any situation before making a move. Clair wondered briefly why she wasn't good at chess.

Around eleven o'clock Emily laid out blankets on her floor, and they both drifted off to the sounds of Emily's fish tank aerator. It reminded Clair of the coffee machines when they were percolating the morning brew, and she fell asleep almost instantly.

The next morning Clair woke up to Emily gently poking her nose.

"Up and at 'em, sleepy head." She was already dressed, her hair washed, wearing a pair of jeans and a striped white and yellow top. "Mom's making chorizo!"

Clair sighed and sat up. It was the first time she hadn't been plagued by dreams in a long time. She stretched her muscles and realized they weren't sore. How long had it been since she woke up and her muscles didn't ache?

"Wow, Em!" Clair shouted, thrilled. "I feel great!"

Emily tilted her head to the side, one eyebrow raised.

"You slept on the floor and you are this happy? You really *do* need to sleep and eat more, girl. I am going to go make some coffee. Go ahead and get ready in my bathroom. There is a towel if you want to shower."

Clair laughed and got up, walking over to the bathroom that was connected to Emily's room. She had some seriously bad bed head, and her eyes were puffy, but the bags underneath were reduced almost completely. She smiled at herself in the mirror. Even after all the difficult mind training, nutritional eating, and stress, a good night's sleep almost cured her aching body.

She turned on the shower and let it get warm before undressing and stepping in, feeling the heat melt away the last of her tiredness. Clair wondered, while she shampooed her hair and conditioned with Emily's fancy salon products, what Sam and Chris would have in store for her training session tonight. It would be over twenty-four hours since her last session, and Clair couldn't shake the feeling that Sam was going to work her, hard. He would probably make Chris lead her on a ten-mile hike, uphill both ways.

Clair smiled at the thought of telling Chris about the painting. She was sure he would love to see it.

When she was done showering, she dried off, pulled on her jeans from yesterday, and gratefully accepted the black tank top Emily had left in the bathroom for her. Most of Emily's clothes were too stretched out in the chest area for Clair, but tank tops were always conforming to the person who wore them. Clair felt refreshed and ready for the day when she went downstairs.

Emily was in the kitchen with her mother, speaking fast Spanish, the spicy smell of the chorizo bringing a fresh wave of hunger to Clair's stomach. She looked at the clock on the wall—nine.

"Whoa," Clair said, accidently interrupting Emily and her mother mid-sentence. "Sorry, Em, I didn't know I slept in so late!"

Emily laughed. "You needed it! Plus, my first customer isn't until around two o'clock, and if I remember right, you are dating the manager at your work, so you can afford to be a little late."

Clair laughed, filling a plate with food and stuffing it down into her stomach. Emily switched to English, telling her mother about their wine tasting girls' night, about certain pieces of art she had liked as well as the flirtatious bartender.

"That's my mija," Mrs. Sanchez laughed and said with a wink, "breaking hearts everywhere she goes."

After breakfast, Emily drove Clair straight to work, offering to pick her up and take her home afterward, which Clair gratefully accepted. Sam was going to make her hike tonight, she just knew it, and walking home would just take too much needed energy before training.

Even with the morning's breakfast, sleeping in, and missing the training session the night before, Clair walked into work an hour and a half late feeling amazing.

"Oh my gosh, look who's here!" Melody was jeering from behind the counter. "Miss Perfect is late!"

Andrew looked up from where he was making drinks and smiled. "I can't pay you for the time you missed."

"That's okay. I deserve it." Clair smiled devilishly and bounded behind the counter to put on her apron. She took the next drink order and began working next to Andrew.

"You look good," he whispered, smiling at her.

"Thanks," she smiled up at him, grateful that Emily had a spare toothbrush so her breath didn't smell bad. "Who knew the therapeutic effects of a great girls' night and some extra sleep?"

Andrew's smile widened at the enthusiasm in her voice and the skip in her step. He really was a great guy, and an even nicer boss. She needed to make sure to make more time for him, and Emily too. Training was important, but she wanted to have a life.

The rest of the morning went by wonderfully fast, Andrew left for an early lunch with an old friend from high school, and Clair worked alongside Melody until around one o'clock when Melody forced her to take her lunch break.

She walked down Main Street, looking at all the different food stops before deciding on a burrito from a chain restaurant. It was a horrible choice, but Clair enjoyed every single bite, imagining Sam's face as she ate her last burrito of freedom. Clair laughed to herself. He was so health conscious, and so was Chris, for that matter. Both of them were trying to get Clair off caffeine and away from bread. It wasn't like Clair ate that badly, especially with all the physical exercise.

As she was walking, Clair noticed the flower shop and decided to pay Jean a visit. After the incident with the lily, Jean had taken pains to trim the flower and place it in some plant food with water. Clair had been surprised one day to walk into her shop and find it looking a lot better, its scent just as intoxicating as it had been that day in her kitchen.

Jean had said that flowers were hardy things, this one especially, and Clair had left it to her care, only visiting once in a while to check up on it. She dreaded the day when it would wilt, and hoped as she opened the door that today was not that day.

It wasn't.

"Hello, dear," Jean said from behind the counter.

The lily was in the same bright blue vase, its petals looking like a face turned to greet her. She felt a paternal surge of joy as she walked over and stroked one of the beautiful white restored petals. It had regrown its broken leaves, and the stamen had reformed, producing a fine dust of golden pollen.

"Hardy little thing, isn't it?" Jean was admiring the lily. "Just add a little fresh water with some plant food, and nature takes its course!"

"It looks great!" Clair said with a smile. "I think it has less to do with nature and more to do with the fact that you must have a really green thumb."

Jean waved her hand as if to dismiss the thought but blushed beneath her long lashes.

Clair hoisted herself onto the counter and listened to Jean talk about each type of plant as she checked them—ferns and hydrangeas, roses and succulents. Jean had everything imaginable in her shop, and all of them were healthy, with vibrant colors.

"Now these ones," Jean said, gently lifting a small pot from the ground, "were your mother's favorite."

Clair had a hard time swallowing the bite of burrito she had in her mouth. She set it down on the counter and hopped down, walking numbly over to Jean. She was touching a small flower with many fan-like petals, each coming together to form a small ball. Clair leaned into the pink petals and sniffed. They smelled like summer—warm, light and airy.

Clair stroked the silky petals.

"These are carnations," Jean said, watching Clair. "Your mother had me make the bouquet for her wedding. She used a lot of these, all in white with some pink accents. It was beautiful."

Clair looked up to see Jean smiling at her and felt tears coming to her eyes. "I never knew."

Jean grabbed one of Clair's hands, her own eyes misty. "I only knew your mother for that short time right before her wedding. She didn't grow up around here, after all, but she was a beautiful woman with a kind heart."

Clair let the tears fall. She had never asked about her parents' wedding or where they met or known anyone who would have been able to tell her anything about them. Dotty was a private person, and Clair knew it hurt her to even talk about her son, ever since the accident, and mostly Clair let it go. But a piece of her always wondered about them, struggled to know them somehow.

"Thank you, Jean," Clair said, hugging the woman briefly before looking down at the carnations again.

"You're more than welcome." Jean turned to grab a flower canister, pointing at the different pots in the room. "Mind helping me water some of these bad boys?"

"Sure," Clair laughed, wiping the last of the tears with the back of her hand. Jean knew how to take an emotional situation and make it light.

They watered the plants for the rest of her lunch break, talking about the different types. Clair helped to trim the gerbera, large flowers that looked like mutant daisies, and to water and repot the *Penstemon cobaea* or Showy Beardtongue, which Jean nicknamed Big

Mouths. They were deep purple flowers that opened up like small oval bowls. She put her finger in one of the flower's mouths and laughed a bit at the childish act.

Clair felt close to Jean. She was one of the only people who knew her mother from all those years ago, and even though it might sound silly, Clair felt like she could be with her mother through Jean.

A few minutes later, Clair went to gather the rest of her half-eaten burrito next to the lily, intending to head back to work, when she got a strong blow of its scent, and recognized it. The lily smelled like Chris—smelled like the quiet part of the forest where they would train. Looking at the flower, Clair was reminded of the painting from last night by the anonymous artist, and those yellow eyes staring out from the bushes.

She almost dropped the burrito.

They were always training in the same place in the forest at the bottom of the bowl. When she had first met Chris, he was there in that same place, almost as if he had appeared out of nowhere. There were never any birds or animal sounds in the bottom of the bowl, and that feeling.

"I don't know what is with the plants, but they have been growing so well these last few weeks!" Jean was taking off her soil-soaked gloves and setting them in a pot beside the door along with her tools.

Around the same time as I brought the lily into your shop . . . Clair thought.

Chris said that minor angels had a purpose and that somehow Sam hadn't found his purpose. But Chris had mentioned something about waking up next to his.

"Thanks, Jean," Clair said in a daze, trying to collect her thoughts.

"You okay, dear?" Jean looked concerned.

"Oh, yes," Clair said, straightening her face into a smile. "Thank you so much for telling me about my mother."

Jean smiled and hugged Clair again before she walked out the door.

Clair didn't head back to work and didn't go home. She walked along Main Street in the opposite direction of where she was supposed to go, thinking.

There was a reason why Sam and Chris were so worried, why her blood was angelic. It was like the truth was just out of her reach, on the cusp of her mind. She rubbed her temples and tried to lay out the pieces again, ordering them over and over in her head in a way that would make sense. There were only a few things she knew for sure:

She had angelic blood, blood she wasn't supposed to have. Chris and Sam were minor angels bent on finding a purpose. Dotty was upset about the flower, but people always said she used to have the most beautiful garden in the entire town.

Clair reached into her pocket to search the Internet on her phone, before she remembered it was still dead. What was that passage again?

There was only one class in college on the Hebrew Bible, and Clair thought she was knowledgeable enough before the class that she rarely attended. The modern world had its own view of the Tanakh—most students calling it the Old Testament even after the professor became red in the face telling them that it could only be considered the Old Testament in conjunction with a New Testament, and that the Hebrew people didn't *have* a New Testament.

In fact, Clair had learned that the Hebrew Bible was actually a written masterpiece of many different authors combining the history of the Israelites from multiple generations and time frames. Clair wasn't sure what she believed in relation to the faith significance of that fact, but one thing was for certain: everyone knew the story of Adam and Eve, in the Garden of Eden.

Clair didn't realize she was running until she reached the other side of town, crossing through the back streets and alleys behind Main Street, hair flying behind her in brown wisps. The sun was setting to her left. How long had she been walking?

She reached the forest's edge and plunged in the direction of Chris's house. Chris and Sam should be there by now. They were supposed to have a lesson tonight, but Clair had other things in mind. It was time they told her the truth, everything.

She almost ran into Sam halfway to Chris's house.

"Where's Chris?" she asked, panting, when she saw Sam standing alone.

"I don't know. I thought he was with you."

Clair shook her head. "No, I was at work today. I have some questions for you two." She was staring at him, body tired, mind trying to keep the pieces she found together as tight as possible.

Sam raised an eyebrow but didn't object. Instead, he pulled out his phone and handed it to Clair

"I hate this thing. You figure out how to call him."

Clair dialed Chris's number and waited. She thought the phone would go to voicemail, before he picked up on the last ring. His voice sounded hoarse, and he was breathing heavily.

"What's wrong, Chris?" Clair was immediately worried.

"I got child abducted," Chris said, a slight irritation in his voice, "by your grandmother."

Clair stared at Sam, who looked puzzled in front of her, and related the message, blandly, as if she wasn't quite processing it. Sam's face grew dark.

"Sam looks pissed," Clair said, still shocked, and she heard Chris give a hard laugh.

"Well, yeah, I can't say I'm thrilled," Chris said. "She wants to talk to him."

Clair deftly passed the phone to Sam, who took it, placing it to his ear. He never said anything, his face blank. She could hear a voice on the other end giving instructions, but she couldn't make out the words.

"Alright," was all he said as he hung up and pocketed his phone.

"What's going on?" Clair still felt like her mind wouldn't catch up with what was happening around her.

"A trade of hostages."

Emily

Emily went straight to the coffee shop after her last hair appointment. When she walked in, Andrew was mopping up the floors, and only a few people were still milling around.

"Hey, Andrew," Emily said, walking over to the register and picking up a wrapped biscotti from the counter. "Where's Clair?"

Andrew stopped mopping and looked up at Emily.

"I thought she was with you."

"No," Emily laughed, taking a bite. "I was supposed to pick her up and drive her home. Maybe she just walked without telling me."

"I don't know," Andrew said, leaning the mop against the wall and walking over to where Emily was eating. "She left for her lunch break and never came back . . . I assumed she would call, but she never did, so I thought she would be with you—some girl emergency?"

Emily straightened up, the biscotti almost fully eaten. "No," she said, thinking about the possibilities. "Maybe she just ducked out for a hike with that Chris guy."

Andrew narrowed his eyes and then corrected himself. His feelings about Chris were just too obvious.

"I thought that too," he said, flipping the sign on the door from Open to Closed. "But he came in here looking for her around two o'clock. She hasn't been answering my phone calls or texts either."

Emily felt the hair rise on the back of her neck. What if Clair was in trouble? Hadn't she said something about her phone being dead?

"I'm going to call Dotty," Emily said, walking outside. "If Clair went home, Dotty will know. I wouldn't worry too much about her, Andrew. This is a small town. I'm sure she just lost track of time."

Andrew nodded but didn't look convinced.

"Will you let me know if you get in touch with her?"

"Of course!" Emily said with a wave of her hand, exiting the shop into the warm summer night. She dialed the number in her phone for Clair's house, listened to it ring, and then hit a robotic voicemail. She hung up.

It wouldn't do any good leaving a message. She was sure Clair would call one of them soon, but just as she was deciding to go and make sure Clair made it home, she got a text from Mike: "Come to bar—need to talk."

CLAIR

Sam told Clair that Dotty would release the barrier on the house long enough for them to pass through, for the trade. Clair decided she should walk in front of Sam, just in case her grandmother had plans to take Sam out.

"I think you should actually pretend to be my hostage," said Sam. They were at the edge of the forest, and she could see Chris tied up in a chair, through the kitchen window.

"How does that hold him?" Clair found herself asking.

"I don't know. He might be faking it," Sam said, glancing at Chris while he fastened a rope around Clair's wrists, gently. "But it could also be spelled. We'll see when we get in there.

"Check your ropes."

Clair pulled at the bindings and found them secure, which wasn't comforting should things turn sour. But she truly didn't believe Dotty was the enemy in this situation, unlike Sam, who was taking every precaution. The only person Clair was worried about was Chris.

"Good job," she said, feeling the ropes tighten as she struggled against them, burning into her wrists.

"Don't struggle too much," Sam said, rubbing the raw red parts. He whispered something, and the stinging subsided a bit.

"Thanks," she said, feeling like this was the stupidest situation in the world. Her grandmother had kidnapped an angel, and another angel decided to play along in order to have a conversation.

Sam took a deep breath and walked Clair in front of him toward the front of the house. They would be entering through the front door, as Dotty had dictated, where they would then walk into the kitchen. Clair hoped she hadn't sprayed angel repellent or something.

As they approached the edge of the property, Clair could feel something surrounding them, every step pushing them further into a bubble-like elastic in the air. It felt hard to breathe and even harder to walk through, but Sam held tight to her arms, pushing them both along until they emerged from the bubble.

They had been in the barrier.

"You don't normally feel that," Sam whispered, his breath labored. "I don't think I would have gotten through if I wasn't touching you."

Clair wondered briefly if that had been a part of Dotty's plan.

The door opened, and Dorthea stood, hands at her sides, staring at the two of them as they walked up the path.

"Clair," she said, concern in her voice, "are you okay?"

"Yes," Clair said, trying to throw some fake fear into the mix. Sam squeezed her arm, and she knew it wasn't working. "Everything is fine."

Dorthea backed away from the door, and they entered the living room. Walking backward, Dorthea led them to the right and into the kitchen. Clair had never seen her grandmother look so fierce. She was almost proud. And then she saw Chris.

The kitchen window hadn't done the ropes justice. They were wound tightly around his entire body, a glowing presence emanating from the straps at his wrists, ankles, and neck. He was sweating profusely and breathing hard.

"Grandma!" Clair shouted, watching her grandmother jump into a fighting position at the shout until she realized it was Clair who was speaking. "How could you do this?"

Clair was outraged, her fake fear turning into real anger. Dotty's face showed concern, and then her eyes narrowed in suspicion.

"Clair, what is going on here?"

Clair looked from Chris to her grandmother. Sam squeezed her arm. The plan, must stick with the plan.

"Grandma," she said, "I need answers."

I don't think either of them could have anticipated what Dotty did next: in one second she was looking at Clair, in the next, giant ropes like the ones holding Chris fell from the ceiling above Sam's head, wrapping around his body and throwing him to the ground.

Clair was stunned. She looked behind her to where Sam was wriggling, back to Chris, who was still seething in pain, and then to the triumphant look on Dotty's face.

"Sorry about that, dear," Dotty said, walking over to Clair and undoing the ropes on her hands easily. "Didn't want to have you looking up and spoiling the surprise."

The edge had gone from her voice, and she was relaxing visibly. Clair still had her mouth open.

"Grandma," she said, rubbing her wrists and turning to face Dotty, "I need you to give me some answers, and *not* hurt my *friends.*" Clair gestured to Sam and Chris.

"I have seen how friendly they are," Dotty said, walking over to the wooden table and gently touching the spot of blood stained into it. "This is yours, isn't it?"

"Yes," Clair said, standing up straighter.

"Why did they do this to you?" Dotty asked, her eyes bouncing from Chris to Sam for a fraction of a second before returning to Clair.

"I did it," Clair said, glaring at her. "My turn: are you really my grandmother?"

"Of course!" Dotty said, shock on her face and hurt in her voice. "Of course I'm your grandmother! These . . . *things* have tried to get you to turn against me!"

"No, they haven't!" Clair couldn't help the anger in her voice or the octave. This was supposed to be a peaceful negotiation.

So much for that.

"Chris"—Clair gestured to him—"and Sam"—another gesture—"have been *teaching* me how to be *what I am.*"

Dotty stared at Clair, mouth open. "You have been learning, with *them*?"

"Yes," Clair said, throwing her hands in the air. Taking a deep breath, Clair walked over to the side of the table across from Dotty, closer to Chris. "Why didn't you tell me. If I'm yours, why wouldn't you tell me? I deserved to know!"

"No, Clair," Dorthea said, moving a few inches away from the table. She took a deep breath and looked at Sam and Chris. "Their life doesn't have to be yours. You don't have to fight like they do."

"So you do know, about everything . . ." Clair felt her heart sinking. A piece of her had hoped, even still, that Dotty was an innocent bystander, or at least uninformed. It hurt to realize that she had been deceived her entire life.

"Yes," Dotty said, sensing her pain. "I knew you had the possibility . . . of being what you are." She was being elusive, and Clair suspected it had something to do with Chris and Sam listening.

Clair took a deep breath to clear her mind and tried to bring things back around.

"Grandma, these are my friends"—Dotty started to protest, but Clair continued—"angels or not, and I would appreciate it if we could all talk as rational adults."

"They could kill us at any minute!" Dotty looked stricken. "You don't know what they could be capable of!"

Clair walked over to Chris, who looked dangerously close to passing out, and touched his brow. He had a fever, and the ropes were burning holes in his skin.

"Grandma," she said, "Please. Trust me."

Dorthea narrowed her eyes. She glanced again from Chris to Sam and muttered a curse under her breath.

"These ropes will be hanging above your heads the entire time! Should anything seem to go wrong, they will come down—and this time, they will keep contracting until you're dead."

With a snap of her fingers, the ropes flew up to the ceiling, and Clair immediately turned to Chris. Somewhere in her peripheral she saw Sam rise from the ground, the ropes dangling like a menacing snake above his head. Chris was winded, but unhurt. When he opened his eyes he looked better, the fever in his forehead lessened as soon as the ropes were gone.

"Thanks," Chris said, getting to his feet unsteadily. Clair wrapped an arm around his waist and felt the blood in her veins course faster.

Now is not the time to be shy, she thought, before turning to face Dotty.

"Grandma, Sam needs to look at the books in the antique shop."

Clair didn't phrase it as a question and didn't wait for a response. Nodding to Sam, she helped Chris through the hallway to the door. A second before she touched the handle she wondered if it was booby-trapped, but it opened easily enough. Clair flicked the lights on. Everything looked normal.

Books upon books were strewn within the tight space, mini walls making a maze throughout the shop. Clair led Chris to the large desk in the center of the room, papers and books strewn open across it. For the first time, Clair saw something that looked suspicious. In the book that was closest to her was a picture of what looked like rope floating, written in another language.

A slightly hysterical laugh escaped Clair, and she could feel Chris look down at her as she called to Dotty sarcastically over her shoulder. "This doesn't make you look like a witch at all, Grandma."

Dotty muttered something, walked around to the open book, and eyed Sam, who stood off to her left looking from the book to the ropes above his head.

"So," Dorthea said after Clair had seated Chris in a chair opposite the desk. "What do you want to know?"

Clair sighed and thought for a minute. There were so many questions in her head she could barely contain herself, but before she got the chance, Sam spoke.

"You aren't angelic, are you?"

Dotty directed a piercing gaze in his direction. "No."

"So how did you come to possess Clair?"

Dotty straightened further, chest puffing out. "I did not *come to possess her*, Neglig." Sam's eyes widened a bit at the word, but Dotty continued. "She's my granddaughter. By blood."

"What does *Neglig* mean?" Sam looked at Chris. It was the first time he had spoken. Clair was glad he asked. She was wondering the same thing.

"It means negligent one, a slang term for a minor angel used by the higher-ranking angels."

Chris still looked puzzled, so Sam continued

"The higher-ranking angels use the term because we were human, then created into angels after death—a death we created. We aren't fully angelic and are the least expendable. But to them, we dishonored our rights as humans and don't deserve to exist."

"Oh," was all Chris said, but Clair spoke up.

"If you're not angelic, Grandma, how're you able to use magic?"

A small smile reached Dotty's lips. "Your grandfather taught me a bit," she said, throwing a triumphant smile at Sam. "Just enough to protect us."

"My grandfather . . ." Clair repeated. All she knew about him was that Dotty never knew him, not really. She had always told Clair he had been a fling after her brother James had died.

Dotty looked at Clair, her eyes sorrowful. "I never had a brother, Clair."

SAM

Sam thought the night had gotten wildly out of control, and didn't like the fact that ropes were hanging above his head.

"Dorthea"—he looked straight into the older woman's eyes—"James was your husband."

Clair looked off at a wall on the opposite side of the room, her face a mask. It must be a lot for her to take in, Sam thought, but there would be time for her to adjust. There were more pressing matters.

Dotty turned to Sam, the words spilling from her mouth.

"James said that he had been given a chance to live, to have a human life with me . . . but we were always in danger. Things were . . . *called* . . . to his blood."

Dotty was defensive and getting more agitated by the minute, Sam could tell, but he needed more information.

"So you pretended he was your brother," said Chris, who was leaning against the side of the desk, his wounds from the ropes almost healed.

"Yes," Dotty said, glancing at Clair. Her face was still closed off, staring into nothing. But it all needed to be out in the open now.

"So," Sam began, trying to dictate this odd story, "James was an angel, probably seraph, who was made human." Sam looked at Dotty, who shrugged, before continuing. "Who was maybe made human and was allowed to live with you, until he died?"

"It was a closed casket," she said, looking at the faces before her. "James would . . . walk in the forest a lot after we moved here. He would be gone for days sometimes. He said he was walking with a friend." She stopped for a minute to inhale deeply, obviously trying to stay in control. "And then one day, he didn't come back, and I knew he was gone."

A hushed silence fell over the room. Sam gave Chris a knowing look.

"Like Enoch," said Clair, still looking at nothing.

"Who's Enoch?" said Chris.

"It's not important," said Sam, who was glaring at Dotty and tapping the ragged old book open on the desk. "Did you ever use the magic in these books, besides now?"

"No," she said holding her elbows and looking from Sam to Chris. "I never did much of anything about the magic. James said it would be better if I didn't know, and I took him at his word. Plus, I didn't want to draw any attention."

Sam stared at Dotty, but after a few seconds of silence, he sighed and shook his head.

"I believe you, but with all of these books in here . . . you must have looked after James left."

"Of course I did." Dotty stared at Sam. "This is my grandchild. Of course I wanted to make sure I knew as much as I could in order to protect her."

"So the force around the house," said Chris, "that was you. You put something around it to keep evil away?"

"No." Dotty folded her arms, indignation across her face. "I put up the barrier to hide us from *either* side."

Chris must not have considered that, because he looked at Sam, worry in his eyes. "Would anything come here, for Clair?"

Sam leaned over the book, eyes staring past the page.

"I don't know," he said at last. "Maybe, depending on her origin . . ."

"Clair is not the devil's daughter. She is my granddaughter!"

"Yes," said Sam, walking around the small table and standing face-to-face with Dotty. He was a good foot taller than the elderly woman, but she met his gaze with proud anger. "But who were Clair's parents? You had a child. Where is it now?"

"Clair," Chris said, turning to her, "I think it's best if you go to your room."

Sam and Dotty looked from Chris to Clair, but neither disagreed.

"No!" she said. "I deserve to know."

"Not right now," Sam said. "Go upstairs."

Clair was clenching her hands into fists, and her face showed signs of fighting. Then she relented, stomping through the door and slamming it shut.

Chris and Sam glanced between themselves and turned back to Dotty. She deflated instantly, her whole body sagging back into an age much older than her years. She turned around, gently touching one of the worn tapestries hanging from the wall.

"I tried so hard with him," she began. "After James died, when I found out I was pregnant, I scoured the books to see if it was possible, and the only reference I found was the Nephilim."

She turned around, anger in her eyes.

"They were described as monsters—half human, half angel—strong beings who were killed in the flood. I wasn't sure if anyone would come for him, so I did everything I could to ensure no one ever found out what he was."

"So," Sam said, "you hid him here, with the same spells you used to hide Clair?"

"Yes," she said. "But . . ."

There was a short silence while Dotty wiped a tear from her cheek. She was a proud woman, and very strong, but this subject was difficult.

"Did it not work, Dorthea?" Chris said. Sam wondered why he was using her full name, possibly as a way to get on her good side or a sign of respect. The way Chris was looking at Dotty confirmed the latter.

"No, it worked," she said, eyes misty but no longer crying. "But he couldn't handle it . . . Elijah was his name. It was too much for him. He was so torn . . ."

"I know this must be hard for you," Chris said, "but if you could just start at the beginning . . . what was too much for him?"

Dorthea inhaled and shakily exhaled.

"When he was a baby, and he was the most beautiful child, everyone said so . . ." She looked at Sam and Chris, a sad smile on her face. "He had an aura about him, like James.

"No one in town could know whose child he was, so I lied." Her face turned pink, and she smiled sheepishly. "I told everyone I had a one-night stand and got pregnant. And people believed it! I was able to sell some of the gold in the shop—the artifacts I knew didn't have magic—so I could close up and not have to work."

"So no one would enter," Chris said, putting the pieces together.

"Yes," she said. "I just started studying the books and didn't trust anyone. As I learned more, I realized that the spell James cast around the house kept us safe . . . and Eli was always so friendly with everyone. He led a pretty normal life and made people feel good about themselves . . . Then one day, he met Hannah."

"Clair's Mother?" Chris was inspecting one of the glass baubles hanging from the ceiling. It was a good method for giving a subject space, and Sam wondered where he had learned the technique or if it was instinctual.

"Yes," Dorthea said, walking to an armchair and sitting on the edge of it, hands in her lap. "She was such a lovely girl—quiet, but with Clair's shape and nose."

Dorthea smiled at the thought.

"Clair said her parents died in a car crash." Sam needed to know exactly what happened in order to begin training Clair the right way. "Is that how they died?"

"No, it's not."

There was a long pause. Chris quit playing with the glass bauble and sat down in a wooden chair, resting his head in his hands. Sam walked around the desk, looking at all of the papers and books.

"He didn't die, did he?" Sam said. "Did he kill Clair's mother?"

Dotty was looking at the ground, eyes somewhere far away.

"I don't know. They found the car in flames, and Clair was left on my doorstep the same night . . .

"I don't know what happened."

CLAIR

lair moved away from the crack under the door and tried to fight the pain creeping up her chest.

Her father murdered her mother.

Or might have.

She ran out the sliding back door and into the cold night air. It shocked her system, but she didn't care. The tears were flowing down her cheeks while she tried to pull her thoughts together.

What was she? She should have been relieved that she wasn't some spawn of the devil, but if her father had really killed her mother . . . what if he was still alive? What was she going to do?

Clair heard a twig crack, and spun around. Chris was standing in the backyard, hands in his pockets. He had stepped on the twig on purpose.

"Go away, Chris!" she shouted at him.

"You know I can't do that," he said, eyes too caring and too deep. "Right now it might not be safe for you to be alone."

Clair turned her back to him and faced the trees. It was a beautiful night despite her mood. The stars were out, and she could hear an owl in the distance. She shivered.

Clair almost jumped when she felt the jacket placed over her shoulders, but she was getting used to Chris. She inhaled and exhaled slowly.

"Did you know I was listening?"

"Yes," he said, somewhere behind her to the right. Her senses were getting better because of the training. Clair didn't really want to thank Chris right now, though, so she pushed the thought from her mind.

"Did Sam know?"

"Probably," he said, shuffling his feet.

She turned to face him. "How could she not tell me?"

Chris met her eyes, and she saw a pain there she hadn't expected. "She loves you, Clair. She doesn't want to see you get hurt."

Clair turned away and looked at the stars. So many dots. So many lights, she corrected herself. All of them up there for years and years, traveling miles to earth, until they extinguish and a new light is born. Clair thought that hearing her father might still be alive would bring her happiness. Instead it just brought her more pain.

"You see that one?" Chris said, coming closer. He leaned in next to her, his right hand outstretched, pointing toward three dots in a line. "That's Orion. You can only see him in summer, at least from here, because he disappears during the winter to go south where it's warm."

Clair didn't understand why Chris cared so much about Orion. "It's just three little stars."

"But it's not, Clair," Chris said, letting his arm drop. "The three dots are only Orion's belt, and the surrounding constellation is all of Orion."

He turned to face her, his gray eyes shining, his face so close to hers.

"Sometimes, something that seems inconspicuous can bring together something extraordinary."

They were so close. Clair didn't care about the constellation, didn't want to think about her father's possible homicide, her grandmother's lies, or the fact that she was an angel. In that moment, all she wanted to think about was how close Chris was to her, his eyes staring into hers like she was the most important thing in the world, his warm breath on her face.

She leaned in and tentatively touched her lips to his. His body tensed, but he didn't pull away.

His lips were soft, and he tasted like strawberries.

When he didn't push her away, she kissed him again, more urgently, sliding her tongue into his mouth, placing her hand on his chest and feeling him mold into her body as he began kissing her back, putting his hands through her hair and pulling her close while she ran her hands up his back.

She felt a fire inside her ignite—as if all her power was rushing through her body, unconstrained, free. Chris was her spark.

And then a flash seared white-hot across her mind, and she was staring at a wasteland of fire; Chris was dead on the ground, and she was covered in his blood.

Clair yanked herself away, shock and fear in her eyes.

"What do you sense?" Chris was on alert, breathing heavily, looking around the backyard for a nonexistent intruder.

He didn't see the vision, Clair thought. He didn't see it. She was in shock.

Chris shook his head, realizing there was no danger.

"I . . ." He was still breathing heavily, his eyes blazing in the light from the stars. He shook his head, looked at Clair, turned, and walked back to the house.

Sam came to the back door just as Chris pushed past him. He must have felt the tension, because when he turned to Clair, there was contempt in his voice. "Get back in the house and go to your room."

Clair was too shocked to move.

What the hell just happened? she thought miserably.

EMILY

mily was debating whether or not to go and get Mike on the other side of town. She went to the bar to meet him after he texted, and found him in the storage closet, smoking.

He offered her the joint.

"Seriously?" she said, voice loud. "You said we needed to talk, and all you really want is to get *high*?"

"Shh!" Mike said, laughing. "We don't want Joe to hear . . ."

He leaned in close and shut the door, leaving them in darkness except for the low ember glow coming from the lit end of the joint.

"Mike," Emily said, sighing, trying to disengage her emotions and put on her counselor hat. "I don't understand why you are being so self-destructive."

"I'm not. I'm being fun," he said, taking another long pull.

Emily couldn't understand him, and she finally realized she didn't want to. She was done, more than done—she was pissed. For the first time since they had been dating, even after all of the crap Mike put her through, she was truly white-hot angry. But she didn't explode.

She was quiet as death.

"Mike, we are done."

She left him in the closet, alone. If he was going to throw his life away, that was his problem, not hers, and she would not stay aboard a sinking ship.

She had tried to help him over and over again, but she just couldn't anymore.

She drove home and sat alone her room, looking at the ceiling and feeling miserable, the darkness outside a mirror to her own thoughts. She heard her cell phone ring on the nightstand and leaned over to pick it up.

"Hello?"

"Hey, Emily." It was Andrew. He sounded worried.

"Andrew, hey, what's up?" Emily swung her legs off the edge of her bed.

"Have you heard from Clair? I keep texting her but haven't got anything back."

Emily had completely forgotten about Clair. She checked her texts. Nothing.

"Nope," she said. "I'm going to call her and Dotty again right now, though."

"Okay." He sounded deflated. Emily knew Clair had been giving Andrew the runaround about becoming official for a while now, but she was sure Clair liked him well enough.

Something wasn't right.

"Clair has been a little off lately, Andrew," she said, "but I'm sure everything's fine."

"Yeah, sure, you're right." He sounded a little better but still unconvinced. "See you at bowling tomorrow?"

Emily knew it was Clair he wanted to really see at bowling tomorrow, but she appreciated Andrew too.

"Yes, for sure, dude." She put more excitement into her voice than was necessary, in an attempt to make him happy. What was up with Clair lately?

"Okay, cool," he said. "Bye."

"Bye."

Emily stood up and dialed Clair's number. It rang a few times before going to voicemail.

"Clair, it's Emily. You have been acting weird lately, and Andrew is worried—so am I." She grabbed her jacket off the back of the door. "I'm coming over."

Click.

CLAIR

Just as Clair reached the stairs, a loud banging came from the front of the house. She reached the door first, Dotty, Sam, and Chris right on her tail.

"Clair!" Emily was shouting through the door. "I see lights on. I know you're there! We need to talk."

Clair glanced at Sam and Chris before opening the door.

"Hey, Em," she said, smile in place.

Emily walked in, eyes shifting from Chris to Sam, and then to Dotty, who stood in the kitchen doorway.

"Who is he?" She gestured to Sam.

"That's Sam, one of Chris's friends," Clair said, gesturing first to Sam then Chris.

Recognition dawned on Emily's face, but it was quickly replaced with scrutiny as she looked Chris over.

"You don't seem so tall to me."

Clair forced a laugh, trying to ease the visible tension in the room. She forgot that Emily had never actually seen Chris, even though they talked about him on occasion. "You are taller than me, Em. Anyways, everything is fine. Chris and Sam were just leaving."

Chris moved to shake Emily's hand before walking past her to the door, and Sam muttered, "Nice to meet you."

Everything would have been fine if Emily wasn't so observant. Just as Sam reached the door, the ropes, which had been following above his head around the house, dropped to the ground.

Emily froze—mouth open.

It took a lot of convincing, but Clair finally managed to get Emily to sit down while she explained, Sam complaining the entire time about humans being unaware for their own good.

Once she finished relating the entire story—from meeting Chris, to the test Sam put her through, to Dotty and the fact that her great-uncle was actually her great-grandfather—Clair sat back against the living room sofa and looked across at her friend.

"So," Emily began, stiff on the edge of the sofa, hands on either side for a quick escape if necessary. "You are both angels?" Her eyes darted between Chris, who was sitting in the smaller chair across from them, and Sam, who was leaning against the stairway banister. "And you are half angel?" she said to Clair.

"Part," Clair said, wondering about exactly how much angel blood she possessed. "Not half, just part."

"But part seraph," Emily's eyes grew wide. Clair was surprised it meant something to her. "That's the highest rank, Clair—Catholic school," Emily said with a shaky laugh, seeing the shocked look on Sam's usually smug face.

"Well," Dotty stepped in, looking her age for the first time ever. "It's getting late, and I think it would be best if you two left."

Sam nodded to Dotty but cast a furtive glance in Emily's direction, before walking out with Chris, who hadn't looked at Clair since they were in the backyard.

She sighed when the door closed.

"Emily, I think it would be a good idea for you to stay here tonight," Dotty said, looking at Clair.

Emily nodded. Dotty said goodnight, walking up the stairs to her room.

Clair turned to Emily.

"I'm sorry I didn't tell you sooner," she said. "I really wanted to. I've been dying to have someone else to talk to."

Emily gave a half smile and exhaled deeply.

"I know it is a lot to process. But think of it this way," Clair continued with a slight laugh, "at least you know I'm not doing drugs."

"Em," Clair said, turning her head toward her friend where they lay, hours later, awake and unable to sleep on her bed. "I kissed Chris."

Clair watched Emily's eyes widen in the darkness. "When?"

"Just before you came over." Clair looked back at the ceiling. They had discussed everything over the past few hours. Clair answered as many questions as she could, and Emily was taking the whole thing better than Clair could have imagined.

She pressed her palms into her eyes. "After I listened in on the conversation about my dad, I ran outside, and Chris followed me . . . and I just . . . did."

Emily continued to stare at the ceiling, her brows pinched in thought. Clair was just glad she wasn't judging her—she felt bad enough.

"Well, how did you feel . . . when you kissed?"

How did she feel? It had all happened so fast. When she thought about it and was honest with herself, she knew she had found Chris attractive, knew she loved being with him and learning from him. They had become more than friends—they shared magic together, a whole other world Clair never knew existed, a whole part of herself she was just beginning to understand but wanted more and more of every day.

But she had always viewed Chris as off-limits, as if even he knew it wasn't something that was done, some secret code that angels didn't date, didn't love. But then he was there, with her, standing so close and looking for all the world like she *was* the world. She had felt on fire. Like her heart had expanded to twice its normal size as all of her senses came alive, her body pulsing with a new kind of understanding about her power. Clair had experienced sex and love, but this was different. This wasn't something as simple as the physical or emotional bonds she had before. Kissing Chris was like waking up from reality into a dream, where anything was possible.

And then the vision happened.

Clair dropped her hands, tears slipping down her cheeks. How much more could her friend take? Should she share the vision with Emily, after everything?

Emily wiped a tear from Clair's face.

"I know you must feel guilty, about Andrew, but if you have feelings for Chris . . ."

"It's not fair to Andrew, but it's not about him either." She told Emily about the vision of Chris dead on the ground and being covered in his blood.

"And that happened while you were kissing?"

Clair nodded.

"Wow," Emily said, surprising Clair again with how calm and collected she was being about everything. "I only have sci-fi to go off of, but it sounds like a vision to me." Emily turned on her side to face Clair. "Is that why you're so torn? Not because of Andrew, but because you think you can't date Chris and you want to?"

Clair felt even worse but nodded. It was the truth. Her first thought hadn't been of guilt about Andrew but sadness that fate had shown her so much hope and then such a deep loss all at once.

"Well," Emily continued, handing Clair a tissue for her now streams of silent tears, "the counselor thing for me to do would be to have you and Andrew discuss what happened tonight, but the best friend thing to do would be to let you decide if you want to tell him."

Clair looked at Emily, mouth open.

"The way I see it," Emily continued, looking at the ceiling, "you had just been through an emotional roller coaster, and Chris was just there. If it had been Andrew, you might have done the same thing, but with him."

Clair felt in her heart that it wouldn't have been the same, but Emily made a point. Would she have reached for Andrew if he had been there? Was her action truly based on emotional trauma?

She felt her heart contract.

Sam

Sam finally found Chris sitting alone at the bar, about ten empty shot glasses in front of him. Joe, the local bartender, was listening to him carry on about some type of plant.

". . . but it only grows in *summer*," Chris was saying, swishing a glass filled with amber liquid around while talking with his hands. "Some plants are just so mysterious."

Joe gave a grunt and watched Sam approach.

"Are you drunk?"

"Can we get drunk?" Chris slurred, looking slowly up at Sam, down at the glasses, and then back to him. "Maybe I am!"

"Bloody hell," Sam sighed as he sat down next to Chris, thanking Joe for watching him and ordering a Jameson on the rocks. Joe nodded and walked away.

If this young angel was supposed to be his apprentice, things were not starting well. "It takes a lot, but *yes*, obviously, you can get drunk."

"I don't think I have ever been drunks," Chris said, making a castle with the empty shot glasses in front of him. "I mean, I *know*, I have never been drunk, *you know*, this time around." He winked. "But even though I don't *know*, you know, about the other one, I don't think I was drunk then either."

Chris finished the castle, looking solemn. They sat in silence for a few minutes while Sam sipped his drink.

"Does it ever get easier?"

Sam didn't know what to say. Easier? No, it never got easier. More tolerable maybe. Chris was watching his face as he thought.

"So that's a 'no' then," he said, sighing and signaling Joe for another round.

Sam took a long draw of the Jameson. He had picked up the taste for the liquor in Ireland, back in the first century of his new life where *he* had first learned he could get drunk. Sam looked at Chris and couldn't help but empathize with him. The journey of a minor angel was depressingly difficult.

"You want to hear the story of when I first got drunk?"

Chris listened to every word as Sam related the bar in Cork, the wild dog, and the Scottish man who had accidentally landed on the wrong island, which was extremely bad luck back in the thirteenth century. They laughed and drank and laughed some more, and for a brief moment, Sam forgot about the possible danger ahead.

Joe brought them both waters and told them he was closing. Sam walked Chris back to his house, and on the way decided it was time to start a sore subject.

"You have to let her be, Chris," he said, watching Chris attempt to stuff the key into his front door.

Chris turned to him. "She kissed me."

Sam knew something had happened in the backyard but hadn't expected that. "Still," he said, "you are not a seraph, and just because James got away with human romance, we are only just beginning to understand this new process."

Chris stepped into the house, flicking on the lights and heading toward the fridge.

"What process?" he said, grabbing a fistful of ice and throwing it into a glass, a few of the blocks missing and falling to the ground.

"Well," Sam began, "the eternal powers don't make mistakes. This must be some type of rule we didn't know about."

Chris sighed, filled his cup with water, and dropped the dirty floor ice into the sink where it broke and fell down the drain.

Poor boy.

If this girl Clair never came home, he could have lived out his purpose in this small town peacefully, never getting involved in the eternal matters that Sam himself tried to avoid.

"Well," Chris said eventually, moving toward his small room. "I think I've had enough for one day. Sleeping well in the spare room?"

"Yes," Sam said, moving toward the sofa and sitting down. "I plan on going to the store for some supplies tomorrow, and to visit the antique shop."

Chris raised an eyebrow at him. "Getting started right away then?"

Sam thought back to his time in Lebanon before this adventure began and wondered how much time he had left to fulfill his purpose.

His eyes grew distant.

"The present is all we have."

The next morning Sam woke with the sun and realized, with a bit of a shock, that Chris was already awake and watering the plants in his backyard. For the past few days, Sam had gotten used to rising a good hour before the young angel.

Sam watched him through the window in the spare bedroom. The small room had a twin-size bed frame and an armoire. Sam decided he would get more at the store today than spare sheets. As Chris said, he had only been living in this house for two years without working, living off his crops and what he could sell. There was no way he had any money saved. Sam, on the other hand, had been alive a long time and was able to afford whatever he wanted.

Moving away from the window, he walked to the kitchen, feeling the cold tile sink through his socks. He liked the house. The open space of the kitchen connected directly with the living room and dining area. And even though it was small altogether, it felt right, somehow—homey and comfortable despite the lack of furniture.

Sam crossed to the window and looked out into the woods. Who knew how long he would remain here. Clair was certainly an interesting pupil. She struggled and fought against the idea in the beginning, but was quickly progressing. Even with her lack of upbringing in the art, she was able to intuitively guess her way through the exercises. It infuriated him how easy it was for her blood to react to the power. So far Sam was only testing his own theories: how long the effect of fasting would last on her blood, how fast her body could react to proper breathing. And even though Clair didn't like the slow progress, the tougher training required patience and a determination of mind and heart that he wasn't sure she possessed yet.

The sun was just breaking through the trees, filtering light gray into the sky, when Chris came into the kitchen.

"Good morning," he said, moving toward the fridge and grabbing out a large bowl filled with brown eggs. "Hungry?"

"Always," Sam said, moving to the table. Chris began making omelets filled with peppers, spinach, and cheese.

"I thought you didn't eat anything you didn't grow," Sam couldn't help but mention, tasting the sharp cheddar in the omelet.

"I try not to," Chris said sheepishly, "but cheese is just too damn hard to make."

Sam laughed. Once they had both eaten, Chris went back to business.

"We still have to figure out what to do about The Gate," he said, grabbing their plates and bringing them over to the sink to wash.

Sam hadn't forgotten. The Gate was still on his mind, but he didn't think it was in much danger with two angels to guard it. However, with Clair and The Gate so near to each other, something was sure to notice.

"You're right," he said, standing and joining Chris at the sink. He grabbed a towel and started drying the plates. It was odd for him to be doing household chores after so many years alone spent in hotels or with people to wait on him. But there was a warm understanding and sense of familiarity between them, and Sam found himself enjoying their task.

"One problem at a time, I suppose," Chris said, handing the last fork to Sam.

"Yes," he said, "one thing at a time."

Once they finished, Sam walked into town, enjoying the weather. It was odd that, given the proximity of the house, Chris was able to walk everywhere in town. It was a good four miles to the nearest property line, and then another two into the main center where the stores could be found. But if Chris really did live off of his own crops, he must not walk into town too often.

Sam entered the nearest furniture store, an overpriced mom-and-pop shop with friendly workers. He supposed the instant service, along with the knowledgeable assistance, was worth the extra amount of cash on each piece.

Sam ended up buying a steel-gray low profile sofa, two leather lounge chairs, geometric rugs, tufted leather bed frames with pillow-top mattresses for each room, and all-black accessories: a few large mirrors, low profile artwork, and smaller pieces of furniture that didn't match, as well as an ornamental floor-length mirror with burnt oak edges. It reminded him of a mirror he'd stolen from a nobleman during the War of the Roses in the mid-fifteenth century, and was just for fun.

The shop also had an electrical section, so Sam purchased a new fridge with steel doors and a matching dishwasher, a washer and dryer, toaster, heater and a generator to run all of the smaller appliances until he could find the nearest electrical company and start service in the house.

The clerk, who had excitedly tallied up Sam's loot, calculated out the price, and Sam paid the woman using his debit card. Sam hoped the use of his card wouldn't prompt The Covenant's interest.

"Alright, you are all set!" the woman said excitedly. "Where should we deliver the items?" The curiosity in her voice was tangible.

Sam hadn't considered this part. He wasn't sure if Chris wanted his exact location known, and now with Clair, it was extremely important that they involved as few innocents as possible.

Sam looked out the store front window.

"Don't worry about the delivery," he said, throwing his most charming smile at the clerk. "I have a better idea."

Clair

Clair woke up the next morning to the smell of bacon and coffee.

She wondered briefly if she was dreaming. Leaning over and opening her eyes, she discovered Emily was no longer in the bed next to her, midmorning light pouring through the lace curtains from the open window.

Had it really only been last night that everything changed?

Emily was now aware of what was going on, and Clair let the positive feelings wash over her; she could share all of her life with her friend again. She was hopeful. It was like fate had smiled down on them, because without Emily, Clair felt very, very alone.

Thinking about hope made Clair think about Chris, and her heart gave a painful squeeze.

How could she have done that to him? Or Andrew, for that matter. She felt horrible for kissing Chris, but also for just standing there and letting him believe she didn't enjoy it.

Because she had.

Kissing Chris was like opening a part of herself she never knew, a powerful part that had a strength she didn't think possible. But it was also extremely frightening. Clair lay awake last night, after she heard the soft sounds of Emily's snores, thinking that the vision must have been a warning—against that type of power. Because it had to have come from her blood, must be something about being a seraph, or whatever she was, that made dating Chris impossible and even dangerous.

Clair stretched, placing her hands above her head, tensing all of her muscles and feeling the tightness in her breath before slowly releasing, loving the way it helped her fully relax.

So much had happened in such a short amount of time, but she needed Chris in her life as much as she needed Emily, Sam, and Andrew. There was a reason why they were all together, and Clair was a firm believer in facing things head-on.

She needed to call Chris.

Reaching across to her side table, Clair grabbed her phone from off the charger. She had nine texts from Andrew: "Are you okay? Emily can't find you." "You didn't answer your phone are you okay??" The last one was from an hour ago: "Hey, are you alive? Please call me."

Clair felt her heart squeeze again. She hadn't even thought of texting Andrew last night. She was the worst friend—girlfriend? She wasn't sure—ever.

She sent him a quick text: "Sorry, just woke up. Long night. Family drama. Everything is fine, sorry I worried you both!" Clair hoped the explanation would serve for the time being while she dialed Chris.

She listened to the phone ring three times, heart beating. When he finally picked up, he sounded groggy. Did she wake him up?

"Hey, um, Chris," Clair stumbled, kicking herself inwardly, "I was wondering if you had some time . . . to talk today?"

What was wrong with her? It wasn't like this was the first time they had talked on the phone, and now she was acting like a twelve-year-old, stumbling over her words.

"Hey Clair," he said, his voice growing less hoarse. "Yes, sounds great . . . Want to meet at the training spot around noon?"

"Yes, sounds good," she said. "Thanks."

There was a pause.

"No problem."

She clicked off the phone and sighed. What the heck was wrong with her?

Her stomach gave a low grumble that demanded she pursue the smell of bacon downstairs. Laughing to herself, Clair jumped off the bed and walked down to the kitchen, where she could hear Emily and Dotty talking.

They were both seated at the small table, with plates of scrambled eggs, sausage, and bacon, and a pot of coffee was freshly brewed on the counter.

Emily looked at Clair over her mug. "Morning, sunshine."

It was so normal that her heart leapt. It was like nothing had changed, and the possibility that she had been dreaming her life away the last few weeks filled her with a sense of freedom. Until Dotty turned around in her chair and smiled at Clair. She looked tired, but ultimately more relaxed and resigned to their current situation after a good night sleep. But it was there, in her eyes. They brought Clair down to earth, back to reality; her eyes showed the same apprehension Clair felt in her entire being.

Normal was over.

"Morning," Clair said, walking over and hugging Dotty from the side briefly before trudging over to the counter to grab a mug. "You made coffee?"

"Well, Emily made the coffee," Dotty said, taking a bite of bacon.

"I found the machine in the cabinet, dusty as heck, and decided to use that packet of coffee you bought ages ago," Emily said. "It's pretty good still."

Clair had forgotten about it. She bought it when she went job hunting, and ever since starting work *at* the coffee shop, she didn't need to make coffee at home like she had thought—especially since Chris and Sam told her to stop drinking it, even though she didn't.

Clair made a plate and leaned against the counter. The eggs had cheese and pepper mixed in, just the right amount of spicy. They were wonderful with the bacon. She sighed, and Dotty and Emily laughed at her.

"Hungry?" Emily said, eyeing Clair.

"Yeah, I guess I was," she said, looking at the two of them. She didn't want to start anything, not yet, but she was dying to make sure everything that happened yesterday wasn't a dream. "Heard anything from Sam this morning?"

Dotty made a huffing noise and bit off another piece of bacon. "Yes, had the nerve to call me at six in the morning!"

Emily laughed. "Yeah, but you were awake."

"So?" Dotty said, making an indignant face. "He isn't very good with the phone. I may not be good with it either, but I am still better than Samuel. He almost made me go deaf when he screamed hello!"

All three of them broke out laughing. It was so nice, Clair felt hope spring into her chest. She didn't know why, but it was like they were all connected now, and everything in her life felt like it was in balance.

Except for Chris—and Andrew.

Emily must have seen the change on Clair's face because she asked her what was wrong, to which Dotty looked over, curious.

Well, she wanted everything out in the open, didn't she?

Clair told Dotty about kissing Chris, and then told both of them about how she had called him to set up a meeting to talk today. She also told them about Andrew's texts and about how she felt like a horrible person for kissing Chris and not thinking to call Andrew last night.

Emily creased her brows, and Dotty cocked her head to the side, lost in thought.

"So," Clair said, looking at the two of them and wishing someone would say something, "any words of advice?"

Emily looked back at her coffee and then up at Dotty, who shrugged.

"It's your life, Clair," Dotty said. "I don't think we should completely trust these two yet, even though they seem honest."

"I think it's a good idea to talk to Chris, as long as you have made your mind up," Emily said, concern on her face, "about not wanting to date him."

"It wouldn't be right, to Andrew . . ." Clair said, looking at the tile on the floor. There was a repeating pattern she hadn't noticed before.

"Plus," she continued, thankful the two gave her space to think, "everything with the vision, and the fact that, no, however much I want to trust Chris and Sam we don't know everything about them, makes it plain that Chris should not be an option."

Clair hoped she hadn't given anything away. She was always a realistic person, but she would not, and could not, deny the way she felt about Chris. Hopefully by telling herself and others the realistic negative facts, she would convince herself that it was a bad idea.

Emily nodded, and Dotty smiled.

"Well," Emily said, standing and pushing in her chair, "thank you for breakfast and the conversation, Dotty, but I have to go get ready for work this afternoon. Clair, let me know when you have your next training session. I want to come watch."

"Of course," Clair said, hugging her friend and walking her to the door.

"Also," she said, stopping just outside the entry, "I talked with Dotty about looking through the books in the antique shop. I had a crazy Catholic upbringing, and I'd like to help with the research."

"Sounds great!" Clair replied, happy that she would be seeing Emily again so soon. The two hugged once more before she bounded down the steps.

Clair waited until she heard Emily start her car, before returning to the kitchen. She poured herself another cup of black coffee before turning to face Dotty.

"So," she said, watching Dotty stare deeply into her tea, "we still need to talk about last night."

Clair felt like a parent, standing there accusing her grandmother of stealing the family car.

Dotty's eyes moved to meet Clair's, the action distant. Clair knew this was going to be hard, knew that she should never have been listening at the door, but she didn't care. She needed to know—beyond reason, beyond doubt—she needed to know about her parents.

Dotty slowly took her glasses off of her head, placing them neatly on the table. She rubbed her eyes. "Yes, we do."

It took all the strength Clair had to be patient and wait for Dotty to speak.

"I am assuming," she finally said, glancing up at Clair with a sly smile that lacked humor, "that you were listening to us last night?"

Clair nodded and took a sip of coffee.

Dotty sighed.

"Clair, what you heard . . . about your parents' death . . . it's all I know." She looked up at Clair, her eyes shiny. "I told them everything, and I am telling you the same thing now. The car was on fire, and you turned up on my doorstep that same night."

"But there had to have been bodies," Clair said, watching Dotty flinch. "When the police showed up, they had to have found something."

Dotty shook her head, staring back into her tea.

"The fire consumed everything. They couldn't tell. You've watched new-age television Clair, the fire destroyed anything that was in that car." She looked up, obviously trying to hold back tears. Clair felt like a monster, but she needed to know, was so desperate to know. Dotty continued. "It took a lot of lies for me to convince the police that your parents had left you with me, before going out that night."

"But what about my father?" Clair cut in, loudly. "What happened with him? *Did* he kill my mother?"

"I don't know, Clair! Can't you see that it's hard enough for me to tell you that? That I don't even know if my own son became a murderer?" Dotty stood, rather quickly, and walked over to the sink. She placed her hands on the edge of the counter and leaned heavily on them. "I loved him, Clair. He was so . . . beautiful. I could never imagine him as . . . as some monster."

Clair felt the distance between them widen, threatening to break them apart. Dotty had raised her, taught her how to survive in the world. She was the only family Clair had ever known.

Clair was at war with herself emotionally.

On the one hand, she knew she was angry—angry with Dotty for keeping this information from her, angry about her parents, angry about this new life she had stepped into without being given a choice. Clair knew she could hold onto her anger—righteously keep it close to her heart where she felt it blooming, creating a wall around herself to keep the world out, to push everyone away.

Darkness began to cloud her eyes, and she felt the light in the room grow dim. A cold was seeping into her heart, and it scared her.

She shook her head to clear the darkness, and tried to take a step back mentally for a moment to imagine what Dotty might be feeling. It was different for Clair; she never knew her parents, never met them, or even had pictures of them. But Dotty had raised her father, knew Clair's mother . . . it was a type of loss Clair had yet to experience. She shuddered at the thought of Chris from the vision.

The wall broke, and Clair walked the long distance to stand behind her grandmother, all the emotion she had kept tight in her chest coming loose.

"I'm sorry," was all she could manage as she placed her hands on Dotty's shoulders, burying her face in the back of her shirt. Clair used to do that as a child, smelling the jasmine-scented soap that stuck to her clothes.

Dotty reached a hand around and placed it over one of Clair's, wiping tears from her face with the other.

"It's all right, dear," she said, patting Clair's hand. "But we have more important things we must focus on right now."

"Yes," Clair said, her voice muffled from the shirt and her own watery eyes. "We do, don't we?"

Dotty turned to face Clair, eyes red and moist, the concern within them heartbreaking.

"I thought it was a dream, this morning," Clair spilled out. "I thought we were normal. That things were normal. I've felt so distant from you these last few weeks. I never want to feel that way again."

This time Clair buried her face in the front of her grandmother's shirt, soaking it with the tears that burst from her. She didn't even know if she was crying from relief, crying for fear, or crying because she was just overwhelmed. But Dotty was always the only one Clair could cry with, could be completely herself with, would allow herself to show moments of weakness.

After what felt like forever, when the tears subsided, Dotty put a hand to Clair's chin and lifted her head up.

"I know, dear, I know. But if anyone could do this . . . if anyone was meant for something great like this, it's you."

Clair could only stare into those loving eyes.

"Could you do me one favor, though," Clair said, leaning back. "Don't tell Sam about me crying."

They both laughed.

An hour later Clair put on her hiking shoes, meticulously tying the neon laces she bought a few days before. It was still a half an hour from noon, but she needed to start moving, her muscles itching for the strain as she began the climb into the forest.

It was only when she reached the top of the hill and looked into the bowl that she remembered yesterday and the thoughts she had on her walk.

Could that really be Eden?

It didn't look like anything different, didn't seem mysterious aside from the quiet she knew was waiting for her. While her mind reasoned, she walked downward, listening to the sounds of the creek and the calls of the birds.

She found him in the forest, lying on a patch of grass in the sun. There were no shadows under his eyes, but he seemed a bit off.

"Before you say anything," he began, one arm slung over his eyes while the other he held up to stop her. "I want to apologize."

Clair stopped dead.

What?

She wasn't sure if her brain had stopped working along with her ability to walk. So she just stood there, mouth open, and like an idiot let him continue.

"It's not like I didn't know you were dating Andrew. I knew, and it's not even my place to have a relationship with you, or anyone, and I should have been more aware of the . . . friendliness of our relationship."

He put his hand down and opened his eyes, the bright light illuminating his gray eyes. "I had no right to . . . become as close to you as I did, and I apologize. I want to be able to retain a friendship with you."

It was like he had rehearsed this speech, the words coming out methodically.

All of a sudden Clair felt like a child.

Chris was more mature than she gave him credit, more mature than Clair felt in her own twenty-two years. There was no hidden emotion in his eyes. No longing or sadness. Chris understood and accepted his decision, and was determined not to do it again.

Clair didn't know what to say. She had come here to apologize to him, to make up some excuse for her behavior—anything but telling him about the vision. But now she was upset.

"Okay . . ." was all she could manage.

Why was she upset? She just got what she wanted: a clean way back to friendship. But Chris had made the decision for her, without even hearing what she had to say. She felt the loss like a weight in her chest.

None of it, like everything else, had been on her terms.

Clair felt dumped. And she felt something else: a bit of resentment.

"Okay . . ." she said again, narrowing her eyes and speaking with a bit more malice than she should have. "What's wrong with you today? You seem off."

"Well, for one thing, I'm hungover." He laughed.

Clair couldn't help the way her mouth fell open.

"You're what?" she said, walking over to where he was lying in the grass, and studying his face. He did seem different, his skin a little less vibrant today. For someone who only ate healthy food, the liquor must have been quite a shock to his system.

"I said"—Chris opened his eyes, laughing, and stared up at Clair—"I'm hung over. It's not pleasant."

Clair couldn't help but laugh at him, with his tousled hair and white T-shirt. "It's not supposed to be pleasant."

She had to remind herself that things were supposed to be strained between them. But somehow, they weren't. They weren't being awkward around each other.

Chris smiled at her, and she looked off into the forest, remembering her second reason for coming to talk with him today.

"I know why we always train here," she said, watching his eyes widen. "Why it's so quiet, why nothing lives here."

He got up slowly and started walking around her, his eyes never leaving her own. It was predatory—something she had never seen him do before. It unnerved her.

"It has something to do with Eden," she said, following his gaze and feeling her heart beat faster. Everything came tumbling out. "Either this is Eden, or it's a part of it, or something—but I just know that it's true. This place . . . there is magic here."

Chris stopped pacing, and Clair realized she had been turning with him while he circled her, placing himself between her and the deeper part of the bowl.

Smart man, she thought bitterly. Did he think she would try to get past him?

"I'm impressed, Clair," he said, hands at his sides, body tensed. "Have you told Sam what you discovered?"

She felt on edge herself, not just because of the way he was looking at her, like a predator ready to defend its kill, but because she was growing more and more angry with him, hurt by the idea that she would try to steal something from him.

"No," she spat, tensing herself, remembering her training. She could almost feel the anger heat her blood. "I just wanted to tell *you*!"

He relaxed instantly, his eyes showing shock. Clair felt her own body respond. Taking a deep breath, she steadied her nerves and could almost see smoke come out with her air.

Chris sighed and rubbed his hands through his hair.

"I'm sorry, Clair," he said, throwing his hands up and then pocketing them with a grunt only men master. "This has been my purpose, for so long . . ."

He was looking at her with those deep gray eyes, longing and sorrow flooding his soul. He looked so conflicted, she had the instinct to touch her hand to his face, to soothe the emotions playing around in his eyes.

But she held back. It wasn't fair to him. Or Andrew. She must remain in check if she was ever to have a working relationship with Chris.

She broke her gaze from his, giving him space and staring at a nearby tree. "You've never spoken about your purpose," she began, reaching up to stroke one of the large green leaves and wishing inwardly that it was his face. "This is it?"

"Is what it?" It was a question, but just barely. She looked back and found his eyes blank and staring at her.

She just knew: he couldn't tell her, she had to guess.

Clair squared her feet with her shoulders and faced him. "You are a guardian . . . of Eden."

Chris smiled, his eyes lit with that inner light she loved so much. She couldn't help but smile as well.

"I had to guess, didn't I?"

She thought it was weird, them standing there, talking about purpose, about *his* purpose, which was larger than life itself, laughing. It was so easy to be with Chris that sometimes it scared her and thrilled her all at once.

"Yes," he said, walking toward her. She felt the space between them like an electric current, and he stopped in his tracks, brows creased and smile replaced by a small frown.

As quickly as it had come, it left, the ease of their friendship, changing into something neither of them was willing to admit, or could admit. Clair cleared her throat and started searching the area behind Chris with her eyes. It looked normal.

"So," she said, flicking a quick glance in his direction but unsure of her ability to hold his gaze. "How does it work?"

"How does what work?" It was a real question this time.

"I thought Eden was near Israel," she said, glancing at his face for a hint. "According to the Jews."

"It is," he smiled, "according to the Jewish people."

"What about according to you? According to angels?"

His eyes narrowed, and his smile grew larger and more playful.

"Well," he said, laughing, "now Sam won't be the only one to give you homework."

Clair felt her mouth drop. "What?"

"Go and read the story, Clair," he said, shooing her with his hand before lying down in the grass again and closing his eyes, his mouth curved in a triumphant smile, "and then we'll talk about it later."

She was amazed how fast the instinct to step playfully onto his chest and knock the wind out of him came to her. But she didn't. Instead, she resigned herself to grabbing a handful of leaves from the nearest tree and chucking them at him, causing him to laugh and her to grin.

"Fine," she said. His eyes were still closed, and she felt denied of them before leaving. "See you later."

As she walked out of the bowl, she knew he was watching her, and her spine tingled at the thought.

Sam must be doing something right, she thought as she reached the ridge. Her senses were becoming *very* defined.

EMILY

mily decided that if Clair was a magical creature with angel friends, then she was going to become someone who could be useful in that world.

In fact, she spent that whole day at work feeling rejuvenated; her life was intertwining with something special. There were a few moments in the day where she tuned out the usual gossip and daydreamed about the possibilities ahead. If there were angels, then there could be more magical creatures.

As Emily was finishing up with her last customer, Sam walked into the shop and sat down in one of the wicker chairs, looking completely out of place. Emily watched Rita walk over to him, her "new customer" smile in place.

"Hello," she said, "how can I help you?"

"Trim," he said, with a frown and a hand gesture in Emily's direction.

"He said he wants a trim," Rita repeated unnecessarily after she crossed the room to Emily, sending a peeved glance at Sam. "He seems like a jerk. Do you know him?"

"Unfortunately," Emily said, leaning the broom, which she had been using to sweep up hair, against the wall and walking over to Sam. "What do you want?"

"A haircut."

Emily would have thought he was handsome if she didn't know what he was really like. He was tall, with a square chin and high cheekbones, buzzed light brown hair, and blue eyes, and an accent to stir even the most pessimistic heart. But Clair had told Emily stories of how cold and distant Sam could be, instructing without emotion like some machine bent on breaking Clair into submission, as if she were some wild animal.

Emily didn't like the way he was staring at her now, like she was some puzzle to be worked out or thrown away. If it was just them in the salon, Emily would have told him to go away, but pride and curiosity won out.

"Fine."

She led Sam to the back, told him to sit in one of the wash chairs, and placed a towel around his shoulders. Leaning his head back, she turned on the water and was testing the heat when he finally spoke.

"You are taking everything from last night a lot better than I would have thought."

"Is that a compliment?" Emily lathered her hands with shampoo.

He didn't respond.

She began massaging the foam into his head. The action made her feel uncomfortable. She always loved being able to ease tension from lives with a good rinse before a cut, but this was different. This was Sam, an angel.

As she was rinsing valuable conditioner into his already short hair, he spoke again.

"No, it was merely an observation."

He was so unnerving she finished washing his hair, wrapped his head in a towel (which was completely unnecessary) and walked him over to her station.

As she was buzzing his hair a fourth of an inch shorter than it was when he arrived, Emily began to relax. She felt better when she didn't have to look at him face-to-face, preferring to throw glances only every once in a while at his deep blue eyes in the mirror.

"I would like you to know," he said as she was running the buzz cutter around his ears, "that I do not like you being a part of this business with Clair, and think it best if you stayed out of it."

She almost snipped his ear with the clippers.

"What?"

He turned in the chair, the black hair guard creating a blanket around his body.

"I don't want you to be a part of Clair's angelic life. I understand," he said, looking around the salon, "that you are a part of her *human* life, but since you are human, I think it best that you stay friends with Clair outside of her other responsibilities."

Emily knew she was staring at him, and only barely realized that the buzz cutter was still on, vibrating in her right hand.

She didn't know much about Sam, but her instincts were telling her he was not the type of man to be crossed. He had been around a long time, according to Clair, and even though Clair was only beginning to tap into her powers, Emily was pretty positive that Sam had a few tricks up his sleeve and was not afraid to use them to get his way.

She took in a deep breath and let it out slowly, deciding.

"No," she said, flicking off the buzzer. There was a short pause where they both stared at each other.

"No?" he said, staring into her eyes.

"Yes, Sam, I said *no*." Emily was trying to keep her voice even, staring straight into those deep, and now angry, blue eyes. "Clair is my friend, and I will be by her side through all of this, whatever that means.

"In fact," Emily continued, hearing the strength hit her voice and fill her with courage, "I'll be attending as many of her training sessions as I can and will look through the books Dotty has to *help* Clair."

When she finished, he just stared at her, his face never changing.

Eventually, he got up, threw a twenty on the table in front of her, and left without looking back.

Emily decided that was as close to a truce as they would ever be.

CLAIR

Andrew really liked video games.

Clair went over to his house the next day to spend some much-needed one-on-one time with him. She found him seated in front of a console, the sniper in his character's hand taking out diplomats.

"Hey, Clair," he said, a little distracted. "Grab a seat."

She knew she didn't deserve star treatment after the way she had handled yesterday. So Clair resigned herself to watching Andrew kill assassin after assassin.

She enjoyed the strategic necessity involved with the RPG. The main character needed to break through a line of other assassins in an attempt to save someone (usually a man, thank you very much princess types). Andrew was swift in execution, and when the game gave him the choice to be either the good guy or evil, he chose to be good, which Clair considered a plus.

Once he finished the level, he saved his game, turned off the console, and turned to face her. His smile was in place, but just barely, and even though he didn't say it, Clair knew Andrew felt bad for making her wait while he finished the game.

"Hey," he said. He was leaning over in the office chair, his forearms resting on his thighs, with his hands clasped together. He looked like such an adult that Clair felt another wave of guilt; she felt like a child who had stolen the last cookie meant for a grandmother who also happened to be dying of cancer.

Instead of replying, Clair got out of the beanbag chair, leaned down in front of him, and, taking his face in her hands, touched her lips to his.

He was warm, and she felt the electricity flowing through her body when he began kissing her back, his anger and resentment forgotten from the day before.

It only briefly registered in her mind that this was a cheater's way of getting out of an argument, but it worked for both of them.

When they stopped making out, Andrew had his carefree nature back in place, laughing.

"You do know that's cheating, right?" Sometimes Clair wondered if everyone in the world besides her could read minds. The thought must have shown on her face because Andrew laughed and pulled her hand through his, interlocking their fingers.

"I know something bad happened yesterday," he said, stroking her palm with his thumb. She felt her skin tingle. "Do you want to talk about it?"

No, Clair didn't want to talk about it, she realized. She had wanted to include Emily on her new-found heritage, but not Andrew. It wasn't because she didn't care about him. In fact, Clair was almost sure it was because she cared too much for him; sharing that side of her life with Andrew would take all of the innocence out of their relationship, somehow. Clair would never risk deterring the natural happiness that he exuded, bringing joy to everyone around him.

No, she decided. She didn't want to talk about it. But she would need to talk about something, because she cared for Andrew, was dating him, and even though they weren't officially in a relationship, she still felt guilty about kissing Chris.

So Clair lied.

"I just," Clair began, looking up at the ceiling and easing some emotion into her voice, "I found out that my parents died in a car crash last night, officially, when I was going through the antique shop and found their records . . ." Clair watched Andrew's eyebrows knit together.

"But I thought you knew they died in a car crash?" he said, not unkindly.

Clair had been prepared for this response, and the lie came easily, surprising even her.

"I did know, but what I didn't know when I saw the death certificate was that my mother was only a few years older than I am now." Clair thought of the saddest thing she could, bringing some fake tears into her eyes. "Underneath the certificate was some of her old things, and I was angry with Dotty for keeping them from me."

Andrew stood up and took Clair in his arms.

"Oh, Clair, I'm so sorry."

Clair felt horrible and surprised that she was able to complete such a daring lie, but it was worth it—they would need it. So she continued.

"So I confronted Dotty about it, and we fought—we never fight, you know—and then everything was okay. But it was just hard. She is the only family I have. Emily came over last night when I didn't answer, and she's going to help me look through the shop for more boxes . . . anything to help me find some connection to them."

It was brilliant.

Perfectly and positively helpful, to the point where Clair thought even Sam would be proud. It would account for why Clair and Emily would be spending more time together at her house, and it was just personal enough that Andrew couldn't feel offended when Clair asked for more girl time.

"Thank you, Andrew," Clair added, still feeling a bit guilty, "for listening, and for being such a great friend."

She pulled back from his hug and looked into his deep brown eyes. He was smiling supportively. Here was one of the nicest guys in the world, and Clair couldn't help but feel like she was wasting him.

"I really like that game," she said, changing the subject and looking toward the console. "How far into it are you?"

That sent Andrew into a detailed explanation about the main character, the plot, and the basic strategy he implemented. They talked video games for a little while longer before Clair suggested a movie, to which Andrew heartedly agreed. Since both of them needed to be at work early the next morning, they decided to go watch an action flick.

Andrew put up a good fight, but Clair paid. She enjoyed paying for things. Plus, it was the least she could do for lying to him. This wasn't the fifties, and she wasn't some romantic. In the end, he gave up, thanking her for the ticket and splurging on a large buttered popcorn, which they shared throughout the over-the-top movie.

Andrew was the perfect remedy for the abnormal story Clair seemed to be in; she couldn't help but feel he was her Jacob. The only problem was that there was an Edward, and unlike Bella, Clair just couldn't see her story ending with a two-year-old and a cottage in the woods.

At the end of the night, and, in keeping up with their current arrangement, Clair drove Andrew back home and walked him to his front door, grinning.

"I had a lovely night tonight, Clair," he said in a high-pitch voice, twisting an imaginary curl before rolling his eyes and shaking his head. "I can't believe I let you do my job tonight."

"It's not your job," Clair said, smiling. "We can treat each other sometimes."

"Yeah well," he said sliding closer and wrapping his arms around her waist. "I still have a lot of work to do if I ever want to tie you down and make you my girlfriend."

His look was playful, but she got the message.

"I just don't know if I am ready for that, Andrew, to be official and all . . ." she began, watching his guarded expression. "Especially when you're my boss . . . think of how the people in town would gossip!"

Andrew laughed, and Clair joined in, grateful that the tension had dispersed from the air. She really wasn't ready for a relationship—kissing other men meant that she wasn't.

"Fine, I relent," he said, "for now."

He was staring into her eyes, and she knew he meant it—he wasn't done trying. He pulled her into a long kiss before letting her go.

Just as he reached the door, he turned around.

"Oh!" he said, facing her. "What are you doing tomorrow morning?"

Having a long hike before another breathing lesson because I'm an angel . . .

"Going for a hike with Chris, and then rummaging through the shop with Emily," she said, watching his eyes narrow slightly at the mention of Chris's name. "Why?"

"I was wondering if you wanted to come to church with me and my family."

"Church?" she said, staring at him. *What?*

Andrew laughed at the surprise in her voice.

"Yeah, church. You know, where they talk about God?"

Clair laughed.

"It's not really my thing, Andrew," she said, scratching her shoulder. The topic was making her uncomfortable.

"Yeah, that's okay," he said, and she could tell he meant it. "I was hoping you would tell me about it, sometime?"

"Tell you about what?" she asked honestly.

"Well," he said, smiling gently, "people who don't believe in God, or dislike church, or have some stigma against religion, tend to have a story about *why*."

He smiled so sweetly she couldn't help but nod.

"I'll tell you, sometime."

"Alright," he said. With a final smile in her direction, he walked into the house.

That night Clair drove home feeling confused.

On the one hand, it had been a long time since her experience with the club in high school, but on the other, church wasn't something she felt she needed in her life. Church was for people with problems, looking for a group of people to join them on a journey they believed would eventually lead them to an eternal peaceful life. Clair's life had never been peaceful, and she didn't like the idea of living forever. For one thing, what would you do? The visuals of heaven painted on canvas were fruity, at best, and the visuals in the actual texts throughout multiple religions were scattered, all self-centered around the individual receiving whatever they wanted for forever.

This concept, to Clair, seemed very un-self-sacrificial and entirely unlike what the Bible says on how to live *before* eternity, which typically demanded that a person's entire life be lived in sacrifice. It seemed highly unlikely to Clair that eternity, should there be one, would involve laziness, when in life that same God demanded everything.

Clair was pondering this concept when she walked into her house twenty minutes later to find Dotty standing on a ladder in the middle of the living room, taking a duster to some cobwebs.

"Grandma," Clair said, sprinting over to hold the ladder, "what do you think you are doing?"

"Well," Dotty said, glancing down at Clair before continuing her relentless pursuit of the abandoned homes, "the ropes had me looking at the ceiling a lot more the other day, and there're a significant amount of webs. It's disgusting!"

Clair couldn't help but laugh.

"Don't do stuff like this on your own! You could have fallen . . ." Clair didn't like that idea at all, but Dotty just laughed.

"Clair, you wouldn't believe some of the—"

But just then there was a loud knock at the door, before it opened and Chris stuck his head through.

"Hello," he said, peering at the two of them. "Sorry to barge in, but Sam said it was important that he check something in the shop. Is that okay?"

"Don't ask them if it's okay!" Sam shouted just outside the door, obviously impatient. "Just go inside!"

Chris rolled his eyes, sending an apologetic look in their direction before walking in, Sam hot on his tail.

"Dotty, I think I've found—" he stopped for only a second, seeing Dotty on the ladder, before continuing "—I think I've found something interesting regarding The Gate."

CHRIS

hris watched as Clair rounded on Dotty.

"You knew about The Gate?" she said, shock and hurt passing across her face.

Dotty creased her brows.

"I was going to talk with you about it tonight, Clair," she began, concern in her voice. "Sam and I discussed it earlier today, when you were with Andrew."

Chris felt the anger rise in his chest, and subconsciously flexed his right hand into a fist before releasing it. He shouldn't be reacting this way, didn't have a right to react that way. He kept repeating the thought over and over in his mind.

"How do you know about The Gate, Clair?" Sam said, moving the book from under his arm into his right hand.

"I *guessed*, Sam," she spat, before turning back to Dotty. "Why is it," Clair continued, looking from Dotty to Sam, "that I'm always the last one to find information like this out? Especially when it deals directly with *me*!"

Clair stood there, eyes burning. "From now on, *I* know. I get told, immediately—anything new, anything important. I'm a part of this!" She was alternating her stare between the three of them, an air of confidence and authority Chris hadn't seen in her before. "And *you will all* make sure I'm informed."

Chris felt the bones in his chest quiver. He wondered if it was from remnants of the anger he felt with himself for how he had reacted, hearing that Clair had been with Andrew, or because, in that moment, he was afraid of her.

Then, as soon as it came, the feeling left. Chris watched as Clair relaxed, her shoulders slumping. Clair shook her head and turned to Dotty. "I'm sorry I yelled."

"It's okay, dear," Dotty said, the smile crinkling around her eyes. "I think it's time we all sat down to discuss what we are dealing with."

Clair nodded, following Dotty through the hallway toward the kitchen. Sam placed a hand on Chris's shoulder and waited for the women to disappear through the door, before speaking.

"So," he said, looking at Chris, eyes narrowed, "*I* don't have to *guess* who told Clair about The Gate."

Chris held Sam's gaze. "She really did know. I don't know how she knew, but she did."

Sam stared at Chris for a few more seconds, most likely trying to see if he was lying.

"Be that as it may, this is getting more and more challenging. I don't like having Clair involved, or Dotty, with The Gate, but given their . . . heritage . . . it makes sense that they'd be necessary. Emily, however, is a human and shouldn't get involved."

"Emily is her best friend, Sam," Chris interjected. "If you tell Emily she can't be involved now, when she already knows everything, Clair will resent you for it."

"There are ways to make it as if she never knew."

Chris thought about that for a moment. It wasn't a skill he had ever possessed, or even imagined. Most of the time whenever he learned a new ability, it was by accident. He had only discovered his ability to move the air when he got frustrated with a stubborn weed that kept growing in his backyard.

The fact that Sam would even suggest erasing Emily's memories filled him with a righteous fury.

"Sam, you won't get anywhere with Clair by creating boundaries around her," Sam started to protest, but Chris held his hand up. "I know you're the superior, but I also know you felt what just happened in here . . . Clair will not be stepped on or pushed aside, which is how we're training her to be." Chris paused for a moment to watch Sam's face. He wasn't protesting, only thinking. So Chris continued. "I think the best thing for Clair is to have her friend, and let the pieces fall where they will."

A few seconds of silence passed. Sam looked at the floor, his hand stroking the five o'clock shadow on his chin before he looked up at Chris, resigned. Chris nodded, and the moment passed.

"Are you two coming!" Clair yelled from the kitchen, the impatience clear in her voice. Chris chuckled, and Sam narrowed his eyes.

"That girl . . ." was all he muttered before walking toward the kitchen.

Dotty was sitting at the small wooden table, one hand holding a flower-embellished teacup while the other was flipping quickly through a tattered book with small writing. Clair was leaning, arms crossed, against the counter. She glared at Sam when they walked in.

"I just got a text from Emily," she said, the anger returning to her voice. Chris had to stifle a laugh—the irony of the situation was just too much—but he ended up making a sound between a cough and a hiccup.

Clair directed her attention to him, but before she got a chance to pounce, Sam cut in.

"I did see Emily today in the hopes of keeping her out of these affairs, since she is a human and things could become . . . complicated." He paused to stress the importance of the word before continuing. "But I agree with Chris, who just spoke for your cause moments ago, which is no doubt the reason why he just gagged on his laughter, that it might be beneficial for you to have a peer-like companion to process with." Sam looked to Dotty. "Not to say that you are insufficient, Dorthea."

Sam said this with such seriousness Chris was tempted to break out laughing completely, but Sam continued. "However, should any harm come to Emily, the fault is on your head Clair." There was finality in Sam's voice that had the laughter dying in Chris's throat.

Could there be a chance that Emily was now in real danger?

"Now," Dotty said, finger scanning a passage from the small ragged book, "let's discuss what we know. Sam, I know you were in the antique shop quite a bit today. Is that book in your hands important?"

"Relatively. Constellations and signs for the summer that could help us determine the significance of the spot where it stopped, but it wouldn't answer the question."

Clair looked frustrated again, so Chris turned to her. "Did you read the passages?"

"Yes," she said, standing up straighter.

"Alright," Chris said, glancing from Sam to Dotty, who stopped talking and looked at them. Chris knew this was not his time to lead, that Sam was in charge, but he wanted to hear it from Clair; he wanted to know what her mind had unraveled on its own. "What have you learned?"

CLAIR

"Well," Clair began, unfolding her arms and sensing the tension in the room, "I discovered that the first three chapters are about God, who creates the world in seven days, including the universe, oceans, sun, moon, animals, and then humans."

"Yes," Chris said. He was meticulously running his finger over the tile on the countertop. "There are multiple writers with different interpretive names for the different metaphors of the Ultimate Good, which I encourage you to call him from now on." Chris paused and eyed Clair, who didn't protest, and then glanced at Sam, who nodded approval, before continuing. "As that is what he is, and by calling him that, you relinquish most of your previous conceptions of his character, which in turn helps you to see more clearly."

"Makes sense," Clair said, raising an eyebrow and watching Chris stroke the counter, wondering if it was a nervous habit. She certainly felt nervous, talking about things that were just stories, weren't real, but now ultimately seemed more important—and true. "Also, from my classes in college, I learned that the Old Testament is actually known as the Tanakh, to the Hebrew people, and can only be called the Old Testament in relation to the Christian religion, which has a New Testament. The Old Testament is also missing some books from the Hebrew Bible."

"Every religion has its own views on the Ultimate Good," Sam spoke for the first time, his voice deep, eyes staring into Clair's pointedly. "And I mean *every* religion."

Clair narrowed her eyes then looked back to Chris, who had his brows creased. Sam resumed staring at the floor.

"So," Chris continued, cocking his head to the side, "what did you find out about Eden?"

Clair considered the question, thinking back to the passages she had read and reread before seeing Andrew. Clearly everyone in the room had heard the story of Adam and Eve in the garden.

Clair sighed and told the story that must have been told a million times.

"God—the Ultimate Good," Clair corrected herself, "created everything in the first chapter of Genesis, including humans. Then, chapter two of the Hebrew Bible restates the creation of humanity, how he created Adam from the dust of the earth and breathed into him the breath of life.

The Ultimate Good let Adam name all the animals he had created, and in the end found that Adam was lonely." Clair paused for only the briefest of seconds while the thought hit her that Adam, who was the first being on earth, could be lonely in the presence of something that, according to the story, was the most interesting thing in the world. "So the Ultimate Good had Adam fall asleep, and created Eve from his rib."

"And Adam said, 'This is bone of my bone and flesh of my flesh. And she shall be called woman, for she was taken from man.'" Dotty quoted the scripture, sending a chill down Clair's spine. Chris turned his eyes to her, sorrow in their depths, while Sam continued to stare at the floor, a deep scowl on his face.

Clair looked at her grandmother

"Please continue," Dotty said.

Clair took a deep breath and tried to remember what happened next. "But Adam and Eve were not alone in the garden. In chapter three, a snake, known as the devil . . ." Clair paused to watch Chris and Sam.

"Ultimate Evil," Chris said. Clair nodded and continued.

"The Ultimate Evil tempted Eve into eating from the tree of the knowledge of good and evil that the Ultimate Good had forbidden them to eat from, and then Eve gave some of the fruit to Adam, who also ate, and the Ultimate Good threw them out of the garden."

"Details, Clair," Chris said, smiling, obviously impressed with her synopsis. "The 'devil' is in the details."

Clair thought about that for a moment. What were some of the finer points? She had talked about the tree, but she knew there was more than one tree—one for the knowledge of good and evil, the Tree of Life, and others just for eating. Eve had eaten from the tree that God—The Ultimate Good, she corrected herself again inwardly—had forbidden they eat from, at the behest of the devil—Ultimate Evil, she corrected again. Adam and Eve were then thrown out to toil the land, while what had happened to Eden?

"It was guarded," Clair said out loud, "by a 'flaming sword that turned every which way,'" she quoted, staring at Chris. "You don't look like a sword to me."

He laughed, closing his eyes and shaking his head. "There are so many things I could say to that." When he looked at her she felt her heart skip a beat, the raw flirtation was almost more than she could bare here in the kitchen, with Dotty and Sam watching their every move.

"But no," he continued, his smile soft, "I'm not the sword that guards The Gate."

Clair glanced at Sam.

"Neither am I."

A small smile passed across Dotty's face.

"What?" Clair asked.

"Well," Dotty said, looking at Clair, "I never brought you to church or anywhere near any religion because I didn't want you knowing any of it, having any part of it, and you go away to school, and somehow fate throws itself upon you." She laughed, and Clair, who didn't think it was funny at all, gave her a wry smile and turned to Sam.

"Why is Eden here?" Clair said, leaving the concept of the sword for a minute.

"Why it is *here*, I cannot say," Sam began. "There are many areas where The Gate stops. This is just one of them. It is why it has *stayed* here for so long that has me concerned."

Clair took a moment to blink and gather her thoughts.

"The Gate *moves*? Where?"

"All over the world, I suppose," Sam said. "I found one a while back in Russia, and I know there is one in Jerusalem and Pakistan, but I'd imagine there are spots in every major city. But no one knows where they all are. That's the point."

Clair noticed that Dotty was looking at the book in front of her, but not reading, only listening. She wondered if she already knew all of this, from James.

"But how does it move?" Clair continued, brows creasing while she let her gaze drift, thinking of the quiet, deep forest.

"Think about it," Chris said, leaning forward. "The 'flaming sword that turns every which way,' what do you think it means?"

The first image that came to mind was literal. The thought was frightening, but not explanatory enough. The sword was meant to guard The Gate, Clair thought, in the story, but The Gate was actually guarded by minor angels like Chris and Sam. But it moved . . . Clair looked out the kitchen window; the clouds were turning pink and orange on the horizon.

The sun.

Clair hoped that wasn't cheating.

The voice had been very quiet recently, and Clair felt a sense of peace hearing it again. It was her own little piece of insane-sanity.

But it was brilliant: the flaming sword was the sun. It turned every which way around the earth, or at least that was the way it seemed from earth, especially to the writers of the Hebrew Bible centuries ago. The Gate moved with time itself.

"The sun," she said, looking at the three people around her. "The Gate moves based on time. It's brilliant. You knew all of this?" Clair was looking at Dotty, arms crossed.

"Yes," she said, moving her glasses to the top of her head to rub her eyes, "but I only thought it left and then returned."

"Because of James?" Clair said.

Dotty closed her eyes. She looked much older, as if this experience was aging her. "James would tell me he was going to visit a friend, and he would walk the forest. I always let it go. You'll find, Clair, that the less you know about certain eternal things, the better.

He would walk and come back brooding, or elated, or confused. It was like this friend of his was some puzzle he couldn't figure out." Dotty looked back down at the book. "It's only now that it makes more sense that The Gate would stop here, and he would patrol it . . . or go into it."

"Into it? A friend?" Clair said, confused.

Dotty looked at Chris, who met her gaze evenly. "I don't know why it took so many years for you to be sent to guard The Gate. As far as I know, you are the only one to be here since James." Chris nodded, and Dotty sighed. Then she became angry, and her eyes passionately turned to Clair. "Whenever we get close to an answer, more questions come up. We're not *meant* to know these things! That's why I kept you away, because you could spend your whole life searching, and die no closer to the truth than you were when you began. And I don't want that life for you."

Clair was going to speak, but Sam cut her off.

"I agree," he said, and Clair felt her mouth drop open in surprise. He held his hand up to her. "I understand your anger, Clair, but your grandmother is right." Dotty raised her eyebrow at Sam, obviously surprised with the show of camaraderie. "There are never concrete answers with the eternal processes, only more questions. Take it from someone who has walked the earth over eight hundred years: trying to find answers will not bring you peace. However," he continued, throwing a pointed glance at Dotty, "we do need to focus on why The Gate has refused to leave, and the dangers it presents."

"What dangers?" Clair asked, and immediately felt stupid when the others looked at her, concern on their faces. "Don't look at me like that! As far as I can tell, the only *dangerous* thing about The Gate is the plants that seep from it."

"About the lily," Sam said, looking at Clair. "You need to get it back as soon as possible. We don't want any humans becoming suspicious."

"I'll get it," Dotty said, looking at Clair. "Jean was my friend a long time ago, and besides, I'm supposed to have her over for dinner, eventually."

Sam jerked an eyebrow upward, but Clair only smiled. Even in the face of the supernatural, Dotty was making an effort to fit in for Clair's sake.

"Alright . . ." Sam said before turning to Clair. "The Gate draws supernatural attention, attention that could be very, very negative."

He began pacing around the room. "Recently, attacks on The Gate have grown, beginning about five hundred years into my new life, according to the communities of angels I've encountered. They didn't know the cause, but it *is* happening."

Sam looked at Clair who nodded, feeling the air around them grow cold. She hugged her arms to her chest. Dotty stood and walked into the other room. A few seconds later Clair heard the heater turn on. It was the middle of summer and the heater needed to be used. Clair found that ridiculous and laughed, just as Dotty walked back into the room, earning Clair yet another concerned look.

"I just thought it was funny," she said to explain the laugh, "that we have to use the heater in summer."

Dotty smiled.

"I think it has been a long enough day for all of us," Chris said. "We can begin hunting through the antique shop more tomorrow."

Sam nodded, and Dotty went to the wine rack below the counter, grabbed a pinot, and uncorked the bottle, which Clair thought was very uncharacteristic. The thought must have shown on her face, because Dotty started laughing.

"Sometimes, the best cure to a long day is a small glass of good wine," she said, offering Clair a glass. She took it gingerly and looked at Sam and Chris.

"I think we should be going," Sam said, turning to Chris. "Ready?"

For a second Clair thought he might stay, but instead he nodded, bid goodnight to the two women with their wine, and followed Sam out the door.

"Well," Dotty said, seated again at the table, "that was a lot to process."

Clair sat down opposite of her and sipped. The wine smelled like spices and had an earthy aftertaste, warming her from the inside out.

"I would say so," Clair laughed, looking at Dotty. "You knew most of that already, though, didn't you?"

"Yes," Dotty said, swirling the glass by the stem. "But it was never as real to me then as it is now."

Clair knit her eyebrows together, and Dotty continued. "Your grandfather and I, we were . . . special."

"*Obviously*," Clair chuckled.

Dotty rolled her eyes. "Well, there was that too. But we were also in love, a deep love, and when I found out what he was—when he told me—he said he just wanted to move forward, to live and love me as a human. That he didn't want to have his past be his present." Dotty smiled, deep and timeless, eyes far away. "He was always so poetic about his thoughts on life. And I loved him more than I could ever express. So I agreed. We didn't discuss it, and I honestly didn't want to know."

Clair had the nerve to look shocked. "You really didn't want to know about *any* of it? But he must have known so much . . ."

"I know," Dotty continued. "He was very wise, very charismatic, and very, very *mine*." Her smile turned wicked. "I didn't want to think about the idea of the supernatural with him. I was young, in love, and happy. You don't think about negative things when you're happy, only when you aren't."

"True," Clair said, taking another long drink of wine. Dotty gave her a look, but Clair shook her head to dismiss the question. "So what happened? What made you want to know?"

Dotty looked out the kitchen window, her brows knit together.

"A few months after we moved here, The Gate stopped for the first time, and James sensed it." Dotty looked toward Clair. "After that, every time it stopped, he would leave the house to meet it."

"So you think he was trying to get in?" Clair asked, draining the rest of her glass.

"I don't think he was trying," she said. "I think he was succeeding."

EMILY

Sam. Was. A. Jerk.

Emily was instructed to be at Clair's house the next day at six in the morning. Dotty answered the door.

"Morning, dear," she said. She was wearing her pink beanie and walking shoes. "Have fun," she said dubiously before walking out of the house. Emily sighed and ran up the steps to Clair's room.

She was standing in her bathroom, eyes bleary, brushing her teeth. When she saw Emily, she made a guttural sound of hello.

Emily laughed and sat on the edge of her bed.

"Morning," Clair mumbled after she spat.

"Morning!" Emily said, watching her try to detangle her hair with a comb.

Clair narrowed her eyes. "Why are you so chipper? I already told you," she said, grabbing a different comb, "Sam has just been teaching me *breathing* techniques the past few weeks. It's nothing cool."

"I know," Emily said, tracing the embroidery on Clair's bed sheet.

Clair turned around, comb still pulling out tangles. "And?"

Emily stopped fidgeting and looked up at Clair. "Sam needs to know I can handle this. You all do."

Clair stopped combing her hair and walked over to her friend.

"Of course I know you can handle it, Em," she said, sitting on the bed next to Emily. "In some ways you have taken all of this better than I have."

Emily let a small laugh escape her lips. That night had been so surreal. The next morning she found herself confronted by Dotty in the kitchen, with a cup of coffee in her hand she didn't remember making. They had a long talk before Clair woke up; Dotty understood where Emily was coming from, how she was feeling. They were very similarly involved in the situation, and after their chat, Emily had felt resolved that she was meant to play a part in this adventure.

"So," Emily said at last, coming out of her thoughts, "what is on the breathing schedule today?"

"Probably more on how to properly 'inhale and exhale through your nose,'" Clair said with a poor fake British accent.

"Maybe he will have crumpets and tea with us," Emily laughed, speaking in the same fake accent.

Clair snorted as she flung her hair into a messy bun. "I doubt Sam understands what it means to relax."

Once Clair had finished putting on her shoes and shorts, Emily followed her out the back door and into the forest. The morning was brisk as they walked. The plan was to meet Sam at Chris's house, where Sam now lived—or, as Emily like to say, where Sam was bumming it. It was the one redeeming quality Emily liked to think about when she thought of Sam—as a vagabond.

The walk was short but uphill, leaving Emily a little out of breath. She never considered herself fat, but she wasn't the picture of fitness. Sure, in high school she had been able to hold her own, especially in her last two years dancing and doing drills, but she wasn't good at sports and didn't particularly feel athletic in any way.

They came to a break in the forest where a small house stood, circled by short ferns. It was faded blue, with white trim and green accent panels that matched the color of the trees. It would have looked like something from a fairy tale if it wasn't for the large white truck sitting in front.

"Whose car is *that*?" Emily said, exasperated.

"I don't know." Clair walked around the vehicle and peered through the tinted windows, cupping her face with her hands. "Nothing's in it, but this thing's hooked up!"

"Really?" Emily said. "Let me see!"

The girls were still ogling the truck's features—state of the art digital panel with Bluetooth capabilities and who knew what else—when Chris said, "Like my car?" and they both jumped.

"This is *your* car?" Clair said. "Since when?"

"Since yesterday when Sam bought it for me," he smiled, and Clair blushed, faintly. Emily almost knocked her upside the head. She could be so obvious sometimes it was ridiculous. Her face showed every emotion.

"Nice," Emily said as she watched Sam walk out the screen front door. He was wearing athletic shorts and a white tank top that obviously belonged to Chris, because it was too tight for Sam. Emily almost forgot she didn't like Sam, watching the muscles in his arms and abs move beneath the thin fabric. Then he spoke.

"You're late," he said, adjusting the watch on his wrist as he moved toward them.

"How did you buy Chris a car?" Clair burst out, hand gesturing to the large vehicle. "And how did you get it here?"

"Drove it through the forest . . ." Chris said, pointing toward a break in the forest to the right of the house that was obviously made by something like a tank.

"And as to the purchase," Sam said impatiently, "I have enough money, always have, and Chris needs to establish himself as a resident. I'm surprised he got on this long without raising suspicion."

Chris looked sheepish.

"Humans drive," Sam said to him.

Emily thought about Chris. She had never questioned his transportation or anything else. He'd always been just another townie. Emily wondered if she'd missed other magical beings in her lifetime.

Clair was looking from the car back to Chris, and over at the forest, then back to the car. "It doesn't have any scratches on it!"

Emily examined the truck. It still looked brand new.

Chris had a proud smile on his face. "Well, it took a lot of convincing, but the trees eventually moved."

Emily and Clair half ran, half jogged to the edge of the forest where the gap stood, immense. Sure enough, the trees were all there, neatly dispersed, creating a six-foot path of dirt that wound out of sight.

Emily was pretty sure her mouth was hanging open, but she didn't care. "The trees . . . moved?"

Chris looked concerned, but Sam was staring at her, the smile on his face so cocky that Emily remembered to shut her mouth, and corrected herself, putting on a nonchalant face. "Oh, well, I've seen that in movies anyways—nothing new."

"Alright," Sam said, smile gone. "We've wasted enough time. Let's go."

Chris didn't go with them, saying he needed to stay and work on his garden, where he was having some plant emergency. "Have fun!" he said before disappearing around the house. Emily didn't think *fun* was the right word, but everyone seemed to be using it today.

"Where're we going?" Emily asked, and noticed that Clair flicked her eyes to Sam, who looked at her for a fraction of a second before answering.

"We're going to the usual training spot, a quiet place in the forest."

"Okay." Emily was pretty sure she saw Clair visibly relax, and made a mental note to accost her about it later. Maybe there were some spots that were less friendly in this forest. "Lead the way."

It took them about an hour to get to the spot, up one hill and down another until they finally stopped hiking and Emily caught her breath.

"Now," Sam said, sitting in a space cleared of trees. This had to be where they trained daily, because the grass was flattened. "I am sure Clair has spoken with you about our lessons?"

"Yes," Emily answered, sitting down next to Clair with her legs crossed, following Sam and resting her hands on her knees.

"Good," Sam said, a small smile playing on his lips. "Then you won't mind a crash course."

Emily nodded.

Something about the way Sam was smiling made her apprehensive. But she had gone over the breathing techniques with Clair and had even practiced them a bit last night before she went to bed. She was determined to prove herself here, in this arena of angels who seemed to think she didn't belong. Emily damn well belonged wherever she wanted to be.

Sam closed his eyes, pointing his palms up to the sky. A little light was falling through the trees now, the sun playing around the edges of his hands as the wind ruffled the leaves.

"Do as I do," he said, and Emily and Clair closed their eyes, lifting their palms.

"With our eyes closed, we can more fully understand our surroundings," Sam went on, his voice slightly softer. "Feel the heat from the sun on your palms, listen to the slight breeze in the wind, and breathe—breathe in the oxygen that floats around you."

Emily dismissed her first inclination to rebel against this kind of interaction with nature. She had never been a wilderness person, never enjoyed the hippie ideals of connection and life energy that seemed to always link a person with drugs. If Emily hadn't seen what she had, she wouldn't be buying into this whole ordeal. But because whenever she closed her eyes, she saw those ropes fall from the ceiling, Emily followed Sam's instructions and breathed deeply, felt the sun, and listened to the wind.

After about ten minutes—she wasn't exactly sure—of breathing and becoming in tune with her other senses and surroundings, Sam spoke again.

"Now," his voice was even softer, an echo in the forest around them, sending a chill down Emily's spine. "Inhale to your fullest extent, fill your lungs to bursting, and release."

The action sent Emily's body into a tingling sensation, and the sun on her palms was now warming her whole body. She could feel the light breeze cooling her, the play of heat and cool happening over and over again like some natural religious cycle.

They completed these sets a few more times before Sam instructed them to open their eyes. The light was brighter, and it took Emily a few seconds for her eyes to adjust and notice that Sam was standing.

"Now," he said, wicked smile back in place. "We will do some stretches."

Emily looked over at Clair, who shrugged and stood. Emily got the vibe that this wasn't normal behavior, but she and Clair followed Sam through a series of leg and arm stretches for over twenty minutes.

Emily was just thinking that this wasn't the worst way to spend an hour when Sam said, "Ready?"

"Ready for what?" Clair said, shaking out her muscles from all the relaxation.

"Ready for the next phase of training, of course," Sam said maliciously.

Clair narrowed her eyes. "Yes," she said stubbornly. Emily squared her jaw. This wasn't going to be good.

"Alright," Sam said before he jogged away from the training spot. Clair took one look at Emily, who nodded encouragingly before they both began jogging after him.

More like running. Sam's legs took him a lot further and faster than either Emily or Clair, and soon both girls were panting through the forest, up the hill, and then down again, where they reached Clair's house at the edge of the forest, doubled over.

"Down into plank position, girls," Sam said cheerfully, jogging in place before bouncing down onto his hands and toes, holding himself upright. Emily thought she might die, but got into the position and held it for thirty seconds before flopping onto her stomach, Clair following ten seconds later.

"Come on, girls," Sam said playfully, breath even. His muscles didn't even look strained. "You have to at least be able to hold this for three minutes in order to survive the next phase of training. Both of you get back into position."

Emily forced all of her energy into pulling her body from the ground. She was no longer watching Clair or Sam, no longer cared if she was keeping up. This was a personal test, and Emily was going to prove to herself that she could do it. She felt the muscles in her thighs and triceps start to shake, could taste the salt from her sweat as it poured down her face, stinging her eyes, and pooled on her lower back, soaking her shirt. The force of holding herself up from the ground was sending a burning sensation through her arms and stomach, where she was sure her abs were waking up from hibernation.

When Emily hit the ground, after what felt like an eternity, she looked up to find Clair staring open-mouthed at her. Sam was frowning.

"Three minutes exactly," was all he said before getting up and walking away.

Emily turned to Clair with a smile. "Not bad for my first day?"

"Not bad at all," Clair said; her face said she was both relieved and impressed. "Ready for some food?"

Emily stood up and extended a hand to help Clair.

"More than I have ever been in my *life*."

DORTHEA

Dotty found Jean on her knees, shifting dirt from one pot to another in front of a few stubborn patches of hydrangeas.

Even though the two of them were close in age, she couldn't help but notice how much younger and invigorated Jean looked scooping dirt. Dotty just *felt* like dirt most of the time.

"Hello, Dorthea!" Jean said, smile bright. She stood up, removed her gloves, and walked over to shake Dotty's hand.

"Hello, Jean," Dotty said, smiling politely. "It's good to see you."

"It's great to see you too! Or at least, it's great to have you respond to me at all after twenty-some years."

Dotty couldn't help but wince.

Truth be told, after everything that happened with James and Eli, she didn't want to talk with anyone, not even people like Jean who had been kind to her. Dotty pushed down her pride.

"I am sorry about that, Jean."

"It's alright." Jean's face was sympathetic. "Things haven't been easy for you these past few years."

"Easy is dealing with burnt cookies compared to my life," Dotty said, shocked with her own openness.

Jean laughed, and Dotty found herself joining in, enjoying the ease of conversation.

"I love what you've done with the place," Dotty said, looking around the shop and spotting the lily on the counter. "Is that a new stained glass window?"

Jean nodded and pointed out all the new features of the shop, including a timed watering system she had installed herself.

"But the stock hasn't been as good, especially since you stopped keeping your garden," Jean said warmly. "But then Clair brought in that lily, over there," she gestured. "I had hoped it was one of yours, maybe you starting up again?"

Dotty looked over at the lily. Even without any powers, she could sense the magic emanating from it, could see the effect its presence was having on the plants around it.

"No," she said, walking toward the flower. "Clair found it, and I had a bit of an episode, so she didn't want me seeing it again—to preserve my feelings."

Dotty hoped Jean would get the hint.

"Oh, dear, she's such a kind soul," Jean said, walking next to the flower and gingerly touching one of the large white petals. "I suspect you have had a change of heart?"

Dotty couldn't help but notice the glint in Jean's eyes, and wondered if she too could sense the power in the flower.

"Yes, I suppose I have."

CLAIR

"Em, I have to say, I'm impressed."

After the training session, Clair made them a batch of eggs and a large plate of bacon before they went their separate ways: Clair to work and Emily to class. Then, at the end of the day, Clair met Emily at the local burger joint to grab some much-needed bowling fuel. Unfortunately, Clair was only getting a salad because the eggs and bacon from the morning were still sitting happily in her stomach. She thought that must mean part of the training was working.

She never felt so tried in her life.

She was glad Sam was letting up on her fasting regimen—bringing it down to three times a week—but if she had known that he was going to put them both through hell that morning, she wouldn't have bothered getting out of bed.

Clair was, however, in awe with how Emily had done.

"Where did you learn to do all that stuff?" she finally asked, watching Emily eat one of her fries.

"I was in the color guard in high school." Emily shrugged, grabbing another fried potato.

"The what?" Clair said, stealing a fry before taking another bite of her salad.

"The color guard," Emily said, reaching for the ketchup. "The ones on the field with the band at football games."

Clair felt her mouth slack open.

"*You* were a flag girl?"

“Not a flag girl.” Emily narrowed her eyes. “A dancer, with a flag.” She shrugged her shoulders and pointed a particularly burnt fry at Clair. “At least I *did* an extracurricular in high school.”

Clair shrugged.

She never knew Emily liked to dance professionally; her memories of them dancing as girls were filled with NSYNC. Clair mentioned this thought, and Emily started laughing. She was still laughing when Andrew walked in to join them.

“Hey!” he said, smile in place, even after his extra-long shift. Melody had left him in a tight spot again by calling in sick just before she was supposed to show up. If Clair was the boss, Melody would have been canned a long time ago. But Andrew always shook it off as a “Melody thing.”

“Have Tiffany and Alex shown up yet?” Andrew asked, removing his hoodie and placing it on the back of the chair. He stole one of Emily’s fries. She narrowed her eyes at him but didn’t pounce.

“If they were here, wouldn’t you see them?” Emily said sarcastically.

“I don’t know,” Andrew said with a wink. “They tend to disappear to the bathroom at the same time.” He flashed a heart-aching grin at Clair before taking the seat across from her.

Clair liked that Andrew didn’t need to be super affectionate all the time, especially when Emily was still dealing with her Mike situation. As far as Clair knew, it had been a long time since Emily talked with him.

The three of them were discussing which lane to use, when Alex and Tiffany walked in, followed by Chris. Clair almost dropped her fork. Somewhere in the back of her mind, she thanked her luck that she had decided on a salad, because Chris was a terrible liar, and she was sure Sam would ask about her eating habits.

“Hey, guys, sorry we’re late,” Alex said, drawing a hand through his straight black hair and throwing off his leather jacket. “Car broke, stopped working downtown, and Chris here saw us and gave us a jump. Did you see his truck!”

“Yeah,” Tiffany said, pushing Chris into a seat at the table and eyeing him a little too appreciatively. “Our hero.”

"So they invited me bowling," Chris said, glancing at Clair and then to Emily, who smiled and waved slightly before sinking her teeth back into the burger.

"What truck?" Andrew said, staring at Chris from the other side of Emily.

"Chris got a new truck the other day," Clair said, and then regretted it. Andrew directed his attention to her.

"How did you know that? I thought you were with Emily all day yesterday."

"I was," Clair said, taking a sip of her ice water to buy some time. "But Chris texted me a picture of it." Clair looked at Chris, who stared at her but nodded.

"Alright," Andrew said, seeming a bit more relaxed. "What type of truck is it?"

"I don't really know actually," Chris said with a small laugh, picking up one of Emily's fries. Andrew followed the action with his eyes, not missing the familiarity between them. "I just know it gets the job done." Chris finished with a smile.

"Must be nice to have it"—Andrew narrowed his eyes—"living way out where you do. Where *is* that, exactly?"

"It's in the middle of the woods," Emily said offhand, taking a bite of burger.

Andrew pinned his gaze on her. "*You* have been to his house? *When*?"

Emily glanced up at Clair behind her burger, shock in her eyes for only a second.

"I went on a hike with them today, remember?"

"You didn't mention it," Andrew said, deflated.

"Yeah," Emily said, mouth full of burger, "it was nice. Had a good little chat."

She smiled at Andrew when she finished chewing. Chris didn't look worried, but Clair realized she had been holding her breath, and exhaled.

Then Emily continued.

"Yeah," she said, looking at Andrew with a huge smile. "Turns out, Chris and Clair are distant cousins, of sorts."

Clair almost choked on her water, while Chris, whose smile was still in place, stared at Emily with slightly narrowed eyes.

"Really?" said Andrew, the smile on his face a little too smug.

"Yep," Emily continued, turning to her attention to Clair and reveling in her little half-truth joke. "Something on Clair's mother's side. We found it out today, in those letters we've been reading that we found."

"Oh, that's great, Clair!" Tiffany said. "You must be so excited to have found family."

Clair looked over at Tiffany, lost for words.

"Yes," she finally managed, looking at Chris and then to Andrew and Emily. "It's great to have family."

Chris bowled with them for the rest of the night. After Emily's little revelation, Andrew was less competitive and even offered to help Chris with his stance. He did, however, take every opportunity available to slyly touch Clair in front of Chris—from rubbing her arm to an all-out dipped kiss after a strike.

Clair sat down next to Chris after one particularly bad turn where she only knocked down four pins. She watched Andrew pick up a bowling ball and expertly toss it down the lane.

"Well hello again, cousin," Chris said with a small smile.

"Emily has quite a way with words." Clair looked up at him.

"Yes, she does," he said, watching Emily bowl. "It's very funny, and close enough to truth." He was still smiling, but Clair saw the light in his eyes dim. She felt the same, sitting next to him on the bench. They were close enough to touch, but they couldn't—they both knew they couldn't. Clair could feel the energy spiking between them and was surprised it wasn't visible.

"Well," she said, sighing, "at least Andrew will be less suspicious now." The words felt hollow in her mouth. They weren't even having an affair, but she felt guilt coil in her stomach. She was lying to Andrew about everything, lying to Chris about her feelings, and as much as she hated it, Emily had actually come up with a great solution.

"True," Chris said, standing to take his turn. But before he walked away, he looked down at Clair, his brows creased. He looked sad, and for a moment, Clair thought he was going to say something else.

But then he shook his head, smiled, and walked away.

Later that night, Clair lay awake in bed wondering about the lineage of angels.

Even though Emily only said what she did as an inside joke, she had a point: weren't all angels, in essence, related? Could she and Chris actually *be* distant cousins?

Clair rolled over onto her stomach, her face planted in the soft feather pillow.

No, she thought, searching her brain for the answer. Even if it did work that way—if angels had specific blood origins and families—she and Chris wouldn't be related, based simply on the fact that he was a minor angel, not a seraph. Chris was once human and thus was created into an angel. Part of her blood was never human and would be different from his.

So? The voice asked. *Does that make a difference?*

No, Clair thought back, letting out an exasperated breath. *But would it have been so bad if I'd wanted it to?*

There was a brief moment of silence, then: *Choice is entirely individual.*

Clair screamed into the pillow and rolled onto her back.

That wasn't helpful, she thought, kicking her feet out of the sheets and looking up at the ceiling. Sometimes the answers came so easy, and other times it was like watching the same movie over and over again in her head, knowing how it ended but wanting to relive the painful and happy moments, trying to figure out *why* they happened.

It had been hard, those first few months after she transferred high schools, to change her attitude toward people. She was closed off for a long time after the Christian club, refusing to make friends even when she was invited to parties, events, or study groups. She had stayed away from groups, keeping her grades up but never doing anything extracurricular academically or socially.

Emily was right. She was never a part of anything in high school after the Christian club. It wasn't until she moved away from town and went to college that she was able to break free of the shell she had created, making friends and socializing with people who didn't know her story, where she was from, or what she was holding onto in her heart.

Now she was holding something completely different yet just as destructive: her heart yearned for Chris. Her daydreams were of them together in the forest, laughing and kissing, practicing their powers and being completely open. She could never have that with Andrew, could never show him her true self. It was different with Emily; Emily was her friend. But Andrew was supposed to be her lover, and he would never be able to know all of her.

The vision of Chris dead on the ground flashed across her mind, and Clair closed her eyes, soaking in the memory and using it to create a new shell, a new barrier for her heart.

Just before she fell asleep, Clair knew she would dream, and remember.

She was back in the purple forest, the winged angel standing with his back turned toward her.

"It will be time soon Clair . . ."

"Time for what?" she heard herself shout, the feathers already making their way up her face, threatening to suffocate her.

"I cannot stop it . . . it is in motion . . ."

Clair was screaming at him, his voice familiar and distant all at the same time, before the feathers consumed her.

But she didn't wake up.

Her brain fogged, and she saw the world around her as if through a thin layer of water. She could hear voices in front of her, beautiful voices that made her heart swell, the blurred shadows of two people. They were leaned in together.

Then the higher pitched voice touched her hand gently.

"Clair," it said, bright as sunlight. "Oh, my beautiful baby girl . . ."

"Our beautiful little angel . . ." the deeper voice spoke, both figures outlines in front of her as the world on either side of her rushed by—blurs upon blurs like a living painting.

Clair shot up in bed, her heart pounding in her chest.

She had been in the car with her parents; she knew it. It hadn't been a dream at all. Clair had remembered something about the night the car caught flame.

"Can you still see?"

Chris was stretched out on the ground next to her, the morning light casting rays onto his skin, making the white T-shirt glow.

"Yes," she said, looking around. The visions were lasting longer. The more she focused on how to watch the earth, the longer she was able to hold the effects of the fast.

It was beautiful, watching the florescent rainbow aura of the trees sway and caress one another without ever physically touching. It was like a dance. Clair looked to her right and saw a bumble bee, the energy pouring from its wings, the colors like the swirling of a bubble as it flew and landed on a flower. Clair watched the flower give some of its energy to the bee, which took it and flew off, paper-thin wings beating quickly.

Clair smiled and looked back down at Chris. His eyes were open, and he was looking at her in a way that made her heart melt.

She turned away from him just as her sight diminished. She was sure Sam would love to know that informational fact of her blood: that her own guilt killed the power from the fast. She couldn't help it; whenever she looked at Chris, she felt a surge of love she never knew existed, and a fear she had never known—the fear that the vision would come to pass.

Clair decided to tell Sam about the emotional connection with her powers, but he didn't need to know *what* she had felt guilty about.

"Ready to learn something more fun?" Chris said, pushing himself up with his elbows into sitting position. His legs were crossed over each other, the light highlighting a thin layer of hair on his legs. She had always thought Chris was hairless, but found the lack of perfection endearing.

Clair shook her head. He smiled a half smile in her direction, picked up a handful of leaves, and threw them at her.

"Earth to Clair, time to train," he said.

She laughed.

They were back to being friends.

The constant switch was driving her insane. The way Chris moved, talked, and touched her—only to train, only to direct—was still more than she could bear. She thought about the night that they had kissed, daydreamed about it, felt the pull of his energy to hers, and wondered what it would be like if they ever kissed again.

Would she see his death and the blood on the ground, or was the vision simply a fluke?

"So," she said, trying to ease the tension she felt, "how is it living with Sam?"

"It's definitely different." Chris laughed. "But I like it for the most part."

"What do you guys even talk about? Besides how best to torture me in training," Clair added, hearing his laugh deepen. She smiled.

"Actually, we talk about surface things like the weather, the town . . . we each had a lot of questions in the beginning, but now we just sit in silence a lot of the times." Chris knit his brows together, looking at the ground in front of him. "I bet he has a lot to think about . . . having lived so long."

Clair never considered it. She knew Sam was an old fart, living for over eight hundred years, but the weight of what that meant never occurred to her. She found herself wondering if Sam had ever lived a real life—ever was in love, ever had a job. He had to have had a job, her mind reminded her, to be able to buy all the new furniture in Chris's house, as well as the truck sitting in the yard.

"So, you and Sam barely talk even though he lives with you?"

"Well"—Chris turned to look at her, one eyebrow raised—"you lived with your grandmother for a few years and didn't get to know her too well."

Clair narrowed her eyes, feeling a jolt of anger before she noticed that Chris was smiling at her with that closed mouth smile of his, and she realized he was just teaching her, yet again.

Clair sighed and glared at him. "Touché."

His smile widened as he placed his palms faceup on his knees and waited for her to follow.

Back to business.

"Let's start with leaves, Clair," he said, laughing. He always seemed to be laughing at her lately. He got a really good laugh a few days ago when she asked if he could fly. She didn't think it was a dumb question.

"But angels are supposed to have wings," she had said, sticking her tongue out at him.

"Artistic interpretation." He had waved a dismissive hand in the air.

Chris began using the breathing techniques Sam taught them.

It was a silent moment, the first one for Clair in a while. After a few minutes, her heartbeat relaxed, allowing her to regain focus. When she sensed that Chris had opened his eyes, she opened her own.

"Okay," he said when she looked at him, "watch."

Chris grabbed a handful of leaves and put his hands together, creating a bowl with the leaves in the middle, and closed his eyes. Clair watched for a good two minutes while nothing happened, but then he extended his fingers so that only his pinkies were touching, side by side. All of a sudden, Clair could see heat in the air, coming off his palms, like in the desert when objects that are far away become blurred. One by one the leaves began to stir, the warm air from Chris's hands forcing them to rise up and then pulling them down and around continuously, creating a sphere.

"Wow," was all she could say. It was beautiful, the leaves swirling within his hands like a mini vortex.

Chris exhaled, and the leaves stopped moving, gravity pulling them down past his hands to the forest floor.

"Now," he said, opening his eyes again and handing her a lighter, "fire. When you see the hot air, flick the flame and place it in my hands."

Clair swallowed hard, but agreed.

It took a few more minutes for Chris to make the air appear again, but as soon as he did, Clair lit his palms, creating a fireball. She watched as it swirled just above his palms, the flames white-hot blues that slowly changed to oranges before Chris broke the connection at his pinkies, extinguishing the flames and opening his eyes.

There was a moment of silence before Clair said, "Could I do that?"

"When you learn this"—he looked at her, a small rim of sweat on his brow and triumph on his face—"you could *make* the flames."

Clair felt a shiver of excitement flow through her body. She cupped her hands together and began using the breathing techniques to quell the anticipation. Chris moved right in front of her, their knees almost touching, and placed a handful of leaves in her cupped palms.

"Alright," he said, leaning back, "I want you to close your eyes and focus on your palms. Let the air fill you, feel the natural energy floating past you, and capture it."

Clair felt the leaves in her hands, light as air. She felt the air leaving her lungs and the energy of the earth as it pulled and pushed around her as she focused on the leaves.

But nothing was happening. Clair opened her eyes.

"What am I doing wrong?"

"You aren't doing anything *wrong*," Chris said. "It takes time." He reached out and cupped her hands with his own, pulling them together so the creases on her fingers lined up.

Clair felt her heartbeat quicken.

"Try it again." He let her hands go after inspecting his work. "But this time, don't think about the leaves, just the air flowing through them to your palms."

Clair closed her eyes.

This time, she convinced her mind that she didn't feel the leaves at all. That they weren't there. She felt the air around her palms grow warm, then hot, and opened her eyes.

She had a glimpse of the leaves floating a few inches above her hands before they fell. When she looked up at Chris, he was grinning from ear to ear.

She did it.

EMILY

Emily was having an even harder time than usual focusing in her math class.

Not only was math the most boring subject in the world, she now had things like supernatural beings, magic powers, and her best friend to fill her mind, along with her worries about her parents, her boyfriend—if he was still considered that—and her job.

The professor was trying to describe the function of a circle as a geometric shape and how to find its length, or something. All Emily could do was doodle in her notebook and send fleeting glances in his direction to pretend like she was taking notes.

It had been over a week since she had heard from Mike. Emily knew he was alive, at least, because she had been texting Tiffany—who was a regular at the Brown Bear—almost every day to ask if she had seen Mike working. To which she would usually reply, "Yes, saw him today. Girl just come talk to him!" sometimes also followed by a "This is ridiculous Em—call him."

But she just couldn't.

For one thing, the last time she'd seen Mike he was getting high, and the time before that he had bruised her, badly, both physically and emotionally. She knew he was getting deeper into drugs, hanging out with people who were bad influences. While Emily was pretty sure it had something to do with his parents, he never mentioned anything. As far as Emily knew, Mike still hadn't spoken to his parents in the last six months.

The more she thought about it, the worse it looked—something must have happened recently that sent Mike off the deep end. But truth be told, Emily was just scared of what might happen if she *did* confront him about what was happening with him and how he was treating her. They had been dating for over a year now, and until Clair stepped into the picture she was content to play the role of girlfriend, counselor, and parent for whatever Mike needed, but ever since that night at the Brown Bear, when Clair looked at Emily with pity about Mike and his behavior, Emily just couldn't bring herself to be that person anymore.

She was changing, Mike was changing, and they weren't changing together, which could mean that they didn't belong together anymore, and that thought broke Emily's heart.

The professor finished his sentence, and the class began to stir, picking up books and shoving pencils into backpacks and purses. Emily numbly followed, throwing her doodles of flowers into her open binder. She reached for her bag and saw her phone light up. Thinking instantly of Mike she pulled it out and checked the front screen.

It was Clair.

"Hey, Em! Lunch today at 1? Took the day off work. Will talk about it later."

Sighing, Emily threw the phone back in her bag and walked out of class, enjoying the afternoon sunlight. Clair never seemed to remember what days her classes were on, or the times either. But that made sense, Emily supposed, since Clair had just graduated and no longer cared about classes, or homework, or anything else that wasn't angel related.

She got halfway to her art history class before turning around and heading to the parking lot. Clair was an art graduate; if Emily missed anything important, she could ask a professional for help.

It took less than thirty minutes for Emily to get from the small community college to Clair's house. And since it was about thirty minutes until one, Emily knocked on the front door.

"Hey!" Clair said when she answered, moving aside to let Emily in. "I'm glad you could come." Clair was wearing a pink tank top and mid-thigh jean shorts with frayed ends. Her hair, which usually hung past her shoulders, was up in a bun, which meant that she had just gotten back from hiking.

"Yep, I figured if I missed anything you could fill me in on it later," Emily said, watching Clair's face go from confused to shocked.

"Oh, Em, I totally forgot!" She laughed. "You didn't have to ditch class for this."

"I'm sure it's bound to be significantly more interesting," Emily said, trying her best impression of a professor voice. Clair laughed and walked into the kitchen, pulling out chicken from the small fridge and grabbing bread from a cabinet.

"Hungry?"

The two sat and ate, Emily talking about her math class while Clair laughed and agreed that, yes, math was the worst subject in the world. Then Emily asked about what she had learned in training recently.

"Oh man, Em, you have to see," Clair said, eyes bright as she stood and ran out the front door. Emily wasn't sure if Clair meant for her to follow. She was just about to stand up from the table when Clair came jogging back in, hand full of leaves from outside. Emily raised an eyebrow at her.

"You've taken up composting?"

"*No*"—Clair sighed—"something much, much cooler." She moved the food to the side of the table and placed the leaves in front of her. "Now, the last time I did this I was in sitting position and using the correct breathing techniques, but I think I should be able to do it again right here . . ."

Emily watched as Clair cupped some leaves in her hands and closed her eyes. Nothing happened for what felt like forever, and then the air around Clair's hands began to vibrate, pushing the leaves into the air and rotating them in a circle like a mini planet for about five seconds before they fell back onto the table. Emily felt her mouth drop.

"Wow," was all she could manage. Emily thought she was doing pretty well with everything—seeing ropes floating in thin air drop to the carpet, a path made by trees moving, and now watching Clair create a personal wind-ball right in front of her. But every once in a while, Emily was shocked and reminded that this wasn't some game. It was very, very real.

Clair was staring at her, looking worried.

Emily let a small laugh escape her lips, leaned back in the chair, and glanced from the leaves to Clair's eyes, taking a deep breath.

"Wow," she said again, "that's so cool."

Clair broke out into a huge smile and started rambling on about the possible uses for the air vortex, repeating the story about how she and Chris had stumbled upon the bobcat in the forest and how she had watched him use a similar technique but as a shield. ". . . but Chris used it to make a *fireball*."

Emily's head snapped up. "A what? How is that defensive!"

"I don't know how it's *defensive*"—Clair knit her eyebrows together—"but you have to admit . . . it would be a great weapon." The light in her eyes was dancing. Emily didn't like the sound of that but withheld her feelings. Clair was finally excited about what she was, and Emily, although more cautious than Clair, was excited for her.

"That's so awesome, Clair." She smiled, choosing her next words carefully. "Why would you need a weapon? Who could combat an angel?" She hoped Clair couldn't hear the real question behind her words: are we in any real danger, and should I be afraid?

"I don't know." Clair shrugged her shoulders, and Emily felt the breath she didn't know she was holding release. "Sam insisted in the beginning—and Dotty, too, though she's always been skittish—that it *could* be dangerous, being what I am, and for those around me . . ." She looked at Emily. "But we have been doing this for a couple months now, and nothing in my life has been really affected . . . aside from my relationship."

Clair threw her head into her hands.

"I just can't talk with Andrew about anything anymore. He asks me about my day, and I have to lie about everything, making up stories that don't sound remotely interesting. Sometimes I wonder if he believes me or if he just doesn't want to start a fight. Either way, it's becoming harder and harder to lie to him."

Emily felt the same way about Mike, or would have if they were talking at all still. But the counselor in Emily told her to stay on topic.

"Well," Emily said, going for the obvious question, "I know you can't tell him what you *are*, but you could try to find a way to relate to him on his level. What's he really into?"

Clair thought for a few moments then said, "Video games."

"Okay then." Emily tried hard not to laugh. Andrew was always so into those shooter games, just like Mike had been, or was, or whatever. "Well, why don't you try to find a game that is like what you are?"

Clair raised an eyebrow, and Emily decided to elaborate.

"Try to find a game that is relatively magic or religious based, and play the game with him. If you find one as similar to your situation as you can, then you can talk about the game as passionately with him as you would your own current experiences."

"Wow," Clair said.

"What?"

"You are *so* going to be the best counselor ever," she said with a huge smile. "That's such a great idea! Man . . ." Clair stared off into space, no doubt thinking about games she could use for her new little ploy.

"My turn," Emily said, watching Clair snap out of her reverie.

"Mike . . ."

Emily placed her head on the table dramatically, and Clair patted it.

"What *is* going on with Mike?" she said, tilting her head to look at Emily's squished face. "Have you spoken with him at all since that bowling night?"

"Yes." Emily sighed and sat up. "I broke it off with him when he offered me a joint." Clair made a face and Emily continued. "I've been bugging Tiffany to give me information about him when she goes to the Brown Bear, but she's getting annoyed, and I'm just so . . . disappointed with him that I don't know if I can face him."

"Well, not to try to take over your area of expertise or anything, but what are you really afraid of? Breaking up?"

The question wasn't as sly as that of a normal counselor, but it was definitely to the point.

"Yes."

Clair leaned back in her chair, eyes sympathetic, but didn't say anything. There was nothing she *could* say. Emily looked down at the cracks in the wooden table. Either Emily talked with him, and Mike decided to change his ways for the better, or they break up. But if she didn't talk to him, they would break up for the sheer lack of communication.

Emily looked back at Clair. Her eyes were far away, and when she finally looked at her, they were deep with sorrow. "Em, sometimes we just can't be with who we want or can't make them be who we want them to be," she said, placing her hands flat on the table. "Sometimes fate doesn't give a damn about our feelings. But you"—Clair put a hand over one of Emily's—"are a fighter. Sometimes all we can do is fight, no matter what the outcome."

"You're right." Emily felt tears come into her eyes. There were a few seconds of silence before Clair spoke again.

"I'm sorry, but we have to go." Clair lifted half her mouth in a sad smile. She patted Emily's hand, got up from the table, and walked toward the door to the antique shop.

"Where?" Emily asked.

"The shop. Chris and Sam just got here."

"How do you know that?" Emily said, wondering if Sam had some type of dog whistle for whenever he wanted to summon Clair.

"Because the clock just hit two," she said, throwing an annoyed glance at Emily, "and Sam is *never* late."

Dorthea

Dotty never asked Clair what had been happening between Chris and her after that night in the backyard, and wasn't planning on it. Clair had her own life and could make her own decisions.

But the way the two of them were moving around each other this afternoon in the antique shop would spark anyone's curiosity.

Chris, searching the old wood-bound books James had bought somewhere in Moldova from an ancient farmer, would discover something interesting and rush over to show Clair, who would then lean in as close to him as she could without touching.

It was like watching energy charge before a spark, and Dotty worried that it would be Clair who got struck.

Not that it was unusual for a woman in the Douglas family to fall for an angel, but the idea unnerved her nonetheless. She still didn't trust these angels, having never met another besides her own family, and didn't want what seemed like a family curse to fall on Clair. However, in this circumstance, Clair was the one with the power.

"Dorthea." Sam was standing at her elbow, silent as a stone. Dotty felt her body jump slightly and was grateful she wasn't prone to heart attacks.

"I'm sorry." Sam looked shocked. "I didn't mean to—"

"You didn't," Dotty said, glaring at him. "What do you want?"

"In this journal, James wrote mostly in poetry," Sam said, all sincerity gone from his voice. "Poetry, while a decent art, is sometimes difficult to translate into meaningful information."

Dotty took the small black book. It was covered in what looked like taped red lines, all crossing over each other. She began flipping through the pages upon pages of James's handwriting. It was definitely written when they were traveling—coffee and food stains were prominent on many pages from when he would sit and write at breakfast while she mapped out their plans for the day. James always was the most at peace when he was writing, like his worries could be bled onto the page like the ink onto paper.

"Well," she said, handing the book back to Sam, "I can tell you that they were written when we were traveling. That's about all I know."

"James never shared any of them with you?"

"No." Dotty narrowed her eyes. "James was a very private man, and writing was his way of relaxing. I never asked him to share more than he wanted to."

Sam raised an eyebrow but said nothing, walking back toward another row of books. Dotty had to continue to remind herself that Sam was technically older than her by a few hundred years. But he looked so much like a child in his early thirties that she tended to treat him that way.

That and he was smug and deserved some berating, she thought with a wicked smile.

Currently they were looking for any clues as to how James would get The Gate to move. If they could figure out how to move it, they could alleviate much of the supernatural attention it was probably drawing to the town, and to Clair. And the sooner The Gate moved, the sooner Sam would be out of her life forever. Of course, Clair didn't realize Dotty's ultimate plan, but that didn't matter; this whole angel business was not going to steal away another one of her family members, she would make sure of that.

Unfortunately, Dotty had a pretty good idea how James got The Gate to move, and she wasn't about to mention it.

Out of the corner of her eye, Dotty saw Chris making his way toward her, something clutched in his palm.

"Hello, Dorthea," he said, smiling. He really was an attractive young man, with his light gray eyes and dark short hair, as well as a muscular build.

It was no wonder Clair was attracted to him. But Clair had Andrew, and Dotty was grateful, because Andrew was normal.

"Chris, call me Dotty."

"Okay," he said with a smile. "Dotty, I found this and was wondering if it would be alright if I gave it to Clair?"

Chris held out his palm.

In the center was the thinnest cord of gold Dotty had ever seen. It couldn't have been longer than eighteen inches, thin as a spider's web. But it was pure gold—Dotty could tell from the days when she had to pawn off some of the shop items for Clair's college tuition.

"I've never seen it before," she said truthfully. "What does it do?"

"Well, there aren't too many uses," Chris said, picking up the gold string between two fingers. It was almost impossible to see, it was so thin hanging in the air. "But I found a reference to something like this a while back in one of the books, and it said it was supposed to bring good luck to its owner."

Dotty thought that was a load of crap because it had been sitting in the shop since James died and her situation hadn't turned out lucky by any stretch of the imagination.

The annoyance must have shown on her face.

"I mean," he continued, "if you want to keep it that's fine. The book didn't have any specific examples of how it worked, but there is magic in it. You can sense it."

She could.

The string was giving off a faint energy like a battery that had sat in the sun too long—drained but present.

"No, it's okay," she said, wondering where James had purchased it. "Maybe it will work for Clair," she added with a small smile.

Chris broke out into a grin.

"Thanks, Dorth—Dotty. Don't tell her, though, please," he added. "I want to make it a surprise."

He had a very sweet smile, this minor angel.

"Alright," she said, watching him walk away. She looked around the room. Sam was still devouring books in a far corner while Chris went back to looking through a shelf, and Clair was inspecting some of the glassware while talking with Emily on the opposite side of the shop. Emily still didn't know what they were really looking for—she knew they were searching for information about Clair's angelic history, but she didn't know about The Gate. And Dotty wanted to keep it that way.

In any other circumstance, the scene would have looked like a tender family bonding moment—everyone reading or examining artwork.

Instead, the reality was that everyone in this room was in the same danger as James and Elijah were in the past, when things would come after them.

Dotty hoped the barriers around the house would hold, because if she was right, the past was going to come back for her future.

CLAIR

It took a lot of convincing, but Chris finally agreed to let Clair try the vortex with flames.

She had never seen him look so frazzled. She was trying to focus on breathing while he cleared all the leaves from around where she sat, cross-legged, on the forest floor.

"Chris, relax," she finally said after she had begun to feel dizzy. He was muttering things under his breath, and it was starting to annoy her. "It's not like I am going to burn the forest down."

He stopped pacing and looked down into her eyes.

"I'm not supposed to be teaching you this, Clair, so forgive me if I'm a little worried that Sam will find out and kill me."

She raised an eyebrow at him, but he sighed again, obviously exasperated. "You know what I mean."

Clair laughed. She had never seen Chris so upset, but she was too excited to care about his anxiety.

In a few moments she might be doing the first bit of training that would be useful in a fight: a fireball. Ever since she had seen Chris holding his, she had been dying to try it, insisting that Chris show her that very afternoon. He had refused, saying she needed more training on leaves before she could progress to fire. She had been practicing with leaves for over a week now and finally convinced him she was ready when the leaves stayed floating in her palms for over a minute without falling.

"Alright," Chris said, extending a hand down toward her. She took it, liking the way her hand fit within his, the warmth pulling at her heart. She heard Chris clear his throat before he released her and walked over to the creek.

"Chris, I want to try *fire*, not water," Clair said, crossing her arms and watching him place his hands in the water.

"I know that, Clair, for the thousandth time." He rolled his eyes and looked around the clearing as if expecting Sam to come tromping through the forest, finger pointed and scowl in place.

"Chris, Sam is *not* going to find out, okay?" Clair said, throwing her hands up in the air with impatience. "He's studying those old books with Dotty in the antique shop."

"Oh," he said, leaning back so he was squatting next to the creek. He looked almost like a child, his smile turning devious. "Good."

Clair laughed and shook her head, walking toward him. "So what do you want me to do with the creek?"

Chris beckoned for her to join him next to the water. He shifted his weight to his knees and looked her over.

"I want you to keep your hands in the water for about a minute," he said, demonstrating. "It's not too cold right now, but it'll suffice."

Clair nodded and placed her hands in the clear water, palms up. There were little green plants being pulled by the current, and she could see a few water beetles scuttling past. After what felt like forever Chris removed his hands and Clair followed, returning to sitting position.

"It's about manipulating the air, not the flames," Chris instructed, cupping his hands. "Think about the flow of the air, the control. Just like we did with the leaves, we must circulate the air to feed and hold the flame." He looked up into her eyes, worry strewn across his face.

For the first time, Clair realized how scared he was.

"Chris, I can do this."

He nodded, but the worry didn't leave his face. "Alright."

Clair closed her eyes and began the breathing techniques. After a few minutes, when she could feel the air vibrating just above her hands, she opened her eyes, her palms connected, and nodded for Chris to light the air.

Clair watched as the lighter floated toward her hands and a fireball appeared. Clair could feel the warmth from the fire through the air, could sense the power of it as it begged her for oxygen, begged her for release from the control of her hands. Clair was frightened for only a second, but that was all it took. The fire burst through the air pocket protecting her hands, and she felt the flames bite deeply into them.

She screamed.

Chris was up in a flash, grabbing her wrists and shoving them into the relief of the creek, muttering something under his breath. Clair felt the water grow ice cold around her red and blistered hands, quelling the heat from the burn. She didn't realize she was crying until she felt one of his hands on her cheek, wiping away a tear.

"I'm sorry, Chris." She was so embarrassed she didn't want to look up at him.

Clair heard his sharp intake of breath and turned her head to the left, pushing his hand deeper into her cheek. His eyes were alight with anger.

"I thought I was ready," she blurted out, turning her face away again, trying to remove the image of Chris, angry with her, from her mind. "I'm so, so sorry."

"Clair"—the word was a whisper, a silent plea as he turned her face to his, his eyes shining—"don't apologize to me. I'm not angry with you. I'm angry with myself! I never should have let you try this . . . I'm the one who's sorry. Look at your hands," he said, moving both of his to hers and gently lifting her palms from the water.

The air stung, but Chris muttered again, and her hands grew cold. It felt so much better she almost cried again from relief.

"How are you doing that?" she said, watching as he turned her palms, inspecting the damage.

He placed her hands back in the water and ran his own damp hands over his face.

"It's a cooling technique," he said, moving away a bit and looking at her. "No more fire."

"What!" Clair yelled, subconsciously removing her hands from the water and wincing when the air struck them. Chris reached out to grab them, but she flung them behind her back.

"Chris, I have to learn this!" she shouted, shaking her head and trying to ignore the burning feeling that was starting to creep back. "I have to learn something that's useful!"

"Useful?" Chris said. "You think holding a fireball is *useful?*"

"Well I can't *breathe* my way out of a fight, like Sam seems to think!" Clair was so angry she was yelling. She forgot about the pain in her hands, about the way Chris was looking at her. She was upset and tired and embarrassed and everything all at once, and by hell, she was going to yell about it. "All I have been doing, ever since I learned I was some magical spiritual being, is learning how to breathe, when all I have been told is that I might be attacked, or might lead evil things toward myself or the people I love." She threw her hands up in front of her, looking at nothing in particular while she yelled. "And now I finally get the chance to learn something that I could use, really use in a fight, and I mess it up!"

She was staring at the creek and breathing hard, the air leaving her body making puffing sounds on its way out of her lungs. When she finally had the nerve to look back at Chris, he had a small smile in place, and she felt her mouth drop open in surprise.

"What?" she said, a little anger still in her voice.

"Alright," he said.

"Alright, *what?*" Clair said, feeling exasperated.

"Alright, I will continue to teach you the fireball," he said, watching her face change from exasperated to shocked. "But"—he held his hand up—"not until these burns heal, and after my burns heal."

"What burns?" Clair said, concern killing all the other emotions within her as she looked Chris over for red marks.

Chris frowned and raised an eyebrow at Clair. "The burns Sam is going to give me when he sees your hands."

Clair couldn't help it, she laughed.

"Oh, so you think my future punishment is funny, huh?" he said, splashing water from the creek into her face. Clair shook her head to clear the water and gave him a crushing glare.

"Alright"—he laughed—"let's head back to my house and get those hands wrapped up."

Clair nodded and followed him through the forest, keeping her palms straight out in front of her to catch the breeze. It looked ridiculous but felt wonderful.

When they reached his house, Chris opened the door and told her to go sit in the kitchen while he walked outside to the backyard. Since there were no chairs in the kitchen, Clair sat on the counter. She looked around while she waited, and realized that this was the first time she had been in his house with him, alone.

She felt a spike of adrenaline at the thought.

Dotty and Sam were still poring over the books in the antique shop, and since Chris was supposed to be teaching Clair breathing techniques, Sam would assume they had at least an hour left in their lesson, which meant it would be just them in his house for the next hour.

A deep sense of seriousness came over Clair.

Usually when she was with Chris, it was out in the open air of the forest, or with Emily, or Sam, or even Dotty, but never just the two of them in such an intimate setting. Clair found herself wishing that Chris had a dog or something to keep her mind off the facts.

He walked back into the house through the spare bedroom, carrying a bowl made out of a rock, with a small ceramic club-like tool, crushing and re-crushing whatever was inside.

"This should help with the pain and heal the skin." When he looked up, he stopped crushing and stared at Clair sitting on the counter. She knew the tension in the room wasn't just coming from her.

"I thought it would be easier if I sat here," she said with a small smile, trying to push down the awkward feeling coiling in her stomach, "for you to work, Doctor."

She had tried to make a joke, and Chris smiled but stayed where he was. She wondered if he was thinking the same thing she was—could feel the same pull she did.

Clair almost worked up the nerve to ask him, when he looked back down and the bowl and walked over to her, a small laugh escaping his lips.

"I'm no doctor, but I've gotten burned enough to know some good herbal remedies."

Clair sent a puzzled look in his direction as he gently grabbed her hands, inspecting the burns. "When did you get burned?"

Chris had yet to look up and meet her eyes, concentrating instead on the salve he was smoothing into a lotion-like substance. He was almost as tall as she was sitting.

"When I was first experimenting with the leaves and got too close to a candle."

Clair felt her mouth pop open. "You *accidently* discovered the fireball?"

"Yep," he laughed, scooping out a quarter-size dollop of green sludge and gently rubbing it onto Clair's palm. She felt the cooling sensation instantly, as if her hands were tingling with sleep and tiny icicles. Clair sighed and closed her eyes, loving the way the salve dulled the burning, but also the way it felt to have a reason for Chris to touch her.

Clair opened her eyes after she felt both hands covered in salve and found Chris watching her.

"What?"

"It's just . . ." he said, eyes locked with hers, his hands still covered with green. The space between them felt like the fire in her hands.

Just then the door swung open, and Clair felt the air get sucked out of her lungs.

Chris was in front of her in a heartbeat, a knife she hadn't seen him grab poised in his hand as he crouched, ready to strike.

Sam walked around the corner carrying one of the largest books Clair had ever seen.

When he saw Chris, his eyes widened at the scene before him: Clair sitting on the counter with green all over her hands and Chris crouched in front of her, knife ready to strike. Then he narrowed his eyes.

"What are you two doing back here?" he said, closing the book and glancing at Clair, her hands, and then back to Chris. "*What happened?*"

Oddly enough, Chris hadn't relaxed from his crouch, though she could tell he wasn't breathing as harshly anymore, and the adrenaline in her own body was dissipating. Chris sighed and put the knife back in the holder on the counter, ignored Sam's question, and turned back to Clair. He grabbed cloth bandages and began wrapping her hands while Sam just stared at the edge of the kitchen.

Clair, however, from her perch on the counter, had nowhere else to look but in Sam's direction, and the look he was giving her made her feel like her whole face had been burned, not just her hands.

She glanced down at Chris, whose brows were knit together in concentration, then back to Sam.

"Hey, Sam." Smooth, Clair thought, kicking herself inwardly.

Sam walked over to them and looked over Chris's shoulders, getting a peek at the burns, before folding his arms and standing behind Chris.

"Clair, you can go home now," Chris said, swallowing hard. He looked tired and resigned. Clair opened her mouth to protest, but Chris continued. "Come back tomorrow for more salve."

He smiled, and Clair knew they were both thinking the same thing: to make sure he was still alive.

CHRIS

As soon as the door shut, Sam started yelling. "What were you thinking!"

Chris flung his hands in the air, moving past Sam into the living room, determined not to meet anger with anger.

"I was thinking it was about time we gave Clair a reason to be proud of what she is."

"Proud?" Sam said, accent flaring through. It only happened when he got angry. "You thought burning her hands would make her *proud?*"

Chris winced at the thought.

He'd been foolish, he knew, to let her try the fireball so soon into training. But she had been determined, so focused and excited for sessions that he couldn't bring himself to say no.

But when he had watched the fire burn her hands . . .

Chris turned to face Sam, and, resigned for punishment, met his gaze.

"What do you have to say for yourself?" Sam was glaring at him, arms crossed over his chest.

Maybe it was the thought of Clair's burned hands or the way her eyes had met his just before Sam had come home, or maybe it was just the scolding, judgmental look in Sam's eyes; whatever the reason, Chris, who never got angry with anyone but himself, blew up.

"I *have nothing* to say for myself! Can't you see it's eating me up inside? I feel horrible about the whole thing, but you chiding me won't heal Clair's hands and it isn't going to fix any of the problems we're facing!" Chris saw Sam's eyes widen, but continued. "Clair doesn't understand what she is, what could be coming after her, or when. We've been living on constant alert of an enemy we have barely begun to explain to her. Hell," he said, shaking his head and beginning to pace the room, "*I* don't even understand it!"

Chris shoved past Sam, who now had his hands in fists at his sides, to the refrigerator, grabbing out the supplies he would need to make a sandwich, and ranting the entire time.

"So *excuse me* if I wanted to give her hope, or a chance to see what was really involved with being what we are, or whatever," he finished lamely, stuffing a bite of sandwich into his mouth. Chris rarely ate bread and even more seldom did he eat it at night, but he was starving, and he just didn't care about his diet in that moment.

He was still breathing heavily when he noticed Sam sitting at the kitchen table, his hands in a steeple.

The gesture was so fatherly that Chris almost dropped the sandwich. He knew Sam was the elder, was more experienced and knowledgeable about their ways, but he was tired of being treated like a child. He was not a child.

Sam still wasn't speaking.

"Don't look at me like that!" Chris shouted, taking another bite of sandwich and leaning against the seat where Clair had been sitting moments before. It was still warm, and Chris felt another type of heat fill his body at the thought. Sam continued to watch him, and Chris continued to eat, letting his thoughts drift.

He stared at the floor and saw a spot of green salve that had spilled.

When the burn happened, his only concern was getting her hands into the water, of taking care of her; and she had only hoped he wasn't *disappointed.* Clair had attempted a very powerful move and succeeded for much longer than he had when he was first learning—even though he had to learn everything on his own, and usually by accident.

But then, as they were talking and he was cleaning the burns, rubbing the aloe into her skin, she had relaxed, the worry lines on her face disappearing. She had hummed as his fingers rubbed her palms, and he felt right, somewhere deep inside. That intimate moment with

Clair had been the most whole feeling he had ever experienced in his new life. It was as if his purpose was to do just that—to be a balm for her, in any way he could. Chris wanted to walk with her through this journey they had both stumbled upon together, to be there with her wherever she went.

Whenever they were together he could feel the pull of her energy on him, or his on hers, he wasn't sure. And just as he was about to ask if she felt the same, Sam had come barging in and ruined the moment.

Chris looked back up at Sam when he thought that, and found him still staring.

"What?" Chris barked, taking another bite.

"Do you feel better now?" said Sam, the anger and accent gone from his voice.

Chris thought about it.

"Kinda," he said, finishing the sandwich and going for some orange juice in the fridge. Sam waited until he was leaning against the counter again to resume speaking.

"I don't agree with what you did," he said, holding a hand up to stop the rebuttal, "but I do think you have a point."

Chris stared, waiting.

Sam sighed.

"Clair does need to learn more offensive moves, *and* defensive ones. But the best moves require patience, diligence, and an inner development that Clair is, as of yet, unaware of."

Chris relaxed his posture a bit.

"If you think this opinion is inaccurate, please let me know." Sam was watching him through thick lashes. Chris nodded. "Good, then we agree—"

"That Clair needs to learn defense and to be proud of what she is," Chris finished, leveling his gaze with Sam.

After a minute, Sam nodded. "Agreed."

Chris sat across from him at the table. "What would you have done if I'd gotten so angry I kicked you out?"

Sam laughed, something he rarely did, and Chris couldn't help but smile. "Well, for one thing, you wouldn't have kicked me out," Sam said matter-of-factly. "And for another, I would have gone to a hotel to wait out your anger." His face turned from laughter to concern. He leaned back in the chair. "I never thought you lacked emotional control."

"Neither did I," Chris blurted out, a small smile on his lips. Sam didn't look convinced. "I don't usually have emotional problems, or outbursts, or anything," Chris mused, thinking back on the last few years.

Sam sighed and leaned forward onto his forearms, hands folded. "How are you doing, with your emotions about Clair?"

Sam hit a nerve, and he knew it. The concern on his face was obvious and annoyingly accurate. Chris wasn't doing well at all. In fact, when Emily implied to Andrew and Clair's other friends that they were cousins, Chris almost punched Andrew in the face. But instead, he watched the guy circle and touch Clair the entire night, even let him instruct on bowling techniques. As if Chris cared about bowling. It was a stroke of pure luck that he had been around when Clair's friends had needed help and invited him, and it was nice to have an excuse to see Clair outside of practice.

The truth was Chris loved every minute he got to spend around Clair. He felt most alive around her, as if his entire life—well, this new one—was missing air before she arrived back in town. Chris thought they worked well together. And when she had kissed him, that night in the backyard . . .

Just thinking about it brought waves of emotion through him. He had been foolish then, to let himself give into his baser, human emotions. But he had, dragging his hands through her soft hair, loving the taste of her lips, her breath hot in his mouth.

"Chris!" Sam said, making him jump in his chair. "What are you thinking about right now?"

Chris shook his head and lied. "Nothing."

"At least learn to *lie* better, Chris." Sam stood, exasperated, and walked over to the spare bedroom. "You need to remember that we have a purpose here, on this earth," he shouted from his room. "We were not given a second chance to live a second life. We are here to serve, and you must remember that while Clair may be *confusing* for you, she is also . . ."

Sam let the sentence drift off.

"She is also what?" Chris shouted, waiting for a reply.

"She's also something we don't understand, and thus, we must be wary."

Chris was unconvinced, but something about the way Sam said the word "wary" scared him.

"What do you mean by that?"

A few seconds of silence passed before he spoke again.

"Clair is either humanity's saving grace or a weapon for its destruction."

CLAIR

That night Clair and Emily went to the Brown Bear, Emily to face Mike, and Clair for a hard drink.

Emily was shocked about her burns but agreed that it was necessary for Clair to start learning more powerful moves. Emily had suggested the girls' night out, and Clair was grateful to have something to distract her from thinking about Chris.

She just couldn't get past how she felt about him.

Her dreams were becoming filled with thoughts of him—some steamy, others fatal, like the vision—and she was so confused she felt nauseous whenever he was around, like she was keeping some deep, dark horrible secret that needed to be known but couldn't be told. If she told Chris what she'd seen, would he care? Did he have feelings for her like she did for him?

"What're you having?" Joe was wearing a nicer apron tonight than usual.

"Lemon drop, please," Clair said, reaching for her identification. Emily ordered a beer. Even though Joe knew who Clair was, he always checked her ID no matter what, but he didn't check Emily's.

"Joe, you know me," she said, annoyed and exasperated. "Why do you always check my ID? I'm past twenty-one."

Joe narrowed his eyes at Clair before he picked up a wet glass, began wiping it with a towel, and walked away without answering.

"It's okay," Emily said, sitting beside Clair. "He does that to everyone."

"He didn't do it to you," Clair said, feeling childish.

Emily rolled her eyes.

"It was a pity gesture. Mike isn't here," she said, gulping her beer until it was halfway gone. "Joe told me he hasn't come home since yesterday."

"Oh, I'm sorry," Clair said, patting her friends back. "Maybe he just spent the night at Alex's?"

"Yeah, maybe."

Clair was trying to think of something to say that would make Emily feel better, when she felt a pinch on her arm. When she looked down, nothing was there. She was rubbing the spot when Emily said, "Maybe this is fate trying to tell me to just give up."

"No, Em." Clair looked back at her friend. Emily's eyes were staring straight through the wall of alcohol that lined the bar. "This isn't fate, or destiny, or any of that crap. Mike is just out. We'll come back tomorrow."

"Yeah, that won't look pathetic," Emily drawled. Joe silently placed another beer in front of her, as she was draining the first. "Coming here and getting drunk twice in a row just to try to see someone I call my *boyfriend*."

"Em," Clair said, taking a sip of her still full lemon drop martini, "how would he even know you were here tonight? If we come tomorrow, it'll just seem like we're coming for a drink."

Emily didn't say anything, and Clair knew the idea was starting to sink in, like the alcohol in her hand. Emily stood up and excused herself to the bathroom, claiming that a small bladder and beer didn't mix.

Joe walked by, swatting at a bug, and Clair flagged him over. There was a stain on his arm from the dead bug, that Clair didn't look at or mention. Instead, she said something that would have certainly gotten her in trouble with Emily, were she there to hear.

"Hey, Joe, when Mike comes back, could you do me a favor and not tell him Emily and I were here tonight?" Joe raised an eyebrow but didn't protest, so Clair continued. "Emily really wants to talk to him but . . . they're both stubborn, as I'm sure you know."

Joe gave a grunt and nodded. Clair smiled.

He was a pretty nice guy. Thinking about nice guys brought her mind back to Chris, and she frowned.

"Why do you look so down?" Joe muttered.

"Just having a bad day." Clair looked up at him. He was broad and muscular, a tall man with long black hair and tanned skin.

"I think you have done pretty well for yerself, missy," he said, taking Emily's empty bottles and replacing them with a mug of ice water.

"What do you mean?"

"Well, the last time you was here, you drank alone," he said, and Clair remembered when she had just moved back, and how she had met Emily that night. She hadn't been alone for very long at all, actually.

"You're right," she said, looking back up at Joe and smiling. "Thanks."

He gave Clair a flash of a smile and a grunt before walking away.

Clair drove them both back to her house.

She gave Emily her bed and watched her crash into a slightly drunken stupor. Beer must not be her friend, Clair thought, taking the shoes off her sleeping body and placing them at the foot of the bed.

Clair walked downstairs to get a glass of water to place on the side table next to Emily, when she felt an itch on her arm—a fresh mosquito bite was swelling up in a small red mound.

Great, she thought, entering the kitchen.

There was a light on in the antique shop, and Clair walked in to find Dotty, cheeks streaked with tears, reading a tattered old black book covered with red stripes.

Clair had never seen her grandmother cry. Dotty preferred to hide her emotions, and Clair felt like she was intruding on something she wasn't supposed to be a part of.

She silently retreated, walking past the fridge and back up to her room to sleep on the ground.

If Emily wanted water, there was a sink in her bathroom.

The Bar

"Why do you smell of seraph?"

She stayed in the bar until the last of his guests left, watching him. This man before her, he was nothing, but she was so close to the barrier she had almost missed the scent.

It was here, hovering in the air around this place, throughout the whole town. But when she tried to track it she always ended up back where she started, confused and wondering where she was headed.

There was magic here, and a seraph too.

She could have gone straight to The Gate—which, by the scent that filled this town, was staying—but something better was here, a power too irresistible to ignore, a power greater than even Eden.

A seraph offspring.

It had been hundreds of years since she had come so close to one. If she could get its blood into her amulet, she would become invincible.

She would no longer need to steal energy. She could use the power of the blood to fuel her. And after she cut through the barrier, she would have eternity in her hands as well.

Seraph blood would give the amulet enough power to take the world by force.

And this man, standing so close, the blood on his arm calling to her . . .

It was just too easy.

Joe

"Mmmmm."

She was so beautiful, he thought, while his body warned him of the danger, heart thumping and limbs shaking. Even if the mind was deceived, the body held deeper instincts, and his knew that this woman was no good.

"Tell me," she said, her soft singsong voice a breath in his ear, "why do you smell of angel? What do you know of The Gate to Eden?"

Joe had no idea what she was talking about, but he liked it when she talked.

"I dunno what you're talking about, ma'am," he said, using his best courtesy.

"You don't, do you?" She walked the length of the bar, fingers tracing the counter that was still stained with water rings from the night's profits.

As she moved, her hips bounced back and forth. Joe watched the rhythm with hungry eyes.

"Can I get you anyt'ing ma'am? A glass of wine perhaps?" he said, eyes never leaving her hips. "We've some of the best vintage in the north, I promise you that."

She stopped walking and turned to look at him, her eyes blue as the sky and watery like living pools.

"No, wine will not suffice," she said, walking back to the middle of the room where he stood, frozen. "What is it that you desire, Joseph?"

The words came unbidden to his lips. "I desire you, and those hips, and me between you both."

So much for courtesy, said a small voice in his mind.

"Well, I require knowledge that your mind does not possess." She stroked her hand across his face, her touch both ice and fire, leaving a deep burn. "But your blood might have it."

She moved her hand to her mouth, her full lips sucking something red from her fingers.

It was only then that Joe realized it was his blood.

EMILY

mily was furious.

She wanted to be with Mike—to hold him and tell him that everything would be okay. But Sam was standing in front of her, blocking her way.

"You're not the boss of me! I'm not some angel!" Emily screamed, trying to push past Sam to the door. She received a call from her parents early that morning, after they'd heard about Joe's death on the news; they wanted to make sure she was not at the bar last night.

Mike wasn't answering her phone calls, but her parents said that he had been found by the police, high as a kite, at a friend's house.

"Emily, I know this is difficult," Sam said, hands outstretched, ready to grab her should she try to push past him, "but you would be in danger. You've been around all of us too long; you would glow and make an easy target for whatever is out there."

Easy target?

"What the hell is that supposed to mean Sam? You think I can't take care of myself? Well I can!"

She forced herself to his left, but he grabbed her and, gently, pushed her back into the living room and further away from the door.

"Emily, I'm so sorry."

"Stop saying that, Sam!" She didn't want to hear that anyone was sorry for her. Everyone should be sorry for Mike. He had just lost the one family member who ever cared for him. "Get out of my way!"

"I'm so sorry," Sam kept saying, his eyes somber.

"Stop it!"

"I'm sorry."

"Stop, Sam, stop!" She rushed past him again, but this time he caught her and held on, muttering, "I'm sorry, sorry, sorry . . ."

She started to cry.

Her whole body was shaking with the effort to stop her tears; she had to remain in control. She needed to be strong for Mike, and for Clair, who felt responsible. She shouldn't be crying, but she couldn't stop. She couldn't stop crying—for Joe, for Mike, for Clair, for her own helplessness. And the entire time Sam held her and spoke softly to her, sometimes in poems, sometimes in languages she didn't understand. He spoke softly and held her until the tears stopped.

"We can't go to the funeral," she said, after what felt like a long while. It wasn't a question; she knew the answer when she felt Sam's body tense.

"No."

CLAIR

"Healdsburg is still in shock that a local man by the name of Joseph Barber was found dead in his establishment . . ."

"Medical experts determined the cause of death to be blunt force trauma to the head . . ."

"There are still no leads on the attacker, but police are . . ."

Clair flipped through channels, watching the screen change from cartoons, to a tele-novella, to the Bill Cosby show, and then to a showing of Aladdin—"Things are unraveling fast now . . ."—before turning it off and staring at the dark, blank screen.

This was what she had been doing for three straight days.

Clair let her right hand rest on the bed while her left hand cradled her forehead.

He's dead because of me.

Sam and Chris scanned the bar and found traces of a strong evil presence, inhuman, and immediately ordered both Emily and Clair under house arrest. As far as they could tell, Joe had a spot of Clair's blood on his arm the night he was killed—and Clair had a bug bite on her arm linking her to this fact.

"Whatever it is, it's old—older than me," Sam had said after they had returned from the bar.

"That's quite a feat," Emily had muttered under her breath. Sam pretended not to hear.

Clair knew Emily was upset she couldn't leave to comfort Mike or go to the funeral this morning. Dotty had left earlier for it, escorted by Sam and Chris, who were hoping to use her as bait for whatever evil was out there, while she and Emily were forced to wait.

With the TV off Clair could hear Emily crying from the downstairs living room. Clair had been allowed to text Andrew to tell him that she needed space, and not to come over. Emily told her parents she was staying with Clair for a few days, but hadn't heard from Mike even though she was texting and calling him nonstop, with no response.

Sitting in her old room made Clair feel uncomfortable, but she didn't feel comfortable anyway, and she was fairly sure none of them were sleeping. Clair guessed she had slept for a total of three hours in the last three days. And every time Chris and Sam would leave to fortify the barrier around the house or to search for clues at the bar, Clair would watch them go, her heart dying a little on the inside, hoping that they would come back.

Clair felt her skin crawling.

Whatever killed Joe had been looking for her or The Gate, and now someone innocent was dead. Joe was murdered, and he didn't even know anything.

"Clair!"

Clair jumped off the bed and ran downstairs. The shout came from outside. Sure enough, Andrew was pounding on the front door, shouting for Clair to open up. Clair had never heard him sound so angry.

"Andrew." Emily's eyes were wide where she stood in the doorway to the kitchen. "Clair, what if he led whatever is looking for us, here?"

Clair felt her heartbeat pick up painfully. "What should I do?"

Emily took a deep breath and sent a knowing look at Clair, who nodded.

"Just don't leave the barrier," Emily added, moving back into the recesses of the kitchen.

For the second time since she had moved back home, someone was outside her door shouting for her. But, unlike Emily, Andrew was putting them all in serious danger.

Clair inhaled deeply before opening the door.

It was an oddly overcast day, the clouds covering the sun, casting diffused light around the world. Andrew was wearing a black tux. He must have just come from the funeral.

"What do you want?" she said, hands folded over her chest, and face set.

He stared at her, mouth slightly opened, and she kicked herself inwardly for not checking her appearance. She was wearing sweatpants and a tank top, her hair was in a messy bun, and she wasn't wearing makeup, which only accented the bags under her eyes.

But she had to level the emotions she was feeling. She had to do this. She took a second to scan the trees behind him for any sign of someone or *something* watching. She couldn't see anything, but she *felt* it. It didn't follow Sam and Chris, or Dotty. It was out there—somewhere.

Clair wouldn't let it kill him.

"What do I *want*?" he finally said. "It's been three days! You haven't even sent me a text . . . You didn't even go to Joe's *funeral*!"

Clair winced but held firm. He was standing there in his black tux, looking like a sad James Bond. She wanted to close the distance between them, to hold him, to tell him how sorry she was about Joe, about not being at the funeral. But she couldn't. She wouldn't give whatever was out there any reason to kill Andrew. She wouldn't let another person die for her.

So she shrugged, and leveled her voice.

"Andrew, I can't do this anymore," she said nonchalantly, watching his anger dissipate as eyes grew cold. She pressed on. "We had fun, but it's over. It's just too much to handle."

Andrew opened his mouth, then closed it. Clair watched as he turned around, walked to his car, and drove down the road back to town. As soon as he was out of sight, Clair sensed to make sure the evil presence hadn't followed him.

It didn't.

She walked back inside and shut the door.

Emily was staring at her. "You okay?"

Clair nodded and walked back upstairs to her room. She was never going to be okay again.

An hour later Clair heard Emily in the kitchen, baking. Even though sweets wouldn't help, Clair knew Emily just needed to keep busy.

She got up and walked downstairs, smelling the sweet dough and chocolate, and quietly entered the kitchen. There was a batch of chocolate chip cookies on a cooling rack on the counter, and Emily was mixing another batch of something else in a bowl.

"I'm sorry, Em," Clair said, feeling moisture come into her eyes.

Emily froze and set the bowl down, placing her hands flat on the counter. A moment of silence passed between them before she turned around.

"It's not your fault, Clair." Her eyes were misty, but she held them back. "I wanted to be a part of this, and I'll figure out something to tell Mike, when . . . if . . . he asks."

Clair ran and hugged her, getting flour all over both of them while they cried.

"Can I help you start your bake shop?" Clair asked, wiping her eyes and gesturing to the ingredients strewn around the kitchen.

"No, I think I'm okay in here," Emily sighed, putting her hands on her hips. "I'll just bake these and call it quits."

"Alright," Clair said, feeling a bit deflated. "I think I'm just going to check out the antique shop for a bit."

"Okay," Em said, with a small smile.

Clair walked through the kitchen and into the store.

Everything looked different now, foreign and mysterious. The key to whoever, or whatever, was after them could be in this room.

Clair started opening books, looking at parchment, and generally scrutinizing everything. After she had found out she was an angel, she had seen the antique shop in a different light, but not like this; now it was a portal to another world, with the secrets of heaven and hell.

Clair was halfway through a book on demonic references from the reformation when Dotty walked in.

"How was the funeral?" she asked, closing the book and causing a stream of dust to fly up. Dotty looked around at the papers strewn across the desk, and then to Clair.

"It was a beautiful ceremony, but I would have had a bonfire, myself," she said with a half-smile.

Clair reached out her senses and knew Chris and Sam were in the house, most likely eating cookies and talking with Emily.

Dotty cocked her head to the side.

"What?" Clair asked, trying to decipher her strange expression.

"Your grandfather would make that face sometimes," she said, straightening her neck and grabbing a book from the shelf. "What did you just do?"

"I wanted to know if Chris and Sam were here, so I sensed for them."

Dotty made a noncommittal sound and continued flipping through the pages of the book, not reading it, her eyes distant and sorrowful.

"I'm getting better," Clair burst out, knowing her voice sounded pleading and desperate, but she didn't care. "I can protect us." Someone she knew had been killed, because of her, because of The Gate, of what she was, of whatever, and she hadn't been able to stop it. Next time, she would. Next time, no one would die for her.

Dotty looked over at Clair, her eyes watery. "You shouldn't have to."

Later, when they were all gathered together in the living room, Clair told Sam that the evil hadn't followed them to the funeral. She told him about Andrew and about how she could sense the evil near the house. But when Sam went to check, nothing was there.

Chris, Dotty, Sam, and Emily started discussing Joe's funeral in the living room. But Clair didn't want to hear about it, couldn't hear about it. She felt the guilt like a rock in her belly.

So she went to wash the dishes.

Of all the things she could have been doing at that moment, she was standing at the sink in front of the kitchen window, hand washing the mess from the cookies. She had listened for a few minutes about the funeral—about how many people had attended, the flowers, Mike—before walking out and coming into the kitchen to be alone.

It was all so horrible.

Sighing, she placed the last of the bowls on the counter and looked out the window.

It was still overcast, even at midday, the clouds turning the trees a faded green and the dirt a darker brown. Leaves were falling in the slight wind, an off occurrence for summer. Just as Clair was turning to go back into the living room, she spotted an odd-looking tree in the forest.

It wasn't a tree at all.

Standing a few hundred feet away was dark flesh stretched over bone, her sunken eyes boring into Clair's and paralyzing her with fear. The monster could scarcely be called human, with long white hair frozen above her head in waves as if it was blowing in the wind, her hands long spikes of wood and bone stretched over two legs that seemed to be rooted like a tree.

And at her neck, a bright red pendant glowed with golden light.

Clair felt hands come over her eyes and screamed.

"Clair, it's me, it's Chris," he whispered in her ear, his body pressed up against hers. "I'm going to back us away from the window, okay?"

All she could do was nod. Chris pulled them both back to the other side of the kitchen, gently turning their bodies away from the window to face the fridge. She heard feet running from the living room. He removed his hands.

Sam, Dotty, and Emily were all standing at the door, staring at her.

Clair stood there, tears falling down her cheeks and shame filling her heart. Chris walked around to face her, eyes boring into her own.

"Are you okay?" He was cupping her face in his hands. They were wonderfully warm.

She nodded, unable to speak.

"You saw it, didn't you?"

"Yes." Clair looked up to meet his gray eyes. "Did you?"

"No." Chris was breathing heavily, sweat pouring down his face. "I couldn't look, but I just felt you . . . sensed you tense, and I knew something was wrong. I came to check on you." He removed his hands and glanced down at the floor. "But I felt it. It was forcing me to open my eyes, to look, to *see*."

He shivered.

Sam was asking her questions about what she saw, and Dotty walked over to embrace her while Emily grabbed another cookie from the counter and brought it over to her. Everyone was talking at once.

"I don't know what would have happened if I had seen it," Chris whispered to Clair, his eyes a refuge from the storm in her head, "and I don't want to know. No more windows."

"No more windows," she repeated, feeling her last shred of freedom vanish.

CHRIS

hris found Clair sitting in her bedroom, knees drawn up to her chest, with her head resting on them. She was staring off into nothing.

He wanted to run to her, take her in his arms and soothe her, tell her that Joe's death was not her fault—fate had delivered him into the hands of evil, and there was nothing she could have done to stop it. He wanted to tell her that he would protect her from what she had just seen—that evil in the trees—that he would protect her from anything in the world that would try to harm her.

But he didn't.

Instead, Chris walked to the edge of the bed, sat down, and placed his hands in his lap.

"Is Emily baking again?" Clair was still leaning her head against her knees.

"No," he said, watching her, his heart bleeding for her. "She, Sam, and Dotty have moved the cookies into the antique shop and are searching for answers. They want us to join them."

Clair nodded.

Whatever had sensed Clair's blood was most likely drawn to the town by The Gate, but was now looking for her. Chris asked Sam whether or not he thought The Gate was in danger of being breached, but Sam said that Clair's blood, being what it was, would be more alluring, and that the magic Chris had used to protect The Gate should hold until they could figure out what was out there.

"Clair," he said, reaching out to touch her shoulder. She flinched, but he didn't pull away. "You know there's nothing you could have done, to stop what happened to Joe."

Clair looked at him then, eyes brimming with tears. "It should have been me."

"No," Chris said, the sorrow in his voice replaced with furious confidence. "No, it was not supposed to be you. You can't keep blaming yourself for what happened. Grieve his death and honor his memory, but you must keep living—and *fighting*."

Tears slipped down her cheeks, cold and wet where they hit his hand on her shoulder. He was up in a flash, moving closer to her and wrapping his arms around her, burying her head in his chest. He felt complete, and more at peace than he should have felt, given the circumstances, holding her while her crying slowly changed from tears to breathing spasms, shallow breaths, and then quiet.

When she was breathing normally, he pulled her back slightly.

"I have something for you," he said, reaching into his pocket and withdrawing the golden thread. Her eyes widened.

"What is it?" she said, gingerly touching the spider-silk gold.

"It's magic, in a very pure form," Chris said, twirling the string around her wrist three times, making an odd bracelet. "It's supposed to bring positive energy."

Clair looked from the thread to his eyes, tears welling up in her own. "Thank you."

Chris nodded and walked into the bathroom, returning with a few tissues to wipe her eyes before leading them both downstairs to join the information hunt.

EMILY

They had been searching every book, artifact, and paper in the shop for hours. The windows were dark, and the clock said it was well past three in the morning.

Emily was sitting in a large chiffon chair, a pile of open books in front of her as well as some random artifacts from around the world. Sam, Chris, and Dotty were clustered around the desk, piles of papers in front of them. Dotty had her face so close to one that her nose was almost touching the page. Clair was opening random boxes throughout the shop, looking for hidden volumes of information, most likely just to keep moving.

As she let her eyes stray, she wondered how so many things could fit into the shop. The bookcases and tables covered almost every inch of floor, giving the appearance of a hoarder's home. The walls were covered with old maps, photos, paintings, and wall hangings like dead stuffed deer and boar heads.

This was hopeless.

Whatever was out there was sure to get through the barrier eventually, even with Sam's and Dotty's enchantments, and Emily refused to die here in this dusty antique shop.

"Okay," she said, breaking the silence and watching three heads jump. Clair walked over, deep shadows under her eyes.

"Okay what?" she said, dropping a book onto the table in front of Emily. Sam, Chris, and Dotty were all staring at her.

"Tell me again, exactly what you saw."

Clair sighed, flopping into the nearest chair.

"It was like a woman—I'm almost positive it was a woman—but a tree as well . . . demonic looking, with her hair flying above her head as if she was frozen, or under water, or something. She had something gold glinting at her throat."

"Okay," Emily said, "but what are we really looking for? We know whatever she is, she's evil . . . but how would she even know to come looking for Clair here?"

Emily saw Sam and Chris exchange a look, and Clair looked down at the ground. Something was up.

"What are you not telling me?"

Clair sighed and held a hand up to Sam, who was opening his mouth to say something and cut her off.

"She is already involved," Clair said, turning to Emily. "Whatever it is was drawn here by, The Gate."

"The Gate?" Emily raised an eyebrow. "Gate to what? What gate?"

Clair sighed and elaborated.

"Ever since I got back into town, a gate to Eden, which is supposed to rotate around the world, stopped here and hasn't left."

Emily stared. "A gate to *Eden*? Like *the Eden*? Here, in Healdsburg?" She looked at the faces around her, trying to find the joke.

No one was laughing. She looked back at Clair. "A gate to Eden . . . but isn't Eden supposed to be near Jerusalem or something?"

Emily spent the next hour listening to Clair, Sam, Chris, and Dotty explain their purposes, about James, about everything she had been kept from. At the end, when everyone had a chance to explain their side of the story, Clair got up and walked into the house, returning with a huge white familiar lily.

"Oh my God!" Emily shouted, walking over to the flower. It still looked as lively as it had the day they found it, months ago. "This can't be the same flower."

"It is," Clair said, placing the vase on the table between the books. "It seeped through The Gate."

Emily took a minute to process this information.

"If this flower is still alive . . ." she said, thinking out loud. "Does Eden have magical abilities to grow things that don't die?"

"It's possible," Sam said, eyes boring into Emily's. "But Eden was never supposed to be entered after the fall."

"Yes, but"—Emily was returning to her counselor ways—"think of the possibilities! There could be a way to bottle immortality in there!"

"There is more than life there." Sam stood, hands flat on the table, his eyes deep blue pools. "'And unto Adam he gave death . . .' There is a reason why Eden is guarded by minor angels. It's dangerous."

"What do you know about The Gate, Sam?" Chris asked.

Sam looked over at Chris. Emily thought it was weird that no one had asked him that question yet. She would have asked him a ton of questions—about The Gate, about his long life—if they had a real conversation, ever. But they didn't.

"Well," Sam said, sitting back down, "I have never heard of a minor angel entering The Gate, but I think it's safe to say that a seraph could. We don't know if James ever went inside, but the Ultimate Evil was quoted to have been there in the form of a snake, and he was also quoted as being a rank of seraph in the New Testament, before warring with the Ultimate Good."

Chris nodded. Dotty went back to flipping through her current book.

"There are some minor angel histories," Sam continued, hand stroking his chin in thought, "not many, mind you; we aren't supposed to exist. But, as I have said before, the attacks, based on what I gathered from the communities I met, began to increase a few hundred years before I was reborn."

"Was there anything important happening historically then?" Chris asked, trying to puzzle it out. Emily felt her head swimming. "Whatever happened must have drawn more attention to The Gate, or something."

Sam creased his eyebrows but said nothing. Clair sighed and pushed the palms of her hands into her eyes. Emily was looking around the room again, trying to process.

There was a gate to Eden in Healdsburg. It hadn't moved, but was supposed to as a form of protection. Whatever was out there was like a woman but evil, and was pulled to the power of The Gate but distracted by Clair's blood.

Emily sent a silent thank you prayer to whatever God was out there for her sane and strong mind.

As her eyes wandered, she noticed a painting on the wall, half hidden by a bookshelf, and walked over to it.

It depicted a woman lying on a bed of red roses, her auburn hair falling over her bare chest.

"Who's this woman?" Emily asked, pulling the painting from the wall.

Dotty walked over to inspect.

"Looks like some goddess; it was a piece James purchased in Greece."

"What's that around her neck?" Clair walked over and was pointing to a golden snake pendant hanging between the woman's breasts. Her eyes widened in shock. "That's what I saw!"

Sam walked over.

"I've seen this before." Everyone turned their eyes on him. "In Cairo, when I went to look for the Mau, and for you." He looked at Dotty. "It was drawn on papyrus . . . and I have seen another . . ." He was off, throwing books off the table and selecting a small one on ancient Egyptian artifacts, flipping through pages.

He turned the page toward them. It was a picture of the same snake pendant. "It supposedly belonged to a pharaoh but was missing the night he was found dead . . . which was incidentally around the same time as the increased attacks on The Gate . . ."

Sam brought the book over to the painting to compare the pictures side by side. They were an exact match. "A leaf was in the book on this page . . ." Sam pulled a large dry petal from the book and held it up. Clair grabbed it from his hands and walked over to the lily, placing the dry leaf next to the live ones. They matched.

"What if the pharaoh was a seraph," Sam said, eyes boring into the leaves.

"James knew," Dotty said, staring at the match, shock and awe in her voice. "He knew about the pendant . . . about the blood . . ."

Sam walked back over to the desk, throwing more books out of the way, and mumbled, "I thought it was just an accident . . ." He pulled another leaf out of a very tattered, old Bible. "It can't be . . ."

"What, Sam?" Emily shouted, watching his eyes grow wide.

Sam turned to all of them.

"There's a part here that's underlined," he said quietly, eyes distant. "'And when the woman saw that the tree was good for food, and that it was pleasant to the eyes, and a tree to be desired to make one wise, she took of the fruit thereof, and did eat, and gave also unto her husband with her; and he did eat . . .'"

There was a long pause.

"I don't get it," Clair said, looking from Sam to Dotty. Emily was just as lost.

"The evil that's after Clair . . . it has the pendant . . . James knew . . ." Sam was thinking out loud. "He marked the pages with petals from lilies that seeped through The Gate . . . This page is marked, and Clair saw a woman . . ."

"Eve," Chris said quietly.

There was another long pause, where no one breathed.

Emily inhaled deeply. Adam and Eve? Alive?

"James . . . what have you left us with?" Dotty sighed, sitting in a chair, face in her hands.

"Eve," Sam repeated, "using seraph blood, searching for a way back into Eden."

"It can't be Eve," Clair said, echoing Emily's thoughts. "The Bible says that both Adam and Eve died right before the flood."

"It can be safe to say, at this point, that the Bible both says, and doesn't say, *everything*," Sam said, placing the book gently on the desk. "Eve is the one who has been attacking The Gate . . . She's the woman from the painting . . . The pendant must call her to it. It must help her find it . . ."

Emily felt her mouth drop.

Chris was staring at the floor, and Clair was shaking her head.

"It doesn't make sense at all!" Clair said, throwing her hands up in the air. "Even if it *is* Eve in the painting, Eve with the necklace, Eve that I saw . . . how would she be alive? And more importantly, why would she be trying to get *back into Eden*?"

"How she is alive, I couldn't say," Sam said, shaking his head. "There is so much I didn't know before finding you, even in all my years, but Eden—" he looked around at all of them "—Eden holds the tree of *life*, the original way to immortality."

"But she must *be* immortal," Clair spoke up, "to have been alive all these years."

"But she murders," Chris said. "The way she killed Joe . . . when we went to look, it was like his essence had been taken from him. Like the very root of his energy was stolen. Maybe she needs to kill to survive."

Everyone was silent. Emily wondered if Chris and Sam had kept this information from them to spare Clair's feelings. But that didn't matter now. Emily felt like she had just stepped into a horror story. Everything she had been taught in Catholic school went out the window. All the truth she thought she understood was flung upside-down. "We're looking at this the wrong way," she eventually said. "Let's say it *is* Eve. We don't need to defeat her . . . We just need her to *leave*."

"But we can't give her either of the things she's here for," Chris said, looking at Clair. Even though his purpose was to guard The Gate, Emily had the idea that Chris would die protecting Clair.

"I know that," Emily said, "but what about The Gate? What if we got it to move? Can't we get it to move?"

"As far as we can tell, it's waiting for James," Sam said, looking at Clair.

"But he isn't here anymore, and the longer it stays here, the more likely Eve will keep killing people!" Emily shouted, frustrated.

"I need to go to it," Clair said, continuing to speak through the immediate outburst that followed. "Look, we know that James, my grandfather, walked around The Gate before he disappeared. Maybe it just wants me to get close enough to know I'm there . . . or I can show it I'm not James or something—I don't know! But we can't do *nothing*. There's no guarantee it's going to take me like it did him."

"No," Dotty said, holding up her hand. Clair started to protest, but Dotty spoke through her. "You will not risk your life so foolishly. We have enough food left to survive a few more days and figure something else out. Now, I think it's time we all got some sleep."

And with that, she stood and walked out of the shop.

CLAIR

mily was lying next to her on the bed in silence, but neither one of them could sleep. Eventually, Clair felt Emily stand up and walk toward the door.

"Where're you going?" Clair asked the darkness.

"Back into the shop to look some more."

Clair didn't try to stop her. Instead, she stared at the ceiling, feeling the darkness press in around her. When she could bear it no longer, she stood and walked toward the door. When she opened it, she found Chris in the hallway, looking through a book. He looked up.

"Can't sleep either?" she said.

"Too keyed up," he said, rubbing his eyes. "Haven't heard a peep from Dotty or Sam, but I doubt they're sleeping either."

Clair nodded.

"Would you mind . . . ?" she began. Chris stared at her, and she blurted it out: "Would you mind reading in my room? It's just so weird and quiet in this house."

Chris nodded, closed his book, and followed Clair back through her door. As soon as he shut it, the room felt electrified. This was the most private situation they had been in since she had burned her hands, what felt like eons ago.

He glanced at Clair once before lying on the floor next to her bed.

Clair listened to him breathing, the slow rhythm coaxing her mind to sleep.

For the second time in her life, Clair woke up screaming.

In her dream the monster from the window had lured her outside, but not before Clair had killed everyone in the house, watching them die with fear in their eyes.

Chris was up and next to her in seconds. "Clair, are you okay? What's wrong?"

She felt the warm tears slide down her cheeks, and for once was grateful it was dark. She was so tired, so tired of being the reason why people were dying, why their lives were being uprooted and thrown into this blazing fire. She missed what her life was before this adventure began, before she knew she was an angel.

But even in that moment, Clair knew her adventure had begun a long time ago, with another sleepless night and a steaming hot bath.

Clair reached out and found his face. His cheek was warm, but he froze at her touch.

"Clair," he said, his voice a whisper.

"I lied to you, Chris," she said, moving her face through the darkness that separated them. "I love you."

Clair pressed her lips against his, finding her hope and letting it fill her. Slowly his lips began to move against hers, his body sliding easily onto the bed. She let the warmth of him become a spark that grew in her heart, forgetting all the pain, forgetting the battle and the evil that lay in wait. Clair kissed Chris like they were the only ones on earth, as if they could have a future and a life together apart from evil and good.

Chris leaned away first, pulling Clair into his arms while they lay on the bed holding hands in the darkness.

"Clair," he said, pulling her even closer, "I love you too."

Later that night as she lay awake in Chris's arms, still in her sweatpants and tank top from two days ago, she knew what she had to do.

"I have to go to The Gate."

She felt him exhale, slow and deliberate, his heart rate slowing as she pushed herself up from his chest and looked into his eyes through the darkness.

"I won't get taken. Nothing can stop me from being with you now." The moonlight was pouring through the window striking odd angles on his face. He looked like a statue cut from the finest marble. "But you have to let me do this. We can't live like this, and I won't risk anyone else getting hurt."

There was a long period of silence.

"Okay," he finally said, reaching up to touch her face, eyes melting. "But I'm coming with you."

The plan was simple.

In the morning, they would leave, just before sunrise. Chris quietly placed magical seals on the bedroom doors so no one could leave the house, even if they were heard. Clair went into the antique shop and found Emily asleep on a pile of books, drooling, and locked her in. She would be safe.

When Clair came back into the kitchen, she found Chris standing in the center, his white shirt off exposing his broad chest and arms. He was holding a large kitchen knife in his hand, with the hilt extended toward her. She had never seen Chris without his shirt, and immediately wished it was under different circumstances. She eyed the knife dubiously.

"I can't," she said, walking toward him. Chris nodded and flipped the knife around, gently grabbing her hand.

"Look at me," he said, gray eyes holding hers. Clair felt the cold of the steel for an instant before it bit across her palm, blood seeping out through the gash. He dragged her stinging hand down both of his arms, and across his chest before he whispered something into her palm and the pain stopped. Clair looked. The red was gone, but a large scar was left.

They were ready. She looked back up at him.

Before she had time to react, he pulled her face to his, his forehead resting against her own. There were no words.

Then she was running.

The plan was simple: they would each leave the house, running, in two separate directions. Chris would leave out the front door and run toward his house, doubling around to The Gate, while Clair would run out the back door, the quicker way. If the plan worked, Eve would be distracted by the two scents long enough for Clair to reach The Gate and convince it to move.

Clair felt like eyes were on her the entire time she was running, but she couldn't look over her shoulder, not yet. She needed to keep moving.

The wind was whipping unexpected rain into her eyes, and her clothes were stuck to her skin, making the upward run even more strenuous.

When she reached the top of the hill, Clair struggled to see into the basin. The wind was ripping leaves from the trees and throwing them into her face and eyes.

In a less desperate time, her mind would be laughing right now, imagining the weather reporter's face. *"In a shocking turn of events, this freak storm seems to have been caused by a system from the East . . ."*

But the adrenaline in her veins was pushing her forward, increasing her awareness and strength as she plunged downward, running as fast as she could toward the spot she knew too well.

She tripped more than once over a rock or a loose root, but knew she was getting close. When she reached the clearing, she stopped and looked around. There was no sun to light the forest, and her vision was blurred by the rain, but she didn't sense anyone there.

Clair turned to face The Gate.

She couldn't see it, but a faint energy was pulsing right in front of her, quieting the sound of the rain that broke through the trees above and poured down her face.

She walked closer, feeling the energy flow around her, cover her. She felt it in her blood, in every ounce of her being. She wasn't supposed to be this close, wasn't supposed to go nearer.

She was almost through The Gate.

"Clair!"

Clair looked to her right. Chris was sprinting toward her, the blood washed from his bare chest, his eyes wide.

Clair spun around.

Behind her was Eve, the goddess from the painting, in a Grecian white shift untouched by the rain, bright auburn hair whipping around her wild eyes, eyes too alive to be real, too full of malice and hate. The golden pendant at her neck was glowing viscously red in the darkness.

"Seraph," her voice sent ice through Clair's veins, echoing throughout the forest, "I have been waiting for you . . ."

"No!" Clair heard Chris shout from somewhere to her left, but Eve was running toward her, long knife-like fingers outstretched.

Clair felt Chris collide into her left side.

The Gate swallowed them both.

CLAIR

he could feel something cold and moist next to her ear.

It's the forest floor, she thought, feeling the rough earth beneath her fingers. A red-orange light was filtering through her eyelids. But there was no sound.

Slowly, Clair opened her eyes, her cheek still hugging the earth. There was brightness above her, a white blanket that covered everything. She looked at the forest. This was not Healdsburg.

Eden—her mind struggled to remember.

She had been running.

Eve.

Clair pushed herself up onto one hand, adrenaline thoroughly waking her from the daze. She stood and turned in a circle, looking around.

It was like a living painting—the trees were large swirling colors, the plants, though soundless, moving to a breeze that did not exist. It was like seeing through her eyes when she was riding the high of fasting—everything had an aura.

Clair looked at the nearest plant. It was bright green, almost like a fern but with jagged red spikes at the tips of its leaves. Its aura was in a constant state of upheaval between green and brown—dead and alive, dark and light. It was twitching as if it was being ripped apart from the struggle to find balance.

When she had almost come full circle, she saw something else.

In the middle of the clearing was a man.

Naked and crouched as if to hide in the earth, his back arched over his knees, head cupped in his forearms, hands pulling at the hair on his head. He was moving, but barely, the rocking motion a deft sway like the plants around him.

Clair took a step in his direction.

"You are not James." His voice was like bells, chimes, like the wind itself. It sounded familiar and distant all at once. Like something from a dream.

The man turned to look at her.

His face was blank, not contorted in pain as she imagined based on his demeanor. His eyes were expressionless, a deep earthy brown half covered by a black frock of hair.

"No." Her voice was sucked into the air around her, ringing until it died out completely. The breath she released to speak felt taken from her, as if this place was collecting every bit of her life.

Part of her mind was trying to catch up with the present, while the other was accepting and thinking ahead. Was she in the garden? How did she get here? If she was through The Gate, then who was this man?

"Who am I?" He smiled, his lip curving upward, the bells a brighter pitch. "Why not speak openly Clair. I can hear you whether you speak or not."

Clair swallowed. There was something about his face that kept her from moving closer to him.

"Who are you?" she asked, her voice sounding hollow as it echoed throughout the forest.

"I am he who was first."

The man stood, his deep voice filling the shifting world. The earth felt him move, and moved and swayed with him, was of him.

Clair didn't know how, but she just knew.

"Adam," she said, watching him smile.

"Yes."

He was taller than any man Clair had ever seen, his lean body reaching high above her own.

Clair took a deep breath and looked around once more.

If this was Eden, and this was Adam, then Eve must have come through The Gate as well. And if she was here, shouldn't Chris be here as well?

Adam, hearing her thoughts, knit his eyebrows together.

"They are not here, Clair of James," he said, the sorrow deepening the pulse of the forest. Clair looked at him. "My wife will never be here . . . however long she may seek me . . . she will never find what she wants."

There was so much sorrow in his voice Clair felt her body respond with a tear, the reverberation of his emotion flowing through her. It shocked her.

"Do not be afraid young one," he said. "I am the first of you and yours, the first of all. My emotions base your own, and all that will follow until the end of time."

Clair wiped the tear from her cheek. She was in Eden. She had no idea where Chris was, if he was still fighting Eve back beyond The Gate. She was talking with Adam, who was supposed to be dead.

"Death . . ." Adam laughed, slowly moving his head to look around the garden. "There was no death for me, not truly. 'And unto Adam he gave death.' But what is death, young one? Is it not the absence of life, of breath to fill your lungs and food to fill your belly, with sleep to spend the night dreaming?

"No." He was walking toward her now, his height towering over her own. She felt her pulse quicken. "Eve and I will never die, because we no longer live. Is that not worse than death? She will search for eternity, chasing something that does not exist."

Adam sensed the question in her mind before she had processed it. "Yes, Clair, you are here, but where is here? Is not the mind the brightest of them all? Would it not be the best prison for a soul? You stand here and see the garden as a painting, nothing more than the fragments of a blotted dream . . . Does it exist? Do I? What makes something real has no place here, for this place is the beginning of the end."

Adam dropped to one of his knees so that his brown eyes were level with Clair—and she gasped because within their depths, she could see herself, and she looked like nothing more than a scared young girl.

Adam smiled.

"It is good to see our own weakness." His smile vanished into the face of nothingness again, his deep eyes pooling with emotion as he looked through her, thinking back on a memory. Clair felt her heart sink for him. "We were so foolish . . ."

"You and Eve?" The words sucked out of Clair's mouth, but they sounded stronger, which gave her hope.

"We thought we could have the world. It all started so simply, made so much sense . . . a single thought . . . And then power has you. All men seek it." He looked over at Clair, his eyes piercing. "I was just the first of men to take it."

"But Eve was the first to take a bite."

Adam gave a short, bitter laugh, and shook his head, as if to clear the memory. "And what did I do while Eve was tempted by power?" Adam ran his hands up his face and through his hair. "Everyone always forgets my part of the story. I watched while she destroyed humanity."

Suddenly Adam's hands flew to his face, missing Clair by inches, a scream coming from his lips.

"*No!*" he shouted, pulling at the skin around his eyes, his cheeks, his hair. It was like he was trying to pull something out of his head. "Clair . . . you must tell . . ."

But Clair had just enough time to jump out of the way as he jerked onto his back, his legs kicking in all directions while his hands continued to claw viciously at his eyelids.

"When doubts . . . come back . . . to the beginning . . ."

Adam stopped screaming.

He was lying on his stomach, his body relaxed, hands flat on the earth in front of him. He was so still Clair thought he might be dead. She took a step toward him and reached out to place a hand on his back.

Before she had time to think, he had pushed himself from the ground to his full height, gripping her wrist painfully with his right hand. Clair screamed as she heard the bones crunch, and looked up into his eyes.

They were filled to the whites with gold. Clair remembered the eyes from the painting in the bushes. This was no longer Adam.

A shiver ran down her spine. She was staring into the eyes of the Ultimate Evil.

"I have been waiting for you." The voice was deep, no longer a peaceful bell. It was harsh like knives being thrust into metal, a horrible screech that penetrated the forest, driving it into chaos.

"What do you want from me?" Clair shouted, feeling the blood in her veins quake. If she was going to die, she was going to die staring into the eyes of her killer.

"Oh, Clair, this is not surely death . . ." His voice was forcing the world around them into a deeper state of unrest—the plants were eating themselves from the inside out, the trees bending at odd angles only to twist back again.

The world around her was spinning.

Clair felt the breath in her lungs leave her. She was suffocating.

"This is only the beginning . . ."

Clair watched as his jaw unhinged, elongating like a snake to reveal a dark throat too large for any mouth, before she was swallowed into the black.

CLAIR

Clair could hear breathing—in and out, in and out. The breath warmed the cold stone beneath her cheek, so cold it felt wet.

She opened her eyes to the tungsten shades of an orange street light above her, oval shaped and leaning. It appeared to come straight out of history, the ornate metal décor swirling above the light like a small wave ever threatening to crash down upon the bulb and smother it.

Clair stared at the light, willing her body to catch up with her mind. When she regained the strength to move her head, she looked to the right and saw a towering structure of glass and turrets that she recognized but couldn't process. She pushed herself up to sit on the cobblestone ground and looked up at the Notre Dame.

She was in Paris.

Her body reacted almost instantly, the shiver of adrenaline washing down the middle of her spine and out through her entire body.

Clair scrambled to her feet, the memories flooding back to her in sharp, colorful images.

The deep greens of the forest, of Eden. The red blood from Adam's eyes as he ripped his fingers through his skin, fighting to keep the evil from entering the sacred place. Chris, running toward her. Even further back in her memory . . . Eve, the red-haired beauty with eyes like fire that dug into her soul.

Clair clutched her forehead in anguish, trying to keep the memories from consuming her. The pain in her head was so great she felt her skull would burst, that she would have survived Eden just to die outside of it.

But she didn't die.

She heard footsteps somewhere near. They were coming closer. She could hear voices, and Clair struggled to focus, to be ready for another attack.

An older couple came toward her slowly. The man was wearing a gray brood cap with an argyle sweater, his left hand leaning on a cane and his right outstretched in front of the woman, who kept trying to get past him to get a closer look at Clair. She must have been his wife, because they both had plain gold bands on their left ring fingers.

The man spoke to Clair, while she was fighting for sanity. He was speaking French, and Clair couldn't do anything but shake her head, unable to speak through the pain and unable to understand.

Then, as if through water, his voice began to become clear. She could understand him. The pain in her head started to cease, but a dull throb remained.

"Miss? Are you alright?" Clair took a deep breath, the oxygen clearing her thoughts. She looked at the man. He had deep brown eyes and lines in his face from years of happiness.

"Yes," Clair said, her voice echoing throughout the street—or in her mind. She couldn't tell, and she didn't care. She was just glad they were speaking English. "I'm sorry, I'm lost . . ." She wasn't sure what to say. Surely "I just came out of Eden somehow and don't have any money or passport" wasn't a good conversation starter. Clair struggled to think of what to say, and then it hit her.

"I got lost, from my group," she said, the lie coming quickly to her lips. "Do you know where the nearest phone is?"

The man nodded, but his wife pushed forward from behind his protective hand to stand in front of Clair. She was a short woman, portly, with the same laugh lines as her husband. Clair wondered briefly how long they had been laughing together.

"We live right around the corner." Her voice was echoing through the street, and Clair began to wonder whether or not the street was causing the effect or her mind, because the older couple didn't seem to notice. "You can use our phone to call your group."

"Thank you," Clair said, taking another deep breath.

"I'm Monette—" the woman smiled "—and this is my husband, Richard."

"Clair." Clair offered her hand, making sure to keep her left hand pressed to her temple in an attempt quell the throbbing.

"Ah!" Monette exclaimed, making both Richard and Clair jump, the sound of excitement piercing the street. "A French name, I knew it; I knew you must be French!"

Clair creased her eyebrows but smiled. Richard muttered something about a heart attack, to which Monette just laughed and began pushing him and Clair down the street.

"We were out for our nighttime stroll." Monette began speaking again as soon as they started walking, Richard leading at a robust pace for a man his age, while Clair struggled to keep pace with them. Her mind kept echoing whenever anyone would talk, and although the throbbing was a dull pulse, she still felt sick. "We saw you lying on the ground. Did you fall? You were clutching your head so tightly I thought you might be having a fit!"

"Yes," Clair said instantly, "I slipped on the stones. My head was hurting . . ." Clair didn't know what else to say.

Monette nodded.

"Well," she continued, looking from Clair's head into her eyes, "don't you worry. I'm sure I left a pot of hot tea on the stove, and I can whip up something for us to eat until you get into contact with your group. What tour are you with?"

Clair looked around her at the little apartment-style houses that lined the tight dimly lit street, lost for words. She didn't know any of the general tourist group names, and if Monette and Richard had lived in France for as long as she assumed, they would know if she made something up. For the first time, Clair wished Sam was here to help her out.

Then she thought of something quite brilliant.

"I actually came with my uncle."

Clair heard Richard grunt and knew he was listening. Monette nodded but wasn't the type of woman to let the subject drop.

"But I thought you said you were with a group? Are you and your uncle in a group together?"

"Yes"—Clair looked back into her eyes, which in the passing streetlight looked almost orange, the green picking up hints of the lights around them—"but only for the museums. We were supposed to meet up with them again tomorrow. I just . . . left the group today at the Notre Dame, and must have . . . fallen asleep."

Clair could feel her lie slipping through the cracks. Monette raised an eyebrow but didn't ask Clair any more questions. She decided to try to throw a bit of honesty into the conversation.

"My uncle and I, we're distant relatives. We don't see each other very often, and sometimes we don't get along." Clair shrugged, hoping the gesture looked nonchalant as she focused on the path. "I just needed some space to clear my head, you know—distant relatives and family can be quite tiring."

"Yes, yes." Monette seemed reassured. "Family can be quite an adventure!"

"Yes." Clair laughed, the familiarity sliding between them like warm butter. It always amazed her how two people could have nothing in common, no history, but feel a sense of connection based on mutual experience.

Richard turned down a small alcove and stopped in front of a dark wooden door with a brass handle. He inserted a key and opened the door, ushering Clair into the house.

She stepped into a small white hallway, covered with pictures. There was a banister with stairs on her left, leading up to the second floor, and on her right along the wall were two closed doors. Above her head was a silver electric chandelier hanging from the high ceiling, and at the end of the hallway, Clair could just make out a small sink and coffee table in the kitchen.

"Here, dear." Monette handed Clair a small yellow sweater she had pulled from a closet to the right of the door. "You looked cold."

"Thank you," Clair said, tugging the sweater over her head. It smelled like lavender and vanilla, and the warmth from the wool sank instantly into her skin. Their voices were still echoing, and Clair knew that even with the high ceilings, the sound was happening in her head. She didn't mention it.

"Thank you so much," Clair said again, realizing how lucky she was to have found such a nice couple, and trying to hold back the tears she felt pricking at the back of her eyes. She didn't have the luxury of breaking down right now. She had to keep it together.

Monette patted Clair on the back and then muttered something to Richard, who nodded and walked upstairs. Monette led Clair down the small hallway.

She glanced briefly at the pictures on the wall, all family oriented, before she was ushered into a chair at the table in the kitchen. A warm cup of tea was placed in front of her, as well as a sandwich made of wheat bread, cucumbers, turkey, and mayo. Clair took a bite, feeling her hunger for the first time. Monette sat down across from her, a small cup of tea in her hands. She was watching Clair eat, a hint of puzzlement in her eyes, but Clair didn't mind. She just kept eating. The food hit her system, her empty stomach filling, the throbbing in her head dulling as her angel powers kicked into high gear.

Clair could see the aura around Monette, bright and blue and outstretched. She could hear the beat of her heart and the slow, heavy breathing of Richard somewhere upstairs while he rifled through a drawer. Clair could smell the perfume that Monette had placed on her wrists and neck—lavender, like the sweater. But most of all, Clair could see the light in her eyes, bright and full of kindness.

She smiled.

"Is the sandwich good?" Monette cocked her head to the side, a small chuckle escaping her lips.

"Yes, thank you," Clair said, turning to the tea. "I really like your perfume."

"Oh!" Monette said, her eyes widening. "Thank you. I hadn't thought I put it on since this morning."

Clair choked a bit on the bite of sandwich, but recovered quickly with the tea. "I'm partial to lavender."

"Yes, it's a lovely flower," Monette said. "Are you a gardener?"

"No," Clair said, finishing the sandwich and wiping her hands on a small white napkin Monette had placed under the teacup, "but my grandmother was."

Clair saw the sad, small smile on Monette's face and the sorrow that came into her eyes.

"Oh, no, she isn't dead," Clair amended, and Monette looked surprised. "She just stopped gardening. It used to give her so much joy, but ever since my grandfather died, she's let the garden rot."

Clair didn't know why she was ranting about Dotty and the garden to Monette, but she was feeling so full and happy and warm that she continued to think out loud.

"Sometimes I wish she would start to again, you know, for some closure or something, but she doesn't. Sometimes I wonder if she will ever be happy again."

Clair was shocked with herself. She couldn't believe she had actually said that out loud, or that she even felt that way about Dotty. She looked up at Monette.

"Well," the older woman said, "sometimes the things we love remind us too much of a time when we were really happy, and we're afraid to be that happy again, without the person associated with those memories."

Clair stared at the woman before her and had a brief image of Emily at her age, bright and full of advice.

"You're right," Clair smiled. "Thank you."

"I wish my grandchildren thought I was right more often than not." Monette laughed, the lines near her eyes deepening. After that, Monette went into full detail about her family, from her four children to their children, where they lived, what they did, and the things she loved about them.

Eventually the clock on the wall began to chime, a small metallic sound that flowed through the house. It was nine o'clock. Clair felt a yawn hit her lips.

"It's quite late for a woman of my age, and you must be tired." Monette smiled as Clair yawned again. "Why don't you phone your uncle and tell him you'll be staying here for the night."

Clair could tell that Monette was giving her an out, and she gratefully accepted.

"There's a phone in the spare bedroom, first door on your left as you head into the hallway. There should be fresh bed linens, and I made sure Richard put pajamas in there as well."

Monette got up from the table, taking the empty cup and plate from in front of Clair.

"Thank you again," Clair said. "I can't thank you enough."

When she was done rinsing the plates, Monette patted Clair on the back before walking through the hallway and up the stairs. When Clair knew she was alone, she released the breath she had been holding. The effect of the aura had worn off, and she felt tired to her bones.

She got up and walked to the small bedroom. It had a twin bed with a nightstand, a lamp, and the phone. Clair turned on the lamp and shut the door behind her, grateful for the privacy. She wasn't sure how to operate the phone, but she didn't have to worry. Next to it was a small piece of paper with a man's handwriting, indicating the codes for international calls.

Clair paused as she realized that both Monette and Richard must have known that she was lying, and she felt a wave of guilt and appreciation.

Clair grabbed the phone, dialed the international code, and waited for her *uncle* to pick up.

"Hello?" He picked up on the second ring, sounding alert and on edge, as always.

"Sam." Clair didn't know what else to say.

She heard his quick intake of breath, and then a slow release, his tension audible.

"Clair, where are you?" Clair had to give Sam some credit. If the situation were reversed, she would be freaking out on the other end of the line. But Sam was as collected as ever.

"Paris. It's about nine o'clock here. I'm with an elderly couple," Clair started spouting off information. "I just woke up next to the Notre Dame. I was in Eden. All these things happened Sam—"

"Clair." Sam cut her off, and she tried to slow the air going in and out of her chest. "Clair, you're okay. I am going to call a friend of mine. I'll be in Paris tomorrow around noon. Meet me at the Louvre. Sit in one of the benches near the entrance. Do you know how to get there?"

"No," Clair said, "but I can figure it out."

"Good." She could hear the pride in Sam's voice "Clair . . ." There was a short pause before he spoke again, his voice hesitant. "Is Chris with you?"

Clair stopped breathing. Her mind stopped. She heard the word form on her lips but didn't remember willing it out of her mouth. "No."

Silence. And then: "Be at the Louvre at noon. I'm coming to get you."

She didn't sleep well that night.

The covers were warm, the wool pajamas Richard left on her bed were comfortable, and her stomach was full, but her heart was empty.

The next morning, she changed back into her jeans and tank top, as well as the warm sweater. Monette made her some eggs with toast, and Clair thanked her, eating and drinking the orange juice like a zombie, unable to truly function.

Chris wasn't at home. He wasn't with her. Somewhere in the back of her mind, she had hoped he was home, safe. That he had come out of The Gate back in Healdsburg.

But he hadn't.

After breakfast Clair told Monette she would be meeting her uncle at the Louvre and asked for directions. Monette wrote them on a small piece of paper and gave Clair a hug.

"Feel free to come back, anytime," Monette said, her voice echoing slightly. The smile on her face was warm and inviting.

"Thank you so, so much," Clair said, starting to remove the warm sweater.

"No"—Monette stopped her—"keep it. It's cold outside."

Clair felt the tears burn behind her eyes but held them back, taking Richard's outstretched hand one last time before walking out into the brisk morning air.

She wished her mind and heart were in the present to enjoy the splendor of Paris, but they weren't.

Chris wasn't home. He wasn't here. He could be anywhere.

She numbly made her way to the Louvre and turned down the last street to face the museum. Clair stopped in her tracks.

It was a large structure, larger than she had imagined. The building took up over two blocks, U-shaped and easily three stories tall. It looked like a palace, with one giant glass pyramid in the middle.

Clair walked up to the windowed pyramid and looked down into the expansive museum. She couldn't make out any of the art, just the marbled pathway that must flow throughout the space. Passing the pyramid, she found a line of tourists waiting in front of the entrance.

The museum didn't open until ten o'clock, and it was about eight. She sat down on a cement bench not too far from the entrance and stared at the glass triangle as it reflected the light flitting through the thick clouds.

"May I sit here?"

A man sat down next to her. He wore a brown raincoat with black shoes and had long, ruffled brown hair. He looked about forty.

Clair nodded and continued to look at the people passing along the street. She could feel his presence next to her, but he never moved and wasn't carrying a bag or a newspaper. He just sat next to Clair for a few minutes before getting up again and walking away without another word. Clair watched him leave. She looked down at the seat he just occupied, and saw a small manila envelope with her name typed onto it.

Clair looked up again, but the man was gone.

She grabbed the envelope and ripped it open. Inside was about five hundred Euros, a passport, and a disposable cell phone with a number already typed. Clair hit the call button. It rang twice.

"Clair?" Sam sounded like he was in a car in the middle of a storm. Clair felt relief flood through her at the sound of his voice.

"Sam." She sighed, feeling a lot better with the money and passport. "Where are you? Who was that man?"

Sam ignored her.

"I'm almost there. The flight's landing now. I'll meet you in the museum, in front of the *Winged Victory*. Pay with the Euros."

"Okay," she breathed.

"Everything is going to be alright," he said before hanging up.

Clair put the phone in her front pocket and distributed the five hundred Euros amongst a couple of her jean pockets, just in case. She was about to throw away the envelope before she decided to keep it, folding it up and stuffing it into her back pocket. She was still wearing the warm sweater from Monette and began to feel more secure.

When the Louvre opened, Clair paid for a ticket and walked into the museum.

It was huge.

All around her were paintings—Renaissance, modernism, and ancient works—as well as statues by famous sculptors spread throughout the building like mini islands. When she was in college, what felt like a lifetime ago, she would have killed to be standing in this place, so close to history. Now she merely glanced at the works, passing by the paintings with a sense of awe, but with less wonder than she would have felt a few months ago. She was part of history now, not just an observer.

Clair found the *Winged Victory* standing at the end of the eastern corridor. It was at the top of a flight of stairs, situated on a pedestal that reached far above Clair's head. The woman stood, headless and armless, large marbled wings spread out behind her as if to catch an invisible and eternal wind. The sculptor draped the woman in a thin tunic that hugged her breasts and small waist.

She was beautiful, albeit helpless. Clair couldn't help but wonder how the statue represented victory when all she had was the ability to move, not to react or think. Clair thought she might have been reading too much into it.

"Clair!"

She turned around. Sam was striding toward her through the crowd. He was dressed in a black Armani suit, with a red tie. Clair walked swiftly up to him, pausing when they had closed the distance. They weren't the hugging types, and Sam, feeling the same awkwardness Clair was feeling, quickly extended his hand.

"Glad you're alright," he said, giving her hand a good squeeze before letting go.

"Thanks for coming," she said, feeling all too formal. "Who was that man, the one who dropped off the envelope?"

Sam narrowed his eyes, and Clair saw them shift around the room behind her before he answered.

"Just a friend."

Clair didn't believe that was the whole story, but before she could pursue the subject, Sam grabbed her wrist and led her out of the museum, talking fast.

"We leave on the next flight back to the states. Dorthea insisted you call her as soon as I found you, but we need to make sure we check in for the flight. We have about thirty minutes until it leaves. Luckily you didn't come with any baggage."

Clair wasn't sure if Sam had meant that as a joke or not, but neither one of them laughed. Once they reached the entrance to the museum, Sam pushed Clair toward a waiting black limo before opening the door and shoving her inside. He quickly followed.

The limo ride was short and silent, her mind trying to catch up with everything that was happening. Once they reached the airport, Sam ushered Clair through the security checks. Clair wasn't sure whether or not the passport was going to work, but the attendant barely glanced at her information before ushering them both through security. Sam took off at a brisk walk that had Clair jogging to keep up.

When they reached their gate, the flight attendant greeted them and ushered them through the door, shutting it behind them as she did. They were the last ones boarding.

Clair looked out at the ground as they drifted away from Paris, and couldn't help but feel like this wouldn't be the last time she was in Europe.

ACKNOWLEDGEMENTS

There were so many people influential in helping me get through this first book. First off, I would like to thank my aunt, Julie Thomas, and mother, Gina Bradley. We would set "Writing Nights" up where we would get together and read bits and pieces of the book. It was these writing nights that helped me set deadlines for myself, and then it was my mother and aunt who would help me see what the reader would see when reading the book. After almost a year of writing nights, the first draft of *The Gate* emerged and we were all so excited, and I was so grateful. I could not have written this book without their help—without those nights spent laughing at the characters as they came to life, at misspelled words, grammatical errors, and scenes that came together. It was a magical experience, and *The Gate* is only out now because of them. This book would not be published without my amazing editor Stacey, also known as grammargal in Fiverr.com. I would also like to thank Anne Lamott, the amazing author who wrote *Bird by Bird*, the book that I highlighted, marked up, clutched to my chest, and cried with. It was she who said to write the scenes that I could see in my head and have faith that the rest would come together—and she was right! Without that book, I don't think I would have ever been able to just start writing the book. Obviously, I highly recommend it. Next, I'd like to thank my best friend, Emily Drottz, for being the first person to read the book within a week, and giving me feedback and encouragement. My husband, Marc Selwan, for always encouraging me to follow my dreams. Without our love story I could not have written one for Clair. My father, Douglas Blau, for all those trips to the cabin and the forest of my youth, for the rainy day at the cabin when I cried in the jeep at the top of the hill with you and wrote one of the first pieces of *The Gate*, for all the books I have read in my life that pushed my mind, that gave me a world besides my own in which to live, love, and find magic. And now I feel I must just start listing names! My grandmother, Marie Thomas; my mentor, Lisa Winn; Jazmyne Pollard, for reading it in its infancy; my sister, Samantha Short; my brother, Josh Blau; my grandfather, Walt Blau; my stepmother, Jean Donald; and aunt, Janet Atteberry. I have to thank Mike and Brenda Drottz, for being my parents away from parents; my percussion instructors Ed Cloyd, Dale Pauly, Ben Prima, and Alexis Masingill, for training me to use my own powers. Special thank you to Jazmyne Pollard, my personal cheerleader and reading buddy. There are others I would like to thank—people and things that don't even know they contributed, but somehow my mind stole them and made them a part of the book. Thank you.

BIOGRAPHY

Rachel Nicole Selwan graduated from CSU Sacramento with bachelor's in photography and a minor in journalism. She sta writing *The Gate* in 2011, the first book in the series. Rachel h avid love of video games, books, and coffee (sometimes tea, she feels like trying to be healthy). She lives with her husband, and dog, Master-Chief, in Livermore, CA.

Made in the USA
San Bernardino, CA
11 July 2018